THE WAY TO A LADY'S HEART

S0-BOE-759

Both Lord Peter Phillips and Lord Adrian Whitlow most carefully planned their campaigns to conquer the unconquerable Serena.

Lord Peter first set about melting her resistance with the gift of as fine a steed as a superb horsewoman like Serena would desire. He further advanced his chances by making an ally of her innocent younger sister, Verity.

For his part, Lord Adrian employed the full arsenal of polished manners and practiced charm that had won Serena for his late cousin, whom he so closely resembled in startling good looks. To help him further, he made Serena's brother, Peregrine, his devoted disciple.

And all of London society could only wonder which of these two irresistible lords would topple Serena's defenses—with the kiss that would be the ultimate key to her heart. . . .

DOROTHY MACK is a native New Englander, born in Rhode Island and educated at Brown and Harvard universities. While living in Massachusetts with her husband and four young sons, she began to combine a longtime interest in English history with her desire to write, and emerged as an author of Regency romances. The family now resides in northern Virginia, where Dorothy continues to pursue both interests.

⊘ SIGNET REGENCY ROMANCE   (0451)

TALES OF THE HEART

☐ DAUNTLESS MISS WINGRAVE by Amanda Scott   (161459—$3.50)
☐ MOONLIGHT MASQUERADE by Michelle Kasey   (161025—$3.50)
☐ THE INVINCIBLE VISCOUNT by Irene Saunders   (161033—$3.50)
☐ CAPTAIN BLACK by Elizabeth Hewitt   (161041—$3.50)
☐ A SPORTING PROPOSITION by Elizabeth Hewitt   (161068—$3.50)
☐ A DISHONORABLE PROPOSAL by Katherine Kingsley   (160584—$3.50)
☐ THE PLAYER KNIGHT by Ellen Fitzgerald   (160592—$3.50)
☐ MISS CHARTLEY'S GUIDED TOUR by Carla Kelly   (160606—$3.50)
☐ THE SERGEANT MAJOR'S DAUGHTER by Sheila Walsh   (160614—$3.50)
☐ A MASKED DECEPTION by Mary Balogh   (160622—$3.50)
☐ THE NOTORIOUS NABOB by Sheila Walsh   (160002—$3.50)
☐ WILLOWSWOOD MATCH by Gayle Buck   (160010—$3.50)
☐ LADY SARA'S SCHEME by Emily Hendrickson   (160029—$3.50)
☐ MAD MASQUERADE by Barbara Hazard   (160037—$3.50)

Prices slightly higher in Canada

Buy them at your local bookstore or use this convenient coupon for ordering.

NEW AMERICAN LIBRARY
P.O. Box 999, Bergenfield, New Jersey 07621

Please send me the books I have checked above. I am enclosing $_____
(please add $1.00 to this order to cover postage and handling). Send check
or money order—no cash or C.O.D.'s. Prices and numbers are subject to change
without notice.

Name_____

Address_____

City _____ State _____ Zip Code _____
Allow 4-6 weeks for delivery.
This offer is subject to withdrawal without notice.

THE RELUCTANT HEART

by

DOROTHY MACK

A SIGNET BOOK

NEW AMERICAN LIBRARY

A DIVISION OF PENGUIN BOOKS USA INC.

NAL BOOKS ARE AVAILABLE AT QUANTITY DISCOUNTS
WHEN USED TO PROMOTE PRODUCTS OR SERVICES.
FOR INFORMATION PLEASE WRITE TO PREMIUM MARKETING DIVISION,
NEW AMERICAN LIBRARY, 1633 BROADWAY,
NEW YORK, NEW YORK 10019.

Copyright © 1989 by Dorothy McKittrick

All rights reserved

SIGNET TRADEMARK REG. U.S. PAT. OFF. AND FOREIGN COUNTRIES
REGISTERED TRADEMARK—MARCA REGISTRADA
HECHO EN DRESDEN, TN, U.S.A.

SIGNET, SIGNET CLASSIC, MENTOR, ONYX, PLUME, MERIDIAN
and NAL BOOKS are published by New American Library, a division of
Penguin Books USA Inc., 1633 Broadway, New York, New York 10019

First Printing, January, 1990

1 2 3 4 5 6 7 8 9

PRINTED IN THE UNITED STATES OF AMERICA

1

They left the turnpike after Cheltenham and immediately noted a deterioration in the condition of the road. As the lightly built chaise jolted in and out of deep ruts created by the February rains, Serena felt the diminution in their speed and revised her mental estimate of the travel time remaining.

"Hang on to your teeth, Betsy," she advised her companion with a rueful grimace, thrusting out a hand to steady herself against the side panel as the carriage swayed to the right for no discernible reason.

"Yes, ma'am." A grin broke across the rosy-cheeked face of the girl sitting opposite, revealing pretty teeth worth hanging on to. "This is as close as I hope to come to riding on a washboard, I'll allow. How much longer now, my lady?"

"At this rate, more than two hours, I would estimate. Fortunately, there is plenty of daylight left—that is, if one can dignify this gray murk with the term 'daylight'." She glared through the window at the sky, which remained as relentlessly gray and sodden as when they had begun their journey from rural Hereford the previous day. The only change had been for the worse when threatened rain had materialized for several hours both days. They had spent the night in Worcester, falling asleep to the sound of a steady rain beating against the inn windows in a drafty bedchamber made barely habitable by a fitful fire in one corner. Now Serena drew the woolen lap rug more securely about her legs, glad of her sturdy half-boots.

"Lord, how happy I shall be to see the sun again! Do

you think the sky is a trifle brighter in the west than it has been, Betsy?"

"It won't be long now afore it clears, I'm a-thinking," the maid replied soothingly, addressing herself to the underlying note of frustration in her mistress's voice. She studied the cameo purity of the profile presented to her, sensing the suppressed passion in the generally calm, contained face and speculating as to its cause. "Your ladyship must be anxious to reach home again after all this time," she ventured as Lady Whitlaw turned suddenly from her contemplation of the weather and caught her staring.

Serena's brows drew together and her lips parted before prudence intervened to stifle her impulsive speech. "No, I . . . er, yes, of course," she muttered, returning a sightless gaze to the rising ground through which they were now driving. Goodness, but she had nearly confessed just how little pleasure she was anticipating from this pilgrimage to her childhood home. If a lack of congenial companionship over the past months had her poised to confide her misgivings to a servant, bright and likable though Betsy was, perhaps her mother was correct in assuring her this promised visit would do her a world of good.

She had resisted her parent's initial entreaties, not wishing to trade her hard-won contentment for the disordered hysteria that frequently prevailed at Chawnton Manor, but by dint of repeated references to her own ill health and calls upon her daughter's sense of filial obligation, Mrs. Boynton had eventually prevailed. And here she sat, immured in an uncomfortable carriage, being jolted to bits on frightful roads in wretched late-winter weather, the whole experience rendered even more unpleasant by a pervasive sense of foreboding that no efforts of hers could dispel. For the truth was that Serena did not believe the convenient fiction that Mrs. Boynton's fragile health made her long for the comforting presence of her elder daughter. Twenty-one years' intimate acquaintance with the lady had taught her that when all else failed, her mother invariably invoked her frail constitition to secure her ends or evade any duties she considered onerous. No, there had to be more in her mother's mind than a wish to have her daughter dance attendance at her bedside.

A sudden lurching worse than any previous gyrations jerked Serena from her gloomy thoughts of what awaited her at Chawnton. Judging by the ominous cracking sound that preceded the jolting halt of the carriage, the present was about to provide problems enough to engage all her attention.

"Mother of mercy, what happened?" squealed Betsy, clinging to the ceiling strap to keep herself from falling on top of her mistress.

"At a guess, I'd say we've broken something vital, most likely a wheel. Are you all right, Betsy?"

"I think so. You ain't . . . aren't hurt, are you, ma'am?"

"Nothing hurts but my dignity in this awkward position," replied Serena, finding herself on the downside of the severely canting carriage. "Can you open your door, Betsy? Heaven knows where I'd land if I tried to open this one."

The words had scarcely left her tongue when the upper door was pulled open from the outside and the anxious face of the groom peered in. "Are you hurt, my lady, or you, miss?"

"We're fine, Jenkins. Help Betsy out, then haul me up. It's a bit cramped in here."

Once safely on the ground, thanks to the combined exertions of the coachman and groom, Serena had the tainted satisfaction of seeing her prophecy of disaster confirmed.

"That wheel's a goner, ma'am, my lady," said the coachman, shaking his graying head with finality as his mistress bent to examine the splintered remains. "That last hole did for it. I was trying to avoid a diff'rent one and didn't notice that one partic'lar, all filled w'water as it was. I'm that sorry, ma'am . . . my lady."

Serena patted his arm. "Don't fash yourself, Samuel, as our old Yorkshire cook would say. If it had not been that particular rut it would have been another sooner or later. This road is in a deplorable state."

"That it is, ma'am, and it's one I don't know neither. Do you have any idea where we are, being as how you come from these parts?"

Serena surveyed their immediate surroundings, but there was nothing in the vicinity to jog her memory. The curving road ascended as far as the eye could see, and there were no structures visible in the rolling hills to either side. "I haven't been paying close attention, I fear," she confessed. "Have we lately passed through a fair-sized village with a Norman church—a stone church with a square tower?"

"No, ma'am. We passed a few houses a ways back, but there weren't no church atall."

"Then we cannot be far from it. Unhitch one of the horses so Jenkins may ride on. There is a good black-smith there and a small inn on the other side of the village. The landlord will have a gig for hire to take us to the inn while the wheel is being replaced."

An hour later, warmed by most of the contents of a pot of strong tea made by the landlord's wife, Serena sat in the small parlor, her mind once again occupied with speculations about what to expect at Chawnton. Betsy was sitting by the fireplace trying to chase away the remnants of chill from their recent adventure. Bricks were heating within to wrap in flannel for the comfort of their feet on the final stage of their journey. It was warm and cozy in the shabby little room with its scarred Windsor chairs and threadbare carpet, but Serena was seized with a mounting restlessness that soon had her off her chair and pacing. Betsy eyed her mistress with curiosity but held her tongue.

She hadn't long to wait. After bumping into a sharp-cornered table for the second time in one of her tours, Serena bit off an impatient exclamation and strode over to the settle near the fireplace, taking up her pelisse, which Betsy had draped over the curved back to warm.

"I'm going out for a walk," she declared, shrugging into the black gabardine garment.

The maid's eyes flew to the window. "But it could start raining again at any moment, my lady."

"Then I'll turn around and come back," the other replied indifferently, pulling on black kid gloves. "The smith said the carriage won't be ready for at least another hour, and there isn't a thing to read in this miserable establishment."

Sighing, the abigail stood up and reached for her cloak, only to be told kindly that she had best stay indoors near the fire lest she chance an inflammation of the lungs following their recent exposure to the dampness and cutting wind.

"Begging your pardon, ma'am, but your ladyship is asking for just such a misfortune if you go back out into that nasty damp air."

"Nonsense, I never take cold and I must stretch my legs a bit before we climb back into that wretched chaise or I shall go quietly mad—or mayhap not so quietly. You would not wish to be confined in a carriage with a raving Bedlamite, would you, Betsy?"

The young girl responded to the impish charm of her mistress's smile but her own smile faded as she found herself looking at the closing door. Defeated, she sank back onto the settle. There was never much use in arguing with Lady Whitlaw when she had made up her mind to do something.

Emerging from the inn, Serena gave a quick glance down the street toward the village, but checked her step when she glimpsed two women coming out of a shop. She had no desire for any human contact at the moment, however slight. All too soon the family would wrap its tentacles around her, making unceasing demands on her time and patience. She set out in the opposite direction along the road, and after a few hundred feet turned off onto a path that led into the hills.

Fortunately, her traveling dress was cut wider than the prevailing fashion, enabling her to stride out freely as the path became a mere track into the hills. Serena loved this high area of the Cotswolds where she had been used to wander at will during her childhood. She hadn't realized until this moment how much she had missed the hills. Even on a dreary day in late February it was beautiful here, with only a hint of the vibrant green that would blanket the hills in a few weeks. At the moment the land was silent, waiting for the surge of renewed life that spring would bring. There was not a living soul within eyesight, not even a sheep, and she reveled in an almost forgotten sense of physical freedom that burgeoned up in her limbs and burst out in an impetuous outflung gesture of her arms—whether of joy or defiance, she could not have said.

She paused after a few moments to catch her breath, chagrined that her legs could no longer carry her for hours with no effort or effect. Hesitating over which track to take, she spotted movement off to her left and squinted into the distance. After a few seconds she could make out the figure of a man walking with a cavorting dog beside him, and her decision was made for her. She took the track that wound around the hill to her right leading upward. A few moments' climb should bring her to an eminence that would offer a superb view as a reward for her efforts and a visual memory to take with her in the carriage.

Her own harsh breathing and footsteps on the loose gravel prevented Serena from hearing sounds indicative of the presence of another creature near at hand until she clambered up through a break in the limestone ridge just in time to see a young boy disappear over the edge of the flat area on top. Shock and disbelief froze her in her tracks until the boy's cries freed her limbs. She rushed forward across the plateau, slowing as she approached the spot where the ground had seemed to crumble under the child's feet. Her heart leapt into her throat as she peered cautiously over the edge of what she hoped was solid rock.

The child was sprawled on a narrow ledge some five or six feet below her. The ominous sounds of stones dislodging themselves from his perilous perch mingled with the boy's cries. Below him there appeared to be a sheer drop of fearsome height, but she could not afford to dwell on that.

"Hush, boy!" she commanded, forcing a stern tone

through lips that would tremble in spite of her attempt to steady them. "Are you hurt at all?"

"Me head's bleedin' and I want to get off here!" the child shrilled, raising a dirty, tear-streaked face that showed no curiosity at the sudden appearance of another human being.

"If you can stand up—very carefully, mind—I may be able to pull you up again."

"I . . . I'm afeard."

"So am I, but the only alternative is to remain there quietly while I go back to the village to fetch help to rescue you."

"Me pa will whomp me good for comin' up here alone," protested the child, commencing to cry again.

"Then you had best let me try to pull you up. And stop that sniveling, boy; it never helps in the least. All you have to do is stand up and hold your arms up to me. I'll do the rest, and I promise you I am very strong."

Serena found her own attempts at portraying brisk confidence unconvincing, and could only trust a young child's perception would be less acute. It seemed her performance was adequate, however, because the boy slowly gathered his muscles and courage together to make the effort she was demanding. He got to his knees with agonizing slowness that set Serena's teeth on edge, since his movements were accompanied by the distressing noises made by stones coming loose from the ledge and striking on more stones far below.

The boy was aware of this factor too, for he froze on his knees for a time and she had to bully him verbally to bring him at length to his feet. By lying full-length on her stomach, she was able to extend her arms over the edge.

"Grasp my wrists with your hands, boy, and I'll do the same to you. That's right. Do you have a tight grip? Good. Now, up you come."

The words were confident, but Serena found the task infinitely more difficult than she could have imagined. The boy's slight weight seemed trebled from the circumstances of their respective positions, and her arms soon felt they were being dragged from their sockets. Had she been able to brace her feet against something it would have made all the difference, but such was not the case.

"Try to help by putting your feet on the wall as though you were walking up the cliff," she panted, only to have the child fall back with a painful jerk against her arms when more stones were loosened by his movements. For the first time Serena feared that her strength would be inadequate to rescue the child, even while she redoubled her efforts. The thought of leaving him trapped on that crumbling ledge while she wasted precious moments getting help brought a film of perspiration out on her face as she nerved her muscles for another pull.

"Halloooo!"

The welcome call came from nearby.

"Up here, hurry!" she called back, and then bent her attention to calming the crying child while she tried to ignore the pain in her arms.

"Good God, what are you doing?" The voice was just behind her now, hard on the sounds of someone bounding up the way she had come an eternity ago.

"Trying to pull this child back up, but I cannot quite do it alone. Kneel over my shoulders and grasp his wrists while I slide out of your way. A man's strength should be sufficient."

"I cannot use one of my arms at present," came the calm reply. "I am going to grab you with the other one. You just keep a firm hold on the child and I'll pull you backward."

It wasn't the moment for debate. Serena gritted her teeth and hung on like grim death while a muscled arm wrapped itself around her waist and began to exert a strong backward pull that instantly doubled her discomfort. Her agonized breathing made a harsh duet with the man's.

The ordeal was over in less than a minute. As soon as the boy's shoulders appeared, the man released his grip on her and transferred it lightning quick to the child's arm. Serena lay there gasping for a few seconds longer, reluctant to move her arms, which throbbed painfully despite the absence of the boy's weight.

"Are you all right, ma'am? Let me help you up." The concern in the man's voice acted like a spur to a reluctant horse.

"I am quite unhurt, thank you, if one discounts the possibility of several cracked ribs." Serena scrambled awkwardly to her feet, unheeding of the hand held down to her. Thank heaven her legs held her upright. At present they were the only parts of her that didn't ache fiercely. She put up a hand to straighten her hat, which had gone askew during the late rescue operation, wincing at the discomfort even this slight effort entailed. She jumped slightly as the man's dog nuzzled her other hand as if to offer comfort. She smiled down at the spaniel in mute gratitude, but the face she turned to her rescue partner was calm and unsmiling.

"It was merely my misfortune that you can use only one arm, and that one strong enough to crush a bear. I shan't regard a few injured ribs in a good cause, however."

The man had been staring at her in undisguised amazement, but that changed to admiration as he swept off his cap and bowed.

"Accept my sincere compliments, ma'am, on a very brave action. You've saved this lad's life, I make no doubt. That ledge would not have held him much longer."

Serena shook her head decisively. "Not at all. I am persuaded I could not have hauled him up alone. Your arrival was most fortunate. Are you all right, boy?" she inquired, turning to examine the child, who had apparently been struck dumb in the presence of two large strangers.

He could not be called an attractive child at this stage, giving the appearance of a loosely assembled collection of bones, with the thin arms and legs of a preadolescent, inadequately covered by outgrown clothing of good homespun. His cap had been lost in the fall and his straight brown locks were matted with dirt and blood that oozed down his forehead toward one ear.

Serena produced a handkerchief tucked in the sleeve of her gown, but before she could carry out her obvious intention, the boy jerked back in alarm from her extended hand.

"I won't hurt you. Stand still," she commanded in a voice that expected to be obeyed.

At least her voice had that effect on the child, the man watching the tableau noted with some amusement as the boy submitted with pathetic resignation to the indignity of having his wounds probed by a masterful female stranger.

"What is your name, lad?" he asked to divert the child's mind from the unwanted cleaning operation in progress.

"Silas . . . sir." This last was added grudgingly as the boy's intelligent gray eyes ran briefly over the tall, broad-shouldered person of his second rescuer.

"Well, Silas, I trust you realize that you are a fortunate young man indeed. If it had not been for the heroic intervention of Miss . . . of this kind lady," the gentleman amended when the woman ignored the invitation to disclose her identity, "you would in all likelihood be lying on the rocks below with a lot worse injuries than a cut head. What have you to say for yourself? Speak up, lad."

"Yessir, thank you, sir . . . and ma'am," the boy added when the gentleman's aspect grew stern with waiting.

"There, I'm afraid that is the best I can do without any water," Serena put in, having ignored the exchange between the others. She tipped up the boy's chin, which she still held in her gloved hand, and smiled suddenly into the cowed little face. "The cut on your head is not bad, Silas. When you get home your mother will clean it properly. If it starts to bleed on the way home, press this handkerchief to the spot. And mind you keep away from dangerous places in future." She released the child, who smiled back shyly, and applied her practical attention to the chore of brushing off the dirt from the front of her pelisse.

The man, having witnessed the child's antagonism dissolve in the blinding brilliance of the woman's smile, tried again.

"May I introduce myself, ma'am? I am Peter Phillips, presently visiting a friend in the area, very much at your service."

"How do you do," she replied, glancing up briefly before completing the brushing-down of her garments.

"When someone tells you his name, I believe it is customary to reply in kind," the gentleman pointed out.

"Not when there is scant likelihood of those persons ever meeting again," she returned coolly. "I must get back; it is going to rain in a very few minutes. Good-bye, Silas. Good day, Mr. Phillips."

"Actually, it's Lord Phillips, and you must let me escort you back to your home."

"That won't be necessary, thank you, Lord Phillips, but you might escort Silas back home; he's had a frightening experience. Good-bye."

The man and boy left on the plateau stared after her, listening to her fading footfalls as she descended through the gap in the ledge to the track below. It was impossible to tell what was going on in the boy's head, but Lord Phillips acknowledged a veritable parade of passing impressions following his first good look at the person of his fellow rescuer.

The woman's size had struck him initially. It had been like watching an Amazon come into view as she rose to her feet—a beautiful Amazon, he had realized before he could blink in surprise, a beautiful Amazon with incredible dark red hair and clear green eyes set beneath arching brown brows in an oval face of translucent fairness once the high color of physical exertion had receded. Their eyes had nearly met on a level. He stood over six feet tall, which would make her about five-feet-ten or even more. He had never been attracted to large women before, but that had been a very neat waist he had wrapped his arm about just now.

Scarcely had the unknown woman's physical beauty been assimilated before her personality had made an equally decided impression on him. Her candid reference to his disability had been matter-of-fact, perhaps even slightly accusing. Certainly there had been no evidence of feminine sympathy or coyness in her manner, toward either himself or the boy. She had attended to the latter's injuries as a matter of course, brooking no resistance on

the victim's part. Her attitude had been brusque, while
her touch had been tender, a strange combination that
had awakened an interest in the workings of her mind
before ever she had smiled at the child.

That smile in all its radiance had instantly swung his
mounting interest from the character back to the person
of this fascinating stranger, but his subsequent efforts to
put their acquaintance on a more regular basis had been
snubbed with a coolly civil indifference that added annoyance to his other reactions. Obviously she had experienced no reciprocal pull of attraction to him.

Peter's eyes narrowed as he continued to gaze at the
spot where the woman had vanished. So far the lovely
lady had had matters all her own way, but this would not
be the end of the incident if he could help it. He turned
with abrupt decision to the child, who was unconcernedly
playing with the dog.

"Do you know who that lady might be, Silas? Does
she live in the area?"

"I dunno. I never seed her around here before."

Peter compressed his lips, but a drop of rain on his
face brought his attention back to present necessities.
The exasperating female had even been correct about the
imminence of rain. Establishing her identity would have
to wait for a more propitious moment, but he had no
doubts that he would do so eventually. Her accent and
clothing distinguished her as a member of the gentry. His
host most probably would know of her. So singular a
personality could never remain anonymous in this or any
neighborhood.

2

"Where have you been gone to all this time? Jenkins reported the carriage was ready a full quarter-hour ago, and it has been raining for well nigh that . . ."

Betsy broke off her scolding and hurried forward after her first good look at her mistress as the latter turned from shutting the parlor door. "What has happened, my lady? You're pale as a ghost and all wet—is that a *tear* in your pelisse?" The maid was drawing Serena over to the fireplace as she spoke, but the other shook off the hand on her arm and stopped in the middle of the room.

"Did you say the carriage was ready, Betsy? Then we should be on our way at once."

"Let it wait. Another ten minutes won't make a particle of difference one way or t'other. You come over here to the fire and get warm while I try to dry off this bonnet some." She pulled her mistress toward the fireplace and pushed her gently onto the settle, untying the wet satin ribbons of a once charming black velvet bonnet. Still clucking like a mother hen, she then drew off damp kid gloves from the unresisting figure slumping in an uncharacteristic posture of fatigue. With one eye on her silent mistress she used her own soft woolen shawl to blot up some of the moisture on those articles before placing them on the stone hearth to absorb all the heat possible.

"Where did you go, my lady? What happened out there to make you look like this?"

By the time Serena had finished relating the bald facts of the incident in the hills, Betsy's jaw was gaping open, but she soon found words to express her extreme disapprobation.

"Mother of mercy, no wonder you look like something that could haunt a house! Are you touched in your noggin to be hanging over a cliff in the middle of nowhere? You might have fallen to your death, and all for the sake of a ramshackle brat with no more sense than to go where he well knew he shouldn't!"

"You may cease your high flights, Betsy. I was never in the slightest danger of falling—"

"You were on the same cliff that had crumbled under the boy, weren't you?"

"That's quite enough, Betsy," Serena said wearily. "As you may plainly see, I took no harm at all except that I am going to be stiff in all my joints tomorrow, plus a few aching ribs, thanks to his lordship's strong left arm." Ignoring the indignant sniff of her handmaiden, she changed the subject, infusing an artificial brightness into her tones. "Now, I think we must be on our way if we are to reach Chawnton before dark. Thank you for drying my things. I am perfectly warm again, but mind you don't forget the hot bricks."

Another sniff warned Serena that she had offended Betsy by even such a slight implication that the girl might be derelict in one of her duties, but she found it politic to ignore this also. Instead she concentrated on rising to her feet, and could not prevent a tiny hiss of pain escaping her lips as her prediction of future stiffness became a reality.

The maid sprang to her assistance, lending a hand until her mistress was safely on her feet. One glance at her pursed lips and Serena said sharply, "If you *dare* to utter even one syllable of an 'I told you so,' Betsy, I warn you it will be the last syllable you utter in my service, and I won't give you a character either!"

This dire threat had the effect of jolting a reluctant giggle from the young girl, and the two left the inn in perfect charity with each other.

They arrived at Chawnton in the deepening twilight of a rainy winter day. Scattered lights shining from within and lighted torches set around the entrance portico welcomed the travelers. For the first time Serena experienced a thrill of pleasure at this homecoming. Her lips curved into a smile as she recognized the white-haired man who came forward at a decorous pace to open the carriage door.

"Richford, how good to see you again."

The butler beamed paternally. "It's good to see you too, Miss Serena—my lady, I should say. Welcome home."

" 'Miss Serena' will do nicely while I'm here, Richford. And don't look so disapproving. Why should you not call me by the same name as always? I am the same person."

"Are you, ma'am?"

Serena glanced quickly into faded but wise old eyes and away again as the butler handed her down onto the flagstones under the canopy. She had always suspected Richford knew her better than her parents did, and it seemed some things remained unchanged. She hurried into speech. "We are later than expected owing to an accident to the carriage. Has the family dined?"

"Not yet, my lady. Mrs. Boynton told the kitchen to put supper back an hour. She is awaiting you in the family parlor."

Serena abandoned her hope of a few minutes in which to remove the worst of the travel stains and moved her hand to cover the tear in her pelisse. "Very well, Richford. Ah, here is Mrs. Quinton." She kept a smile on her lips during the housekeeper's welcoming speech and then presented Betsy before saying with yet another smile directed impartially at both old retainers, "I know I may safely leave the arrangements for my servants in your capable hands. I'll just go on upstairs to the parlor."

It was a good try, but she should have known better than to transgress on Richford's sense of fitness. "Naturally I shall announce you, my lady," he declared, drawing himself up to his full height, which brought the top of his head to Serena's chin. "If you will be so good as to follow me."

She remained decently cowed until they were in the upper hall, when she ventured to inquire for her mother's health.

"Mrs. Boynton is about the same, my lady."

Serena was puzzling as to whether this euphemism might include the vaporish fits and spells in her bed that her mother had indulged in when last she was at home, and was only dimly aware of Richford's sonorous tones, startling in one of his unimpressive stature, proclaiming:

"The Countess of Whitlaw."

She became conscious of the piano music when it ceased abruptly, but she didn't glance toward the pianoforte just yet. Her fascinated gaze was fixed on the woman who sprang up from a daybed with a glad cry. Heavens, her fragile mother must have put on twenty pounds since she had last been home for her father's funeral two years ago.

"Serena, my dearest girl!"

Still bemused, Serena composed her features into a wide smile and hurried across the room under the benevolent eye of the butler to accept the beringed hands held out to her. She bent down to kiss a lightly powdered and scented cheek. "You are looking very blooming, Mama."

"I wish I could return the compliment," said Mrs. Boynton, holding her tall daughter at arm's length. "You look positively haggard, Serena, and why are you still rigged out in all that black? Your mourning period ended in November!"

Serena shrugged, stepping away from her mother to divest herself of hat, gloves, and pelisse, which she tossed onto the nearest sofa without a glance. "There is plenty of wear left in these clothes. What does it signify what colors I wear?"

"You look like a gaunt crow, that's what it signifies, not to mention giving the appearance of perpetual mourning like those old peasant women on the Continent, when you are not yet two-and-twenty."

Serena demonstrated her disinclination to pursue this subject by turning to greet the girl who had approached silently from the corner where she had been playing the pianoforte. The rigid smile on her lips softened as she examined the pleasing person of her young sister.

"Verity, my dear, I declare you have grown up since I was last here, though you certainly haven't grown bigger," she added with a chuckle, having embraced her delicately fashioned sister. "No one would ever believe we were related. You've turned into a very pretty girl, hasn't she, Mama?"

"Mama says I'll never be beautiful like you, but that I should do very well amongst the common run of females."

Reading the humor in her sister's large blue-green eyes, Serena chuckled again. "Mama confuses real beauty of person, which I cannot claim, with standing out in a crowd, which, without undue immodesty, I believe I may honestly claim to do. It's not every day one comes across a six-foot female with flaming red hair."

"Serena, I *beg* that you will not go around claiming to be six feet tall," protested Mrs. Boynton. "In the first place, it is not true, but more important, you will give people a very odd notion of your personality."

"Do you fear people might think me a braggart, Mama?" Serena asked with a studied innocence that did not fool her parent.

"I cannot think that marriage has had an inhibiting effect on that unfortunate tendency to ill-timed levity that I have often deplored in you, daughter."

"Perhaps not a lasting effect, at least," agreed Serena with a strange little smile.

"Nor should your hair be described as 'flaming red,' a very unrefined color," continued Mrs. Boynton, returning to her complaint. "I am happy to say that none of my children possess that dreadful carroty shade that is commonly meant by red hair. Verity and Peregrine are strawberry blonds, and your hair is a beautiful deep russet shade that is extremely rare."

"I'd gladly trade my strawberry color and its accompanying curse of freckles for your golden-blond hair and perfect complexion, Mama," said Verity with the tactful touch Serena knew she lacked in dealing with their parent.

"Well, it is sadly faded by now," sighed Mrs. Boynton, "but I do believe I may assert without fear of contradiction that mine was truly golden when I was a girl. Your father was wont to liken my hair to new-minted guineas. And you would not still have those disfiguring freckles," she added, addressing her younger daughter, "if you were more regular in your use of asses' milk."

"I think Verity's few freckles are charming. They draw attention to the exquisite shape of her nose."

The younger girl blushed and directed a grateful smile to her sister. "I am so sorry that we were unable to come to you at the time of your husband's death, Serena," she said quietly, "but Mama was feeling too poorly just then to undertake the journey."

"Serena understands that the uncertain state of my health, plus the wretched condition of the roads in winter, made any travel impossible for me, and in any event, I sent Peregrine to represent the family."

"Yes, of course I understood, Mama, and I was grateful for Perry's support. How is he doing at Oxford? I rarely have the pleasure of hearing from him, and such letters as I receive are full of everything other than his studies."

A soft laugh escaped from Verity's throat. "On the evidence of his letters, one would think Perry *had* no studies. But you know, Serena," she went on in a more serious vein, "he never was one to mind his books. You were the only one of us who actually enjoyed our lessons."

"You are talking nonsense, Verity," Mrs. Boynton said. "There is no reason why Peregrine should not go along very well at university. He is not lacking in intellectual capacity; in fact, he possesses more of a quickness of understanding than the commonality of young men."

"It is not his intellectual capabilities we are questioning, Mama, but his application," said Serena.

"I do not see why you should expect Peregrine to apply himself less diligently than other young men in similar circumstances."

"Because up till the present, application has not been Perry's long suit."

"Having lived away from Chawnton for over three years, you are not in the best position to judge your brother's character. He has matured greatly since his father died."

Fortunately, since Serena was already regretting the unintentional challenge to her mother's complacence about her only son's supposed academic prowess, Richford chose that moment to announce dinner.

Conversation at table was dominated by Mrs. Boynton, who kept up a running flow of anecdotal prattle about the residents of the neighborhood Serena had quitted on her marriage. Occasional inquiries and comments from her elder daughter kept her primed throughout dinner. Her younger daughter's contributions were limited to responses to direct questions.

Verity drifted over to the pianoforte when the ladies returned to the parlor after dinner and spent the next two hours absorbed in her music while Mrs. Boynton continued to expound on local affairs. Serena was growing increasingly conscious of her various aches and twinges when her mother released her to her bed at an early hour, citing the need to recover from the discomforts of travel. Pray heaven she remained in ignorance of the extent of those discomforts, Serena reminded herself.

She rose carefully from her chair, trying to conceal alike her gratitude and her physical stiffness. "Is there a horse worth riding in the stables?" she inquired before bidding her family good night.

"Old Jehoshaphat is still there," supplied Verity with a twinkle.

Serena groaned. "An armchair ride at best. Nothing else?"

"Only workhorses and carriage horses. Perry has his mounts with him at the High."

"Verity and I are not fond of riding, so it makes little sense to keep extra hacks around eating their heads off at your brother's expense."

"Then it will have to be Jehoshaphat, if I'm to get any exercise while I am here. Good night, Mama. I'll see you at breakfast, Verity."

The efficient Betsy had done all her unpacking and laid out her nightclothes, Serena saw with relief when she crossed the threshold of her old room. A quick glance about assured her that nothing had been changed in here; it just looked a little shabbier. Someone, most likely Verity, had thoughtfully provided a couple of flow-

ering plants to brighten the room. She made short work
of getting ready for bed, having told Betsy not to wait up
for her, and fell asleep immediately.

On rising early the next morning, she found her arms
were horribly sore and her ribs ached, but no more than
she had expected, and her legs were none the worse for
the unexpected exercise yesterday. Still, it was perhaps
not altogether a bad thing that she would be riding the
placid Jehoshaphat rather than a more lively mount, she
realized, grimacing with the difficulty of struggling into
her riding habit by herself. She decided not to ring for
Betsy. Let the girl sleep a bit longer on her first day in a
strange place.

Betsy found her mistress disinclined for conversation
when she helped her to dress for the day an hour later.
What was even stranger, she submitted meekly to her
handmaiden's scold on the inadvisability of strong exercise following on a physical ordeal such as she had undergone the previous day, advancing only the irresistible
lure of sunshine and the venerable age of the horse in her
own defense.

"Are the servants treating you well, Betsy?" Serena
roused herself from her absent state to inquire before
going downstairs.

"Do not be concerning yourself about me, my lady.
Being dresser to a countess puts me above the salt, so to
speak."

"Is that how you style yourself?" asked her mistress,
amused.

"It wasn't necessary to put anyone's nose out of joint
by being that obvious, ma'am. Every time one of the
others mentioned 'Miss Serena,' I had something to say
about 'the countess' or 'Lady Whitlaw,' that's all."

This time the amusement was tinged with respect. "You
would do well anywhere, I am persuaded, Betsy. You can
read and you write a fair hand, and one never has to tell
you twice how to do something, not to mention that you
have a positive genius for dressing hair. If you watched that
quick tongue of yours more, most likely you could become
a dresser to a real lady of fashion. Would you like that?"

"This position suits me fine, ma'am, and I would not consider I had done my duty if I didn't make a push to stop you from doing foolish things when you take a queer notion into your head, as you must admit you do on occasion."

"I admit no such thing. You were born just plain bossy, that's your trouble."

"And you've got a willful streak in you that can get you into trouble," returned the maid calmly.

"You're incorrigible. I can't think why I put up with your sanctimonious homilies."

"Because you need someone around you who's not afraid to speak the truth to you when you're not in a mood to listen, and you know that."

"Your version of the truth did not necessarily come down from the mountain with the Ten Commandments, Betsy."

Serena flounced out of the room, having had the last word, only because, having seen more dramatic productions than Betsy, she recognized a good exit speech, she decided with a private chuckle as she walked down the stairs to the small dining room.

"Good morning, Verity. That's a pretty dress. That *eau de Nile* hue is very complimentary to your coloring."

"Thank you. You are looking more rested this morning, Serena. Did you go out riding?"

"Yes." There was a pause and Serena looked up to see her sister waiting for amplification. "Verity, why has nothing been done about repairs to the tenant cottages? I rode by them this morning and thought they looked in worse order than when I left Chawnton."

"I . . . I do not know precisely, but I believe that cost is the main problem. I gather the estate was not in good heart when Papa died, and money had to be found this year for Perry's expenses at Oxford."

"Mama's letters are full of how pinch-pursed she is, but then, I have never known her not to be short of funds. But the thing is, Verity, that the earl made a large settlement at the time of our marriage, part of which was earmarked for repairs to the estate."

"Oh. I'm afraid I know nothing of that."

"Of course not, you were a mere child at the time." Serena shook off her serious mood and smiled brilliantly at the sweet face across the table as Richford entered the room bearing dishes of hot eggs and fragrant muffins. When the ladies had helped themselves and accepted steaming cups of coffee, Serena sat back.

"Now that you have become a young lady, tell me, how do you spend your days?"

"There is always something to keep me busy about the house. Mama plans the menus, of course, but I try to relieve her of as many housekeeping details as possible by dealing with the servants for her, seeing that things run smoothly, and arbitrating their quarrels. We do much of the household mending ourselves, and I keep abreast of the tenants' concerns to spare Mama the strain. And I do try to set aside time for practicing my music every day, but that isn't always possible. Naturally Mama likes me to spend time with her. She is very lonely since Papa died, you see, though I must confess I had not realized that they spent very much time together, but I was younger then and must not have noticed."

"I see. And what of wider society? Do you not exchange visits with the neighboring families and attend local assemblies and card parties and other entertainments?"

"On occasion, though quite often Mama finds herself too unwell to chaperone me to such tiring events. The Morrisons still call regularly and the Knightsbridge ladies stop by from time to time, though Mama finds their chatter somewhat tedious, so we do not see as much of them as formerly."

"I see," Serena said again, looking rather intently at her sister.

"And what of you, Serena? It must be dreadfully lonely for you in Hereford since your husband died."

"Oh, no, not in the least. Whitlaw was seldom at home in any case. He was mad for hunting, you know, and was in the habit of joining congenial hunting parties on various estates throughout the season. He was away for weeks at a time."

"Did you never go with him?"

"*I* did not find them congenial parties. The earl and I did not have many friends in common."

"Did you make friends in the neighborhood, then?"

"I fear Whitlaw was not held in particularly high esteem in Hereford, so I did not find myself on visiting terms with the wives of the local gentry. The rector calls frequently, but as he is a prosy bore, I consider his visits in the light of a penitential offering, good for my soul perhaps, but scarcely enjoyable."

"Poor Serena. Then what *do* you do with your time?"

"I ride a lot. I must say for Whitlaw that he was a superb judge of horseflesh. I keep the horses exercised against the time when his heir, a cousin, may decide what to do with the stable. And it was a time-consuming chore to move into the dower house and get the main house in some kind of order for the new earl, though I might have spared my pains, since he has not yet taken up residence. But now I am cozily settled in the dower house, which is a great deal more to my taste than that drafty pile Whitlaw grew up in. The dower house was built less than forty years ago for his grandmother, who everyone assures me was a veritable dragon, but her taste was impeccable, and it is snug and attractively furnished. So do not waste your sympathy on me, my dear; I have no complaints to make. For the last several months my main interest has been in reading and planning an itinerary for my trip."

"Itinerary? What trip is this, Serena?"

"Well, you must remember how I always loved to learn about foreign places when we had our lessons with Miss Eccles. It has always been my wish to travel. I'd like to see the whole world eventually, but initially I will settle for Greece and Rome and Venice. Now that the Corsican monster has been defanged at long last and confined on St. Helena's, it should again be possible to travel in relative safety. I have been reading everything I could lay my hands on about the interesting sites of ancient Greece. In the Whitlaw library there is an English translation of Pausanias' guide to Greece, written in the second century, which I shall take with me."

"But . . . but how can you, a woman, possibly travel
so far? It simply isn't done! People would think you
terribly eccentric, like that Stanhope woman. Mama would
have a spasm—worse than that, it would *kill* her!" Verity
was looking horrified.

"Mama will not approve, but you may take it from me
she will survive. Besides, there is absolutely no reason
for anyone to know or care of my whereabouts. As far as
I am concerned, or Mama, for that matter, the world
may continue to think me buried in rural Hereford. Socially speaking, it is as far removed from the goings-on in
London as Greece is."

Verity continued to look troubled, but the entrance of
Richford again with a message from the kitchen effectively ended the discussion.

Both girls confined their conversation to local subjects
when they walked together about the estate that afternoon, carefully skirting any mention of Serena's pro-
posed odyssey. Verity was sweetly compliant to her sister
with respect to the direction their feet and their conversation took them, but Serena received the distinct impression that she was a bit subdued today. Not that she
had expected bubbling high spirits. Verity had always
been a gentle, quiet child with a yielding nature, and the
current circumstances of her circumscribed life were not
conducive to promoting liveliness. Even so, having duly
taken this into account, she still felt there had been some
slight animation in her sister's manner yesterday that was
missing today. If disapproval of her own unconventional
plans was the cause, then she was sorry for it but had no
intention of conducting her life according to the dictates
of the most hidebound elements of society. Twenty-one
years of conformity was quite long enough. Now that she
had the means to indulge what she considered eminently
reasonable inclinations, she would not be held back by
public censure.

Glancing just then at her sister's firm chin and tightly
compressed lips, Verity sighed and became silent as the
two girls finished their walk side by side but mentally
isolated, each absorbed in her own private thoughts until

one or the other roused herself to make some comment on the passing scene.

It wasn't until after dinner that evening that Mrs. Boynton disclosed the real reason for the urgent summons to her elder daughter. The three women repaired to the family parlor as they had the previous evening, and Verity, as then, seated herself at the pianoforte, instantly becoming lost in the music that Serena now suspected was her consolation, if not her opiate, for the sterility of her days. Her thoughtful glance returned from the figure at the piano to find her mother's blue eyes fixed on her face in a calculating fashion.

"Verity is a sweet child," Serena said.

"She has a sweet nature, but she is no longer a child, and that is the reason a letter would not have accomplished my purpose. It was necessary that you see for yourself that she has grown up. You do not like roundaboutation, Serena, so I'll offer none. I wish you to bring your sister out this spring." Mrs. Boynton had been leaning forward slightly, but now she sat back against the rose-colored cushions of the settee, her eager eyes never leaving her daughter's face.

There was not much to be read on that fair countenance, however. Serena received her mother's demand in unwinking calm. Nor did she reply immediately, and after a prickling pause Mrs. Boynton rushed into speech again.

"Surely you can have no valid objection. Your period of mourning is well over, and by now you must be nigh to expiring from sheer boredom in the wilds of Hereford."

"Is this why you have not pressed me to come home for a visit until recently? Did you hope to see me so thoroughly bored that I'd straightaway agree to your request?"

Mrs. Boynton's eyes fell before her daughter's steady look, but she summoned a hurt expression and protested, "That is scarcely fair. You know you are always welcome in your old home. You might have come at any time without a formal invitation."

"I suppose I might, but in response to your request, I

have in fact three objections. One, Verity is too young at seventeen to be thinking of marriage, so her come-out can easily be put off for a year; two, she is your responsibility, not mine; and three, I have already made plans for the spring that don't include the London social whirl."

"Plans? What plans? Are you thinking of remarrying?"

Serena laughed, but there was more irony than amusement in the sound. "Can you really believe my experience of marriage has been such that I would ever venture into those waters again? No, my plans are to travel, not to marry."

"This whole country has gone travel-mad since the end of the war. It is a lot of foolishness." Mrs. Boynton made a petulant gesture of dismissal with her hand. "To return to the question of marriage; of course you will marry again. What other life is there for a woman? Widowhood is a dismal, unnatural state."

"Is that how you have found it, Mama? Strange, I would have said that you are looking more fit and happy since your release from wifely duties than ever I can remember seeing you."

"You go too far, Serena!" cried Mrs. Boynton, her eyes flashing and her cheeks crimsoning. "I was most sincerely attached to your father."

"Yes, I apologize." There was a trace of weariness in Serena's green eyes. "It is not for me to judge the quality of a marriage. How could I, indeed?"

The bitterness in her daughter's voice caused Mrs. Boynton to forget her grievance for the moment. She leaned forward and said urgently, "Just because you and Whitlaw found you were unsuited, do not make the mistake of condemning all men or the institution of marriage, Serena. There are any number of decent men who would make unexceptionable husbands. If you have made one mistake, well, you will be more discriminating the next time."

"And why, pray, did I make a mistake? You and Papa knew all about Whitlaw. You knew his reputation with drink and women when I did not, yet you *pressed* me to accept his offer."

Mrs. Boynton's hands fluttered in her lap, picking lint from her skirt, and she glanced away briefly before mounting a defense. "Whitlaw convinced your father that he had fallen in love with you. Just because a man has sowed a few wild oats in his youth is no reason to expect he will not settle down and become an exemplary husband."

"Especially if he is rolling in wealth and besotted enough to disgorge a king's ransom to the bride's family to secure their consent."

"There, you have just admitted he was in love with you in the beginning. Why should your father have turned down his suit?"

"Because his character was a byword in the clubs and he did not know the meaning of love—he had a fancy to tame an Amazon, that's all."

"No one forced you to marry, daughter. If you had refused to consider Whitlaw, that would have been the end of it."

"Yes." This time it was the younger woman who looked away. "I was as much to blame as you and Papa. At eighteen I had not yet grown out of foolish romantic notions gleaned from reading too much poetry and too many trashy novels. I didn't know what love was either, but I was most assuredly charmed by Whitlaw's handsome face and dashing manner, and flattered by his determined pursuit and his generosity, as I thought, to my needy family. Oh, yes, I was eager to be convinced that love would follow quickly on the marriage vows. Well, I know better now, so let us not speak any more of remarrying." She brushed back a lock of hair and fixed her parent with a grim stare. "Verity is even younger than I was, and much more gentle and easily hurt. I shudder to think of what would happen to her spirit at the hands of a man like Whitlaw. Keep her home another year before you bring her out."

"Next year may be too late. At least at present I can afford to clothe her for a modest come-out, but the estate may not even be able to stand that charge in a year's time. I was counting on you to provide a house from which to launch her and pay all the other expenses."

"What became of the huge settlement Whitlaw made at the time of our marriage?"

"Your father had more extensive debts than even I knew of. When he died so unexpectedly, his creditors descended on Chawnton like a plague of locusts and hounded me unmercifully. All the money from the settlement and more went to pay old debts. I am not certain there will be anything left when Peregrine comes of age, unless Verity makes a splendid marriage, as you did."

Serena sat in appalled silence for the space of a heartbeat. "You are not going to auction off another daughter to the highest bidder—I won't have it!"

"Then *you* bring her out this year. Once she's settled, I can go to live with my sister Teresa for a spell and lease the estate until Peregrine comes into his majority. Perhaps that way we shall be able to come about." Her piece said, Mrs. Boynton sat back and waited.

A number of conflicting emotions were playing tag in Serena's mind, but surprise was not among them as she sat unmoving, ostensibly watching Verity's talented fingers while mentally reviewing the past few moments. Some part of her intelligence had been anticipating their mother's request since her first sight of her little sister all grown up. She had sniffed out the trap but had not been able to circle it safely. Of course "trap" was too harsh a word; there was no point in overstating the case. Her mother had no legal claim on her finances or personal services; she could still go ahead with her own plans, but it could quite possibly be at the cost of her sister's future happiness. Looking at Verity's dreamy expression as she played the lovely first movement of Beethoven's Sonata No. 14—the one they called the "Moonlight Sonata" —Serena accepted that she could not simply go off and leave this pliant girl to be the victim of her parent's unseemly haste to get her well-married. She'd gladly take Verity traveling with her but knew it would be useless to try to gain her mother's permission.

"Very well, Mama, you win. I'll postpone my own plans and we'll bring Verity out this spring. But," she added, holding up an imperative hand when her mother would have spouted her gratitude, "if I am to bear the cost of this come-out, then I shall insist on having the final approval of her prospective husband." As her mother drew back, hesitating, she repeated, "That is the only condition under which I shall agree. Verity needs a man who will accept her as she is and not try to mold her into a society hostess. Most of all, her husband must not be the kind of man who will set up mistresses and relegate her to an unimportant part of his life. She would wither away under that sort of treatment."

"Your own experience has colored your view of men, daughter. You are still very young and cannot be accounted a mature judge of prospective virtues in a husband."

"You and my father did not demonstrate a noticeable degree of mature judgment in my case. In fact, I do not scruple to say that Whitlaw's generous settlement rendered any other consideration void. If you wish me to assume the financial burden of a come-out, then I must insist that mine be the final choice. Do I have your word on this?"

"He who pays the piper has always called the tune, so I suppose I must abrogate my right as my daughter's guardian," Mrs. Boynton said through tight lips.

"No one, including Verity, need know of our arrangement, but, speaking of arrangements, this discussion may be no more than a hypothetical exercise, since I have an idea it is no easy matter to secure a house in the right part of town for the Season."

"You need have no fears on that head. My friend Lady Silchester has located a suitable house on Beak Street. The price is rather steep but she assures me the furnishings are more than adequate, so we shan't need to bring anything but linens and such articles of our own as we desire to have about us."

"How forehanded of you, Mama. You were very sure I'd agree to your plan," Serena said with a certain dryness that Mrs. Boynton elected to ignore.

"Naturally I had counted on your willingness to help your only sister to establish herself creditably, especially since Whitlaw left you very well-provided-for in his will."

"We may all thank our lucky stars that the very natural reluctance shared by most of mankind to contemplate one's own demise acted strongly in Whitlaw's case, combined with a congenital dislike of the cousin who succeeded him. If he'd had any suspicion that even such a superb rider as he knew himself to be could come a cropper at a water jump, given a sufficient degree of inebriation, he'd have changed that will leaving all his unentailed assets to an unsatisfactory wife. It is at the same time a matter of some considerable satisfaction to me, and a source of guilt, for I certainly was as unsatisfactory a wife as I knew how to be. I assuage the guilt by reminding myself that *someone* had to inherit, and he detested his cousin even more than he did me, since I was only a female, therefore fundamentally insignificant, no matter how irksome."

"You might also remember that it was your father who got him to make that will in your favor before your marriage."

"Oh, I do, though it scarcely compensates for leaving his own estate in such a sad state for you and Perry." Seeing her mother's lips part to defend her late husband, Serena apologized for criticizing her parent, finishing with the cheerful suggestion that they should instead all combine in abusing Whitlaw, who had no one to defend him, and then set about enjoying his wealth.

Mrs. Boynton contrived to look disapproving at this shockingly improper attitude on her daughter's part, but forbore to remonstrate. For one thing, it never did the least good to remonstrate with Serena, who deplored hypocrisy and whose uncomfortable practice it had always been to say exactly what was on her mind in the bosom of her family. Her parent wisely decided to conserve her energy for those moments when it became imperative to prevent her outspoken daughter from carrying over this practice into social situations where her frankness would be ill-received.

3

"It's no use! My hair refuses to behave—look at it sticking out here and hanging limply there—this gown was a mistake, the color is all wrong, and my horrible freckles are standing out like beacons. The kindest thing that will be said of me tonight is that Mrs. Boynton's younger daughter is a nice quiet little thing but rather insipid! Is that a *spot* forming on my chin? Oh, no! That is all that was wanting to turn this evening into a complete disaster." Suddenly the despairing eyes that met Serena's in the mirror were swimming with tears that threatened to spill over.

Lady Whitlaw laid down the hairbrush she had been wielding and stooped swiftly to put her arms around the slim shoulders of the girl sitting on a bench before a dressing table overflowing with salves, lotions, and powders in a half-score of open and covered containers. "Verity, my dear, calm yourself, I beg of you." Serena gave her sister a quick hug before straightening up once more. "Trust me, this is the merest *crise de nerfs*, to be expected before your first big society party, but *not* to be given in to."

There was a playful smile in the emerald eyes that commanded watery blue-green ones, as Serena held her sister's gaze while she methodically disposed of the latter's fears. "First, we have barely started on your hair, which is all shining clean and soft. Betsy will be here in a moment to arrange it, and I promise you she is a wizard at styling hair. Your dress is lovely, as you well know, and that rich jonquil shade, besides flattering your coloring, will stand out in a sea of pale greens, blues, and

pinks. Of a surety there is nothing insipid about that or
about you. It is far better to appear a trifle quiet than to
draw critical attention as a chatterbox. If we are to talk
of insipid, you may pity the really blond girls with their
pale lashes and brows. Your long curling lashes are sufficiently darker than your hair not to require any cosmetic
aid. As for your freckles, though it is a shame to do so,
we can completely hide them with the faintest dusting of
powder across your nose—like so." Serena demonstrated,
and brushed aside her sister's expressed fears that the
wearing of cosmetics would brand her as fast.

"Fustian, my love! It is a far cry from an almost
invisible dusting of powder to a painted hussy. Ah, here
is Betsy," she added as a knock sounded at the door.

Serena gratefully turned the hairbrush over to Betsy
and retired to sit on the corner of her sister's bed to
watch the maid's clever fingers begin sweeping Verity's
silken tresses up to arrange on top of her head in a
Grecian style. She was transported back in time—it seemed
nearly a millennium ago, so much had happened in the
interim—to her own come-out, when she had experienced the same irrational doubts as Verity in anticipation
of her first *ton* party. Of course the nature of her doubts
had been radically different; her concern had not been
that she would fade into the background, either becoming invisible or being considered insipid. On the contrary, she had dreaded becoming too visible by virtue of
her size, and she had formed the uncomfortable habit of
measuring everyone she met, men and women, against
her own stature. She had despaired of finding men tall
enough to partner her on the dance floor without making
them appear ridiculous, and she had shied away from
forming friendships with tiny women whose proximity
would draw attention to her own unfortunate size.

To her amazed disbelief, she had been hailed as an
incomparable, a situation that provided a never-failing
source of private amusement thereafter. Most likely, Verity's fears would prove equally groundless and she would
soon feel more comfortable in society.

The three women had been established in London for

nearly a month. Though Serena had harbored secret qualms about buying a pig in a poke as it were, Lady Silchester's choice of residence to lease had turned out to be more than adequate; if not quite so large as they might have liked for entertaining, at least it was furnished in an innoffensive style they could live with. With no man to act as host, they would not be expected to undertake any very ambitious entertaining, which was one small blessing.

The lion's share of their time since arriving in town had been spent refurbishing their wardrobes. Verity had needed to be completely outfitted in the modest but expensive style considered suitable to girls in their first season. She and Mrs. Boynton spent hours poring over the fashion magazines while Serena organized the London servants hired by Richford and settled the household into a smoothly running routine. By constantly laying stress on her mother's exquisite eye for fashion, Serena had hoped to avoid more than a token share in the tiresome round of visiting modistes, selecting fabrics and designs and, especially, the subsequent hours of tedious fittings necessary to the completion of their orders; but she had reckoned without Mrs. Boynton's tenacity of purpose. Though allowing that black was highly flattering to her elder daughter's coloring, she was adamant that no lingering suggestion of mourning should be associated with her appearance this spring. To keep the peace, Serena had submitted to being measured, fitted, pinned, and prodded under her mother's direction while a wardrobe was assembled that met that lady's stringent standard for what she considered a basic minimum necessary to a lady embarking on a London Season.

Though the painful self-consciousness about her statuesque figure that had tormented her in her teen years had long since given way to a philosophical acceptance of her uniqueness, Serena had never developed much interest in personal fashion. Moreover, she was secretly dismayed at the sudden realization of how many social functions she would be expected to attend if she were to wear all the new clothes now reposing in her wardrobes.

But she had promised, she thought with sinking spirits as she watched Betsy form ringlets to fall from Verity's topknot.

"You are frowning, Serena. Do you not think this style becoming to me?" her sister asked anxiously from her position facing the mirror.

"I was thinking of something else, my pet. I could not be more pleased with that coiffure. Did I not tell you that Betsy was a wizard?" she asked lightly, smiling at the abigail, who was accepting Verity's fervent thanks with a good-natured disclaimer as she finished by pinning a small spray of artificial rosebuds at the base of the topknot. "Mama will be exceedingly pleased with your appearance. Why do you not run along and stun her with your magnificence while Betsy does my hair? I'll be with you both directly."

Four hours later, Serena stood near the flower-studded archway at one end of the long ballroom in the Viscount Silchester's town house in Grosvenor Square, her satisfied glance following her sister's delicate form as she wove between couples in a country dance, the exertion of dancing putting roses in her cheeks. Verity's attack of nerves was long since forgotten in the pleasures of being sought after by a flattering number of partners. She had renewed her childhood acquaintance with Amy and Chloe Silverdale, the two eldest daughters of Lord Silchester, with an exchange of calls during the past weeks, and tonight their brother Andrew had been most accommodating in presenting his friends to her as potential partners. Nothing could have been more fortunate, exulted Serena, for there was no denying that Verity suffered from an afflictive shyness in strange company that she must struggle constantly to subdue. Being eased gradually into a wider circle by the gregarious Silchester brood was just what they had hoped for when Mrs. Boynton and her elder daughter had discussed which invitation to accept for Verity's initial plunge into society.

Serena too had been besieged by gentlemen seeking a dancing partner, but she had laughingly denied herself with the excuse that she was playing duenna tonight. For reasons she did not care to analyze, she had no desire to join the cavorting couples on the crowded dance floor, though she took pleasure in listening to the lilting airs played by a fine group of musicians. Two or three men she had known slightly from the days of her own come-out remained to chat with her after offering polite condolences on her supposed bereavement. She had experienced an unfamiliar awkwardness in their presence. It would seem that, no less than Verity, she must learn—or relearn—how to get along in masculine company. She had been relieved when the men had taken themselves off after a polite interval, though she had been subjected in consequence to a lecture on basic social duties from her surprised mother.

She would be happy to see this evening end. The increasing heat in the ballroom was making her sleepy, which was why she had excused herself a moment ago from the small group of dowagers with whom Mrs. Boynton was exchanging gossip. Perhaps a glass of punch would put a little life back into her. She could slip into the supper room and be back before the music ended.

Serena spun about to put her decision into effect, and crashed into someone heading in the same direction. She put out her hands to steady the small figure that had rocked backward at the impact. "I do beg your pardon. So clumsy of me."

"Not at all. I fear I was not looking where I was going."

The lovely dark girl with the friendly smile was even more diminutive than Verity, and a rueful twinkle crept into Serena's eyes as she confessed, "I feel the veriest monster running you over like that; you are so tiny."

"Not all that small, and I am exceedingly tough, I assure you, ma'am," the other replied, but her smile wavered the next instant when she put her weight on the foot she had been favoring.

"There, I knew I had stepped on your poor toes! Lean your weight on my arm. May I help you to a chair?"

For just a second the girl placed her hand on Serena's arm while she shook her foot vigorously before testing it again. The smile was back as she removed her hand. "No harm done. It just hurt for a second or two. Please, do not look so worried. I don't need to sit. I was on my way to find a cool drink."

"So was I. It is becoming increasingly airless in the ballroom."

"Yes. It has turned into the first real crush of the Season, has it not? Lady Silchester is to be congratulated. My name is Natasha Talbot, by the way—Mrs. Cameron Talbot, to be precise."

Serena responded to the genuine friendliness in the other's smile. "I am Serena Allenby, Lady Whitlaw."

"Lady Whitlaw? I wonder if I may have met your husband?"

Serena could feel her face freeze as she stared into velvety black eyes. Good heavens, could this charming girl have been one of Whitlaw's highborn flirts?

After the tiniest of pauses Mrs. Talbot went on smoothly, "Was he perchance in Brussels last year with the army? I have a vague recollection of being presented to someone of that name." A little wrinkle appeared between her brows. "Or was it Vienna perhaps? My memory of that hectic period is none too accurate, I fear."

Serena had relaxed again under the innocuous flow of words. Her lips curved upward. "I think you must be referring to the fifth earl. My late husband was the fourth Earl of Whitlaw."

"A widow at your age? How terrible for you! I am so very sorry."

Mrs. Talbot's beautiful eyes were full of distress, and Serena hurried into speech to ease the embarrassment of the moment. "No, please, I assure you I am fully recovered. Did I understand that you were in Vienna and Brussels last year? Is your husband a military man?"

"He was until some months before and again after the Congress in Vienna, where he was a very junior member of the British negotiator's staff. He left the army permanently after Waterloo and is now attached to the Foreign Office."

"How very interesting that must be. I must say I envy you your experience of seeing something of Europe despite the wartime conditions. It has been the dream of my life to travel." Serena asked a casual question about Vienna while the waiter in the supper room poured them cups of a tangy red punch. The two young women became engrossed in conversation as they sipped their drinks, until suddenly Serena stopped short, her eyes widening.

"Oh, dear me, how long would you say the music has been finished, Mrs. Talbot? I was so interested in your description of Brussels that I forgot that I am here as a chaperone of sorts. It is a new role for me. My mother is bringing out my sister this spring, and I have promised to take over some of the duties of chaperoning Verity, since Mama's health is not robust. Will you come and meet them?"

"I'd be delighted, and I hope you will call upon me in Portman Square and allow me to show off the new joy in my life, our son, Justin."

Serena smiled in sympathy with the happy pride in her new friend's face when she spoke of her child, and promptly accepted the impulsive invitation as she steered Mrs. Talbot over to the corner of the ballroom where her mother and Verity were seated.

Within a fortnight of their accidental and quite irregular first meeting, the two young women were fast friends. They discovered they shared a certain similarity of mental qualities and aptitudes. Each exhibited a lively intellectual curiosity and a thirst for knowledge beyond the ordinary boundaries of feminine interests. Both tended to become irritated, even mildly outraged by the long-standing limits society set for female education and practical pursuits, and neither was of a temperament that encouraged automatic conformity with the accepted standards of feminine behavior if such compliance ignored mitigating circumstances or refused to recognize the need for specific and individual exceptions.

Their tastes and personalities were not especially alike, though both might be described as rather frank in manner and speech by those ladies more inclined toward ceremony and circumspection. Natasha's impulsivity sprang from a joyous open nature that bubbled forth in her dealings with others. Serena's frankness, in contrast, might have struck some critical ears as being the result of a desire to flout conventional standards, though opinion was divided as to whether she simply disdained the accepted forms or chose this route to enhance a reputation as an original.

In short order the two were spending a significant portion of the daylight hours together. Natasha confessed that she was missing the company of her husband's aunt, who had gone to Scotland for the summer, and Serena was delighted to have an excuse to avoid as many of the shopping excursions her relatives indulged in as was possible without giving offense. Serena had been intrigued to learn that her new friend was a trained ballet dancer who still maintained a schedule of daily exercise and practice. She had been regretting increasingly the loss of her daily riding since leaving Hereford and eagerly accepted Natasha's diffident offer to plan a program of stretching exercises for her.

Three mornings a week found her joining Natasha in a regimen of exercises for every part of the body that seemed odd and quite difficult at first, but Serena was nothing if not persistent, and within a fortnight she was feeling the benefit of increased suppleness and mobility. Her relatives considered that they had benefited too by a decrease in the restlessness that frequently attacked Serena when confined between four walls and forced into narrow patterns of social intercourse. Mrs. Boynton was never entirely free of a nagging expectation that her elder daughter might utter some blighting comment in company that would set up people's backs, but she was quick to note and approve a relaxation in Serena's manner since her association with young Mrs. Talbot had begun.

One morning after they had completed a rigorous routine of stretching movements, Serena flung herself into a capacious chair to cool down her heated body while Natasha practiced her dancing to piano music played by an emaciated-looking lady of uncertain years and effacing manners. She had appeared one day in answer to the advertisement Miss Cameron, who had been used to playing for her niece's practice, had inserted in the papers prior to leaving for Scotland. The accompanist called herself Miss Tottenham, which both girls took leave to doubt, and Natasha confessed that she had never succeeded in drawing more than fragmented sentences from her in the weeks she had been coming to Portman Square.

"She always looks starving to me, poor thing, so I've taken to stuffing her with food after the sessions," she had whispered to her friend before introducing her to Miss Tottenham on that first morning in the large ground-floor room that had been cleared of carpets and most furnishings. "At least now I am satisfied she has some good food inside her three times a week, though it means I have to consume more than I wish myself after exercising."

Serena sat back contentedly, her eyes following the whirling movements of the ballerina as she flashed around the room in a series of incredibly swift pirouettes. She had been astounded initially at the sheer artistry and level of skill displayed by her friend. It had even crossed her mind to wonder whether Mr. Cameron Talbot of the Foreign Office might have found his bride in a *corps de ballet*—something she would certainly have to conceal from her mother if this budding friendship were to continue to flourish without opposition—and had been profoundly relieved to learn about Natasha's Russian grandmother who had taught her to dance. Surely two generations was sufficiently long to erase the stigma of having a professional dancer in the family.

Today Miss Tottenham declined all offers of sustenance, explaining that she must rush to an interview with the parent of a prospective pupil. Both ladies wished her success before Dawson, the Talbots' butler, who had just brought refreshments into the improvised studio, showed the fluttery pianist out.

The women fell on the tea thankfully, and Serena helped herself to a slab of lemon pound cake, refused by Natasha. "Will you be at the Willoughbys' musicale Thursday evening?" she asked between delicious mouthfuls.

"No, Cam has a dinner meeting that night. Charles offered to escort me to the musicale, and if the program had been more appealing I might have been tempted, but I don't really enjoy doing the social rounds without Cam."

"Who is Charles?"

"Charles Talbot, Cam's cousin. He and I are great friends, but the cousins merely tolerate one another, though I am encouraged to think there has been a slight thawing between them of late."

"Is your husband jealous of your friendship with his cousin?" asked Serena idly. The enormity of her *bêtise* hit her at once and she jerked upright. "Please forget I said that. My mother has spent a lifetime trying to get me to curb my unruly tongue."

"You must be a severe trial to her." Natasha's slightly slanted dark eyes danced with amusement, belying her prim words. "It was my fault in any case. My comment invited speculation. Cam and Charles are only a year or two apart in age, but they have never gotten along together from boyhood, though any jealousy is all on Charles's side. It has nothing to do with me—well very little," she amended, looking a trifle conscious and thereby giving rise to additional speculation on her friend's part. "I have been trying to get each to appreciate the good qualities of the other since I met them, but it is slow work to undo the mischief of a lifetime."

"My husband said he and the cousin who is his heir cordially detested one another."

"Are you acquainted with the new earl?"

"No. To my knowledge, he has not deigned to shed the light of his presence on Whitlaw House since ascending to the honors." She shrugged dismissal. "I have been looking forward to making the acquaintance of Mr. Talbot, though."

Serena had previously noted that any mention of her husband brought a glowing look to Natasha's face, as it did now. "Oh, yes. It is the merest piece of bad timing that we have not chanced to meet of an evening when Cam was with me, but as I said, I do not go often into society without him."

"Which practice makes you a rare bird indeed." Serena grinned slyly, enjoying the slight blush mantling her friend's cheeks.

Natasha's eyes were serious as they studied the lovely calm countenance across from her. "Yes," she said, hesitating briefly before plunging, "I have felt a strange constraint about talking about Cam or my marriage to you."

"Have you? Why?"

"Because of your own situation. I would not wound you for the world, Serena, and it seems to be parading my own happiness to be forever prattling on about Cam and Justin."

Serena reacted to the other's distress to blurt out, "Please do not be concerned for my supposed grief because I assure you I feel none. Mine was not a love match, and I feel nothing save the profoundest relief to be out of it. No, that is not quite the whole truth. I also feel very grateful to Whitlaw for leaving me the bulk of his fortune, even though he would not have done so had he had the slightest premonition of an untimely death. I plan to enjoy myself mightily while spending his money," she finished defiantly.

Mrs. Boynton had looked shocked at a similar expression of such unbecoming sentiments. In contrast, Natasha's countenance reflected a concerned sympathy. "He must have hurt you deeply."

For a charged instant innate reticence contended with a newborn need to confide; then Serena lifted empty green eyes to her friend's face. "I disappointed him on our wedding night, and before ever I knew how it happened, the store of good feeling between us—pitifully small, as it turned out—had disintegrated in a puff of smoke."

"Many marriages get off to a bad start in that department, mine included. It is surely not to be wondered at in view of the way young girls are raised to guard their virtue and deny their feelings. It is entirely up to the husband to . . . to initiate his bride gently if he wishes her to share the pleasures of the marriage bed."

"Share?"

"Yes, *share*. You must not think all men are such monsters of selfishness as your husband appears to have been."

"And yet he was notorious for the number of mistresses he kept. These women must have enjoyed . . . I fear there must be some lack in me."

Natasha, reading the self-doubt in Serena's eyes, knew a moment of furious rage against the dead Lord Whitlaw, but she swallowed her bile, merely saying tartly, "A professional mistress, if I may use the term, is a far cry from an inexperienced bride, and she is well-rewarded for pandering to a man's conceit of himself as a great lover."

"But there are some women who are naturally cold and incapable of that sort of emotion, are there not?"

"Certainly, and some men too, I warrant. However, I'd be willing to wager my grandmother's jewels that you are not among their number, though I make no doubt your abominable husband accused you of it." The startled flash in green eyes told her she had guessed accurately, and she went on with gentle urgency, "Serena, there is no experience in the world so wonderful as the expression of physical love between a man and woman who are totally committed to one another."

"I shall have to take your word for that," Serena said with a forced gaiety. "As for myself, however, I shall pin my hopes of happiness on freedom to travel and witness the other wonders of the world."

Natasha subsided in the face of the widow's obvious desire to end the conversation, but a new element of concern was added to her feelings for this bright and ostensibly contented new friend.

4

Thanks to a canceled appointment a few days later, Serena, finding herself with a free afternoon, decided on the spur of the moment to call at Portman Square for a visit with Natasha.

Dawson greeted her with the smile he reserved for privileged visitors.

"Good afternoon, Dawson. Is Mrs. Talbot in?"

"Yes, my lady; she is in the small front room upstairs."

Spotting the polishing rag he was trying to conceal behind his back, Serena gestured with her hand and apologized. "I've interrupted your silver polishing, Dawson. Never mind announcing me, I'll just run on upstairs."

"Very good, ma'am."

She tapped on the door and opened it. Natasha's head spun around from where she sat at a small table desk. Her lips smiled a greeting, but Serena thought she had detected a flash of disappointment, quickly masked. "If I've come at an inconvenient time, I'll go away again directly," she promised with one hand still on the door handle.

Natasha chuckled. "No, no, do not be so foolish. It is not at all inconvenient. You know I am always pleased to see you. It is just that I received a letter from Peter yesterday announcing his arrival today and I thought it might be he."

"And Peter is . . . ?"

"My brother, of course. Surely I told you about him?"

"Yes, but not by name, and of course this is an inconvenient moment for me to turn up. I'll leave now and come back tomorrow."

"You'll do nothing of the sort." Natasha had crossed the room to her friend and now she literally pulled the larger girl away from the door, pushing her firmly onto a chair. She popped down into the corner of a sofa covered in a crimson brocaded fabric that made a dramatic background for her dark coloring and white muslin gown. "My nature is so impatient that I've been driving myself distracted imagining all sorts of disasters that might have happened on the road to delay him. I've even been tempted to wake up Justin to keep me company, except that Nurse is such a martinet about his nap time she terrifies me. Instead, you shall tell me that my fears are foolish and the hours will pass."

"Certainly. Consider it all said. I believe you once mentioned that your brother is a military man. Does he make a long visit?"

"Peter used to be in the military," Natasha said, "and yes, Cam and I are hoping he'll be fixed here with us through the Season at least. He and Cam were friends in the army, you know. It was through Peter that we met. After Napoleon's first abdication, two years ago, Cam sold out, and Peter, who was going to join the campaign in America, asked him to keep a sort of unofficial guardian's eye on me during my come-out."

"I'd say he exceeded your brother's commission."

"Actually, no," Natasha said with the flashing smile that lit up her face. "Peter admitted much later when Cam and I were already married that that was exactly what he had had in mind all along."

"A matchmaker, in fact, and a highly successful one. Is he still himself a bachelor?"

"Yes, and it is more than time that he settled down and set up his nursery. Peter was wounded in the American war and his complete recovery has been slower than one could wish."

"Wounded? Oh, dear, we had better keep him away from Verity in that case. She has an absurdly tender heart, with a penchant for tragic heroes, and he must be far too old for her."

"There is nothing tragic about Peter. He—"

The man who had run silently up the stairs stopped precipitately, his hand on the handle of the slightly open door that had permitted undistorted passage of the feminine voices within. One voice belonged to his sister. The other, with its cool attractive cadence, was also familiar, though he had heard it but once before. A brief look of intense satisfaction crossed Lord Phillips' countenance and was gone. He glanced into the pier glass over the hall table, made an infinitesimal adjustment to his snowy cravat, slapped at a speck of mud on his top boots with the gloves in his hand, and entered the room on a brisk knock.

"Peter!" The petite brunette flew across the room with a glad cry and hurled herself into her brother's arms.

Lord Phillips hugged her enthusiastically, then swúng her off her feet in a circle. "Hallo, baggage, how are you?" Over his sister's head, amused blue eyes met surprised green ones.

"Put me down, you bully," demanded Natasha, beating on his chest ineffectually. "Serena will think you a barbarian."

"Not at all." The gorgeous redhead in the leaf-green walking dress that exploited her eyes and her stunning figure rose to her feet in a graceful motion, gathering up gloves and reticule. "I am happy to see the use of your arm has been entirely restored, Lord Phillips," she added, walking toward the couple near the door.

"Not entirely, ma'am. I still cannot lift much weight with it, but of course Tasha weighs a feather."

Quick comprehension, indignation, and unwilling humor flashed in turn across the lady's features, but she bit her lip to repress the last.

Natasha, sliding out of her brother's loosened grip, looked from his amused face to her friend's wary one. "You two *know* one another? How? When? Why did you not say so?" she demanded of the silent woman.

"You never mentioned your brother's full name, my dear. In any case, we are not acquainted, not really, having met but once, and that by accident."

"And I am at an even graver disadvantage, Miss . . .

Serena, is it? not having deigned to reveal her name at our first meeting."

Natasha was still glancing from one to the other, intrigued by something unusual in the air, but now she took over. "Lady Whitlaw, may I present my brother, Lord Phillips?"

Lady Whitlaw! Peter's eyes flew to the woman's hands as he bowed low. A muscle twitched in his cheek when he raised burning blue eyes to the face that had haunted his dreams for the past six weeks. Of course she had worn gloves during their first encounter, but it had never occurred to him that she might be married. "Your servant, Lady Whitlaw," he said in tones from which all trace of amusement had vanished.

"How do you do, Lord Phillips? May I wish you a pleasant visit with your sister? And now, Natasha, I am going to run away so you may enjoy a comfortable coze with your brother," she added, turning toward the doorway in the face of Natasha's mumbled protest.

Peter reached it first and bowed her through it in his most formal manner. She nodded in thanks, flicking him a quick curious glance before running lightly down the stairs.

"Well, I must say!" Hands on hips, Natasha challenged her frowning brother as he shut the door to the small sitting room.

"So must I. How did you meet Lady Whitlaw?"

"You first, please, since, as I apprehend, you met her first. I have known Serena for less than a month."

Peter rapidly sketched the events of the rescue in the Cotswolds. "And she refused my request to know her identity then with the same high-handed coolness with which she took her leave just now," he finished. "Your turn: tell."

When his sister had related the circumstances of her meeting with Serena, he said dryly, "You were honored. At least she told you her name. Have you met her husband?"

"She's a widow."

Natasha was watching her brother closely but she could

detect no change in his bland expression on receiving her answer. If he hoped a patent lack of response would be construed as a corresponding lack of interest, however, he did not know his sister as well as he thought. Natasha had been well-alerted by a crackling in the atmosphere a moment ago, but she was not so simple as to expect to gain any knowledge of her brother's feelings by direct questioning. Consequently she began to talk of family matters, and her friend's name was not mentioned between them again that day.

Lord Phillips settled comfortably into his sister's household, got reacquainted with his godchild, and began to ease himself into a town routine. He spent as much time with his brother-in-law as Cam's work permitted, and renewed contact with a number of former comrades from his days in the military. Natasha made occasional glancing references to her friend Lady Whitlaw and her family, but he did not reward her efforts by expressing any interest in the lady.

To himself Peter acknowledged a high degree of interest, but unlike his sister, he possessed a cool nature and never made the mistake of rushing his fences. Patience and planning had served him well in his military career and he was prepared to apply those same qualities to the present campaign, though "campaign" was too definite a word at the moment. Suffice it to say that he was willing to await normal development of a closer acquaintance with the lovely lady, given the stroke of good fortune that was her friendship with his sister. He made no effort to call on her, and when, a sennight into his visit, he escorted Natasha to an evening party at which she expected to see Lady Whitlaw, he let more than half the evening go by before approaching the beautiful Amazon. When Natasha headed in Lady Whitlaw's direction immediately on spotting her soon after their arrival, he excused himself to speak to a friend.

Thanks to the lady's superior height, he was able to keep close tabs on her activities throughout the early part of the evening while appearing to be completely absorbed in his own conversations. Men sought her out,

which, given her obvious assets, was hardly surprising.
After nearly nine years in the army and a recuperative
year spent mostly in the country, his own acquaintance in
London was not great, but two hours of observation
showed him that her court was weighted heavily in favor
of men whose dress and bearing proclaimed them men of
the town. He wondered if all that daunting aloofness she
had showed him was deceptive or more pointed against
him personally than he had first imagined, until he made
the additional observation that Lady Whitlaw seemed to
dismiss her admirers with what he could only call admirable dispatch.

"An impregnable fortress?" he murmured to himself.
"Now, why might that be? Unless I am being overhasty
in drawing conclusions on slender evidence."

The young girl with the red-gold hair whom Lady
Whitlaw appeared to be shepherding between groups of
young people occasionally, and whom she did *not* present
to most of her admirers, must be the sister. She looked a
pretty little thing, though at this distance he could see no
family resemblance. What had Lady Whitlaw called her?
Ah, he had it—Verity. Serena and Verity, he thought
with an inward smile for the hopes of unknown parents.

Having spied out the lay of the land, Lord Phillips
arranged to catch Serena unaware as she exited from the
supper room alone for once. He hailed her jovially, as
though accidentally finding himself in her path. "Ah, the
charming Lady Whitlaw. My luck is indeed in tonight.
How do you do, ma'am?"

Serena blinked long lashes at the man making her an
elegant bow. Her eyes narrowed a trifle but she replied
civilly, "How do you do, Lord Phillips? I trust you are
enjoying your stay in London?"

"I generally contrive to enjoy myself wherever I may be,
ma'am, but I thank you for your kind solicitude on my behalf." She was examining his features rather intently, and
he said with some amusement, "Does that hard stare mean
you are questioning my relationship to Tasha, ma'am?"

"Well, you certainly don't look at all like her," Serena
answered frankly.

"Is it not interesting how our minds run along the same channels, Lady Whitlaw? I was thinking earlier that there was little family resemblance between you and your sister. By the way, if we made it clear that my . . . ah . . . deformity was not acquired during the heroic victory at Waterloo but in a losing cause in Louisiana, do you feel it would be safe to introduce me to Verity? Given your involvement with my family, it could prove awkward to pretend I don't exist."

"So you heard that, did you?" In no way disconcerted, Serena continued to survey him critically. "Are you playing on my sympathies now?"

"No, ma'am, for I don't believe you have any," he replied promptly.

"Quite right, so you may discontinue the use of the word 'deformity.' No one would believe you anyway. That faint scar on your cheek gives you a slightly rakish air, but Verity is afraid of rakes, so I shan't object to introducing you if you wish it."

"I do indeed wish it," he assured her, and was pleased to see that his assumed fervor caused her a momentary pang of doubt.

In the event, not the most captious critic could have faulted Lord Phillips' demeanor toward Verity Boynton. His manners and conversation were everything that was exemplary toward a girl in her first Season, and his charming smile quite won Verity's heart.

"Lord Phillips is as pleasant and friendly as Mrs. Talbot, do you not agree, Serena?" she demanded eagerly when her sister came into her bedchamber to bid her good night a few hours later. "I liked him so much."

"He has a most attractive smile," Serena conceded.

"Oh, most definitely. It lights up his face just as Mrs. Talbot's does," agreed Verity, innocently voicing the reluctant observation her sister had made earlier, "but that is the least of it. He is so completely the gentleman, as kind and attentive as if an insignificant girl with little conversation were the most fascinating female in the room."

"You do yourself a disservice, my dear. If Lord Phillips was attentive and seemed pleased with your com-

pany, it was because your company was pleasing to him,"
argued Serena, sinking a desire to brand the glib Lord
Phillips an experienced ladies' man in the stronger need
to reassure her timid sister of her social grace. Verity's
grateful smile was her reward, but Serena went to bed
that night with a deal to think about.

She suspected that Lord Phillips had gone out of his
way to charm Verity as payment for her own lack of
response to his initial attempt to strike up an acquaintance after the incident in the Cotswolds, though she
would be hard put to muster any evidence in support of
this ungenerous theory. He certainly hadn't wasted any
charm on her in their last two meetings, nor sought her
out since learning her identity. Though too wary to take
any of his actions at face value, she could not really
suspect Natasha's brother of willingly hurting Verity.
Watchful waiting would be her posture in future, she
resolved before abandoning thought for sleep.

Serena had ample opportunity to put her vigilant policy into effect over the next fortnight, for they met Lord
Phillips at a half-dozen social events and he never failed
to pay his respects to the Boynton ladies. With Verity he
was flatteringly attentive in a gently playful fashion. While
Serena could not with justification accuse him of trying
to get up a flirtation with her sister, she could not help
but note that he had a convincing line in artful compliments guaranteed to please a shy young girl still uncertain of her own attractions. If Verity happened to be
without a partner at a dance where Lord Phillips was
present, he seemed to materialize at her side to lead her
onto the dance floor. His impressive height and breadth
of shoulder were allied to a natural grace that made him
a most desirable partner. Even the inexperienced girl was
pleasantly aware that to be so often distinguished by the
eligible Lord Phillips added greatly to her consequence,
and she could not help but preen herself a little to her
sister in private. Serena smiled in sympathy and held her
tongue, realizing she had no legitimate cause for complaint as long as Verity did not tumble into love with the
baron.

It would have been a relief to know that her sister merely considered him in the light of an agreeable family friend, but since she could not persuade herself that this was the case, continuing caution on her part was indicated. She was careful not to speak a word against the man, but maintained a steady air of absentmindedness when his name came up that must demonstrate that he was not someone she considered of prime importance in their lives.

Mrs. Boynton was quite as captivated by Mrs. Talbot's charming brother as Verity. His friendly manner toward her was tinged with a pleasing deference and an efficient eye to her comfort when they met. No less than her elder daughter was she monitoring Lord Phillips' progress into their circle, but with the opposite intention of seeing her younger daughter well-established as his wife.

"Though not a brilliant match like Whitlaw, Lord Phillips would be a creditable catch for Verity, do not you agree, Serena?" she asked one evening while they were waiting for Verity to join them before dinner.

Knowing her mother of old, Serena had avoided the mere mention of Lord Phillips in her hearing as a matter of course, but she had not expected this conversation quite so early in the acquaintance. "Lord Phillips is too old and too worldly for Verity, Mama," she said flatly, but Mrs. Boynton was not to be put off so easily.

"Nonsense, daughter, he has not yet reached his thirtieth birthday, according to his sister. As for worldly, what is wrong with that, pray? Would you prefer to see your sister married to a callow youth with no experience of the world, like Andrew Silverdale, who has no conversation and follows Verity around like a puppy dog?"

"Infinitely. From what I have seen of him, Andrew Silverdale is a youth of good sense and fixed principles. He won't always be callow and he will one day be a viscount with a handsome property."

"Silchester is scarcely fifty years of age, and that family is famed for its longevity. Lord Phillips is already in possession of a title and fortune. His sister was telling me about their home in Devon. I gather it is quite a fair-sized property.''

Serena writhed in silent mortification at the thought of her mother pumping Natasha about her brother's financial circumstances, but she knew better than to make any protest, merely saying with finality, "There is no point to this discussion in any case, Mama, since Lord Phillips' behavior toward Verity has not been such as to give rise to speculation about his intentions.''

Her mother would have argued, but Verity's footsteps in the hall put an abrupt end to the conversation.

Serena knew she was on safe ground, for despite her mother's wishful thinking, Lord Phillips' attentions to Verity, while flattering, were not so far of an exclusive nature. She could have told her parent that he was too downy a bird to be easily caught, but it would have been breath wasted; Mrs. Boynton had ever a weakness for believing what she wished to believe. Marriage had cured any tendency in that direction for her, but with some people, her mother among them, hope always seemed to triumph over the lessons of experience. She could only trust that Mrs. Boynton would have the delicacy to refrain from putting ideas of conquest into Verity's head.

It would be a disastrous match on all counts. Had their interests and temperaments been more compatible, the age difference would not have posed an insurmountable barrier to a happy union, but such was not the case. While she loved her sister dearly, there was no denying that Verity's interests were limited to the domestic scene and her music. No doubt there were successful marriages where men of broad-ranging experience were content with women who catered to their creature comforts and remained in their own feminine sphere otherwise, but her exposure to Lord Phillips' temperament warned that he was not such a man.

All her family knew of him was his polished address and accommodating manners rendered more agreeable by virtue of an admittedly charming smile that turned ordinary good looks into something that lingered in one's memory. Lord Phillips showed a different face to Serena, however. Verity's gentlemanly admirer took a perverse delight in taunting Verity's sister by uttering outrageous remarks calculated to provoke her temper or, at the very least, elicit unmannerly retorts. Try as she would to ignore his baiting, she rose to it more often than she cared to admit. It was a severe trial to her disposition to know her reactions contributed to his malicious enjoyment. Such a man would never do for her young sister. Verity, though sweet-natured and loving, was highly strung and her feelings were easily wounded. She would require a constant supply of approval and support from the man she married. Clearly the capricious Lord Phillips was not the man to supply it.

Not only at home was Serena not permitted to forget the existence of the man who had unexpectedly become a thorn in her flesh. With Natasha too was she compelled to dissemble her feelings, for Natasha was prodigiously fond of her brother and Serena had no wish to hurt her friend by expressing any derogatory opinions of Lord Phillips. If she ever did develop any social delicacy or tact, she thought grimly, she would have Lord Phillips to thank for the accomplishment. No doubt it was a most salutary discipline for someone of her rash disposition to be required to restrain her unruly tongue, but she could not be expected to be grateful to the person responsible for her discomfort.

Serena was visiting with Natasha and Justin one afternoon when a crisis in the kitchen required Mrs. Talbot's intervention.

"Will you excuse me, please, Serena, while I see what has happened? I'll ring for Nurse to take Justin back to the nursery."

"Indeed you will not. Justin will stay and play with Aunt Serena, won't you, my lamb?" crooned Serena, taking the chortling baby from his mother.

"Well, if you are sure you do not mind, I'll be back shortly," promised Natasha.

At nine months, Justin Talbot was a lovable but as yet uncoordinated bundle of energy, with his mother's dark hair and, according to Natasha, his father's green eyes.

He possessed unbounded curiosity and a nearly toothless smile that reduced Serena to jelly when he cannily directed it at her. His latest achievement was a vigorous crawling motion that had evolved from earlier efforts that had resembled swimming on land. Tamely sitting on the laps of accommodating persons had consequently lost all appeal.

Having exhausted the limited possibilities of entertainment inherent in Serena's pearls, Justin loudly expressed a wordless but perfectly intelligible demand to be put down on the floor, where his curiosity could be given wider reign. His attendant spent the next ten minutes swooping down from her considerable height to remove from the baby's grasp objects that might be considered dangerous, dirty, or delicate. For the most part, Justin accepted her decisions with unimpaired affability, but at last he let out a wail of frustration at the loss of a particularly tasty morsel of something Serena failed to identify. Shuddering, she tossed the gummy mass into the fireplace and scooped up the protesting infant.

"Shall we go high up, my lamb?" she asked coaxingly, lifting him at arm's length over her head. He squealed with glee at this new vantage point and waved his arms about while his slave obligingly raised and lowered him until the muscles in her arms rebelled. She gathered the squirming little body into an embrace and nuzzled her nose into his neck, setting him to squealing again at the tickling sensation.

The two men who had entered the room toward the end of this homely scene were well in time to witness the baby's revenge as little fingers thrust into his captor's hair and tugged, sending a two-foot cascade of rich russet tresses tumbling halfway down her back.

"Justin, you little imp, I'll never get it back up again!"

"Are you calling my son names, Lady Whitlaw, if, as I assume, you are Lady Whitlaw?"

The gentleman's smiling green eyes met the lady's equally green ones on a level as Serena turned, laughing, and handed the eagerly reaching baby over to his father. "Guilty as charged, Mr. Talbot, but please call me Serena, as Natasha does."

"Only if I may be Cam to you," returned that gentleman gallantly, smiling over his boisterously chattering son's head.

"Oh, what it is to be irresistible to women. Now, *I* have met Lady Whitlaw on numerous occasions without being accorded a like privilege."

Not having noticed him standing silently by the door, Serena started slightly when Lord Phillips began to speak. Faint color stained her cheeks at his mocking words, and she had to bite back a scathing reply, saying merely, "Good afternoon, Lord Phillips."

Cam's initial impression of his wife's friend as a glowing, vibrant personality faded somewhat as the lady's lovely face seemed to freeze in a polite little social smile. He glanced briefly at the mocking amusement on his old friend's face, recalled the drawling tones Peter affected when he wished to conceal his feelings, and wondered what was between these two. "Where is Natasha?" he asked to lighten the atmosphere that had suddenly blown up in the small room.

"She was needed to settle a domestic crisis," Serena replied, her face breaking into a real smile again as she contemplated the appealing picture of a man unselfconsciously holding his child. Mr. Talbot was swaying from side to side in a rhythmic motion, while Justin was absorbed in trying to remove the black onyx pin reposing in the folds of his father's cravat.

"Cam, you're home early. How lovely! And you've already met Serena." Natasha followed her voice into the room, heading straight for her husband, who gathered her into one arm and dropped a kiss on her nose.

"Hello, darling. Yes, Serena and I introduced ourselves over Justin's head. I trust the domestic crisis doesn't mean dinner is ruined again?"

"No, it was just an altercation between a tradesman and the cook, both of whom thought it necessary that I hear their side. It wasn't, but it's all settled now."

"Then Peter and I needn't repair to the club for a meal?" her husband asked teasingly.

"Not without me, at any rate." Natasha wrinkled her nose at him.

Serena had been trying to repin her hair during this byplay, but she was making sad work of it, hampered equally by a lack of pins and the knowledge that Lord Phillips was watching the operation. Natasha glanced her way and laughed.

"You needn't tell me how you came to be in this state. Pulling hair is my son's latest acquired vice."

"Scarcely a vice when the result is so admirable," murmured Lord Phillips, his eyes on the wavy mass that had again descended over Serena's yellow-clad shoulders.

"Yes, Serena's hair is quite beautiful—that extraordinary color!" Natasha affected not to notice her friend's embarrassment as she took her by the arm. "Shall we have my maid do it up for you before you go?"

"Oh, yes, thank you, Natasha. Goodness," said her guest, glancing at the dainty enameled clock on the table desk, "my coachman is due in less than ten minutes."

"Then we won't dawdle. Shall I send Nurse for the baby, Cam?" Natasha paused in the doorway, her hand still on Serena's arm.

"Give us a few more minutes with him, darling." Mr. Talbot sent his wife an intimate smile before turning the wriggling child over to his uncle, whose buttonhole sported a tempting flower that had caught Justin's eye.

After the gentlemen had bidden Lady Whitlaw good day, Peter held his nephew out at arm's length for a moment to say solemnly, "Justin, my dear fellow, I fear you are too young to fully appreciate your good fortune."

"Do I detect a note of envy in your voice?"

"No," denied Peter, eyeing his grinning brother-in-law with disfavor before a reluctant smile crept into his eyes. "Rampant jealousy, more like."

5

His persistence was about to be rewarded, Lord Phillips saw with satisfaction. That striking figure in sapphire blue up ahead walking between two rather diminutive ladies could only belong to the elusive Lady Whitlaw. It was true, then, that sooner or later one met everyone with any pretensions to fashion during the late-afternoon strut in Hyde Park. He reined in his horse to a walk, content now to take his time in approaching the fair Serena and her companions.

Their paths had not crossed since that day last week when he and Cam had surprised her playing with Justin. Until that revealing moment he had nearly accepted the disappointing conclusion based on their previous meetings that the lady's nature belied her vibrant appearance. From the beginning of their acquaintance her determined aloofness had him questioning his initial recognition of an untamed spirit to match her hair. No longer, though. After seeing the joyous warmth in her manner while cuddling another woman's child, he could no longer doubt that her unemotional public persona was a carefully maintained false facade. The reason for the elaborate deception remained obscure to his seeking intelligence, but he eagerly accepted the challenge it represented. He had been intrigued by this woman from the moment of clapping eyes on her, and was more than ever resolved to make her discard her disguise and reveal her true self to him. If he had to forcibly peel her like an artichoke, he would uncover her heart, he vowed, tightening his hands on the reins as he edged closer to the railings.

Happily unaware of the uncomfortable experience in

store for her, Serena heard her name called and turned
her head to greet the man doffing his hat from the back
of a magnificent bay horse. At the moment, her mother
and sister were engaged in swapping pleasantries with
another party of strollers, so she crossed over to the
railings separating the pedestrian path from the Row to
get a closer look.

"What a superb animal, Lord Phillips," she said, smiling up at the rider, her gloved hand going out to pat the
horse's nose. "How old is he?"

"Six."

"Is he a recent acquisition?"

"Lord, no, Fiero carried me faithfully throughout much
of the Peninsula campaign. I couldn't bear to part with
him when I sailed for America, so I arranged to have him
shipped to England in a friend's charge until I could
claim him again."

"I do not blame you for not wishing to lose him; he's a
beauty. Is he Spanish?"

"Yes, and Mameluke-trained. Do you ride, Lady
Whitlaw?"

"I haven't ridden since I left Hereford in February.
Tamely walking in the park like this among so many
riders only makes me realize how much I miss the
exercise."

"Then why don't you ride?"

"Neither my mother nor sister cares for riding, and
since I cannot go myself to Tattersall's to buy a horse
without creating talk, it has seemed easier to simply
forget about riding while we are in London. I suppose I
could rent a mount from one of the livery stables, but
hired mounts are . . ." She shrugged and fell silent.

"If you would trust me to select a horse for you,
ma'am, it would be my pleasure."

A momentary glow came into her jeweled green eyes,
but Serena fell back on form, thanking Lord Phillips
politely but claiming she could not impose on his kindness to such an extent.

"Fustian. I never expected such mealymouthed offer-
ings from you. Where is the imposition when I extended

the offer voluntarily? Or is it that you do not believe I mean what I say?"

Serena blinked at the vehemence underlying his words. Heavens, he actually sounded insulted! She hastened to make amends. "Of course I do not doubt your word, sir; that is not at all what I meant. It is just that choosing a horse is such . . . such a matter of individual taste that I would not wish to burden you with—"

"Suppose we accept that you do not wish to impose on me and I do wish to be of service to you, and go on from there?" suggested Lord Phillips with that sudden total smile that linked him in kinship to his lovely sister. "What are your preferences in horseflesh?"

After a second, Serena returned his smile rather shyly. "I am partial to bays myself, because they are so beautiful, but in the city it is more important that an animal be well-mannered, because there are so many distractions here. I have no preference for a mare or a stallion, but I do prefer some spirit in my mounts. It should be a fair-sized horse too, because, as you have reminded me on more than one occasion, I am no lightweight."

"Now, when did I ever make any comment on your weight? I am not so rag-mannered." Lord Phillips looked pained.

"Do not waste your thespian talents on me, my lord, because I am not so simple as to be taken in by them. You know very well to what I refer."

"To get back to your requirements in a mount," he said, refusing the challenge, "you like a well-trained horse with spirit? I take it you are strong enough to maintain control?"

"I am a competent rider."

He read the confidence in her steady gaze and nodded before greeting Verity, who had just noticed her sister in conversation at the railing.

Three days later, Serena was at breakfast when Richford entered with the announcement that Lord Phillips had called and was waiting in the drawing room. Her eyes went in surprise to the chiming clock on the sideboard as she lowered the piece of toast she had been in the act of raising to her mouth. Only nine o'clock. Certainly no hour to be making morning calls.

"I ventured to suggest it was a trifle early for visitors, my lady, but his lordship felt sure you would wish to receive him." Restrained though it undoubtedly was, Richford's voice still conveyed volumes about his opinion of people capable of committing such a social solecism.

"No doubt he is the bearer of a message from Mrs. Talbot," Serena said pacifically. "This is one of our exercise mornings. Perhaps something has arisen that will necessitate canceling our session."

"As to that, I wouldn't know, my lady, his lordship having declined to entrust me with a message of any sort."

"High-handed, was he, Richford? Sometimes Lord Phillips is inclined to forget that he is no longer in command of a battalion of soldiers. Never mind, I'll see him." Twitching the skirts of her gray-and-white cotton housedress into order, Serena passed out of the room, averting her gaze from the butler's censorious visage.

That Lord Phillips was not acting on behalf of his sister became clear as soon as he had responded to her greeting. "I have something to show you," he said without preamble, pulling aside the heavy drapery that dressed the window where he was standing.

Serena automatically responded to the command in his voice, her mystification turning to enlightenment in a flash as she approached the window. "You have found a horse for me?" she demanded eagerly.

"Subject to your approval, of course. Look." He stepped back to make room for her, but not so far back that he was immune to the slightly spiced floral scent that seemed to emanate from her hair, drawn back today into a simple knot at her nape, which imprisoned the fiery lights somewhat but emphasized the beauty of her clear-cut profile and white throat rising from the soft collar of her gown. The fingers of the hand holding the drapery clenched to prevent an illicit gratification of a sudden driving desire to stroke that lovely throat just inches away. In stark contrast to her haughty indifference in social situations, a vibrant energy radiated from Serena today as she angled her head to peer down into the street.

"Oh, is that lovely chestnut mine?" she breathed, not taking her eyes from the horse being walked by a young stable lad while Fiero was held by Lord Phillips' mounted groom. "I must go down immediately to see him." She whirled away from the window, brushing against Lord Phillips' arm in her excitement. She was half-aware of a strange glint in the bright blue eyes as he challenged:

"Why just 'see'? And, incidentally, the horse is a two-year-old filly—why not try her out?"

"Right now? But I'm not dressed for riding."

"I'll give you ten minutes to change." Peter smiled, openly enjoying the display of uncharacteristic indecisiveness by the young widow.

"Dictator!" She hurled the laughing charge at him while heading for the door. "Don't you dare go away!"

In very little more than her allotted ten minutes, Serena strode back into the room, buttoning a pair of black gloves as she came, her whip tucked under her arm. Peter was given no time to admire the dashing figure she cut in a pewter-gray habit elaborately frogged and braided in black, the military impression further enhanced by a tall black fur shako with a visor that was strapped under her chin and set at a daring angle over one brow. The other brow arced upward when her caller showed no immediate disposition to leave the room.

"Ready?"

"At your service, ma'am." Lord Phillips gathered up the gloves and hat he had deposited on a table while he waited; then he followed his hostess out the door and down the stairs.

Serena's reception of the horse he had selected for her was everything Peter could have wished. She praised the filly's conformation, admired her sleek chestnut coat and soft brown eyes, and laughed delightedly when the animal nuzzled against her shoulder.

"I think she likes me already. What a beauty! Thank you so much, Lord Phillips."

"Save your thanks until you've tried her out," said

Peter, giving her a leg up onto the filly's back. "She was bred from racing stock and has a smooth forward action and a fine turn of speed, but evidently not enough staying power to be successful on the circuit." He watched while the stableboy adjusted the stirrup, then swung himself into his own saddle, all the while keeping a watchful eye on Serena's efforts to calm the fidgets out of the eager chestnut.

During the next twenty minutes he was treated to an admirable display of horsemanship by Lady Whitlaw that put to rest any slight qualms he'd had at choosing a young, high-spirited animal for a lady's hack. She had a good seat, good steady hands, and the strength and temperament to curb any inclinations on the filly's part to balk at the myriad distractions that were unavoidable in the city. They picked their way through wheeled traffic, avoided the numerous tradesmen loudly hawking their wares, from pans to hot pasties, in the hopes of obtaining custom from the servants sweeping the steps and walkways of residential areas, and arrived at the park ready for a brisk canter.

Though taking high-bred exception to some of the lesser creatures with whom she had to share the streets, the chestnut behaved beautifully overall and was, Serena assured him, a soft-mouthed joy to handle. That she was also fleet and enjoyed a good run was apparent as they took full advantage of the scarcity of traffic in the park, brought about by threatening skies, to enjoy a short gallop. When at last they slowed down on approaching one of the more populated paths, Serena's good looks were enhanced by a glow of pleasure that brought heightened color to alabaster cheeks and sparkle to green eyes that were habitually cool and calm.

"That was wonderful!" she said enthusiastically, turning toward her escort with the first completely spontaneous smile he had ever been privileged to attract from her. Even white teeth gleamed between beautifully curved lips. "Thank you a thousand times, Lord Phillips, for finding me the perfect mount. She's a darling and a delight."

Peter could have said the same of the chestnut's passenger, but instinct warned him that a personal remark on his part would instantly banish the spontaneity and replace it with the guarded social manner that so irked him. He curbed his impatience, reluctant to spoil this moment of perfect rapport, and followed her lead. "I trust the filly has exhibited enough spirit to please you? She's still dancing around after that run, and eager for more."

"*Dancer*! That is what I shall call her, despite that alarmingly dignified name you told me earlier." She leaned over to pat the chestnut's neck. "You are hereby rechristened Dancer, my beauty. How do you like that?"

The filly tossed her head with a little whicker that drew a laugh from her rider. "See, she is charmed with the change," she declared, throwing Lord Phillips an impish grin that charmed him to an equal degree, though prudence kept him from delivering himself of a human version of the horse's whicker.

Peter's dealings with the fair sex over the last ten of his twenty-nine years had been mutually enjoyable to an extent that permitted a reasonable degree of confidence in that particular arena, but his conceit was not of such a high order that he made the mistake of assuming to himself any personal credit for the delightful half-hour with Serena in the park. Evidently one had to be an infant or possess four legs to draw forth the warmth he persisted in believing was intrinsic to her character in spite of her dedicated portrayal of a strictly cerebral nature. Nor did he cherish more than a mild hope that their present rapport would automatically carry over to their next meeting.

This was fortunate in that it lessened the disappointment he felt when at a reception later that week he was allocated no more of Serena's attention than any other of the moths that persisted in singeing their wings at the light of her attraction. He accepted his dismissal with the face-saving unconcern he maintained both for his own emotional protection and as a matter of policy. Serena was not to be won by any anguished importuning; her own strength despised weakness, and coquetry was foreign to one of her direct nature.

One concession only had he gained by his service in obtaining a horse for her. He had been determined since the day she casually offered the use of her given name to Cam to secure the same privilege for himself, calmly citing her friendship with his whole family when she puckered up in wordless protest at the first few instances when he called her Serena. After their ride together she no longer bristled at the sound of her Christian name on his lips, but neither did she reciprocate with the use of his own name, a tactical defeat he could refuse to recognize but so far had been unable to reverse.

Peter had still not found a way to penetrate the defenses Serena maintained against forming a genuine friendship the following week, when an unexpected move in the desired direction occurred without any initiative on his part.

Cam having been detained at the Foreign Office, Natasha prevailed upon her brother to escort her to an evening party she had agreed to attend. It was not his idea of an evening's entertainment; small overheated rooms jammed with double their capacity of talking, gesticulating humanity making it impossible to concentrate on one's own conversation would never be his choice of venue for conducting social encounters. There seemed to be a preponderance of the very young and callow in attendance, not so surprising really when he recalled that his hosts were launching a daughter into society. He had met Miss Richardson early in the evening, a sweet-faced young thing with a wealth of brown curls and a tendency to become tongue-tied when a man spoke to her. Five minutes of halting, one-sided conversation had left him looking around for assistance, Natasha having deserted him to answer the summons of a formidable-looking dowager as soon as the reception-line amenities were completed. He trusted he had managed to conceal his relief when the young lady's mother had approached with two likely collegians firmly in her clutches to present to her flustered daughter.

It had been a simple matter to slip away with a bow and a polite murmur as introductions were being made, but a subsequent tour of the crowded reception rooms left him resigned to an evening of boredom. He must be getting old, he thought morosely as he smiled at the tired joke brought forth by a young chub in a shocking satin waistcoat with horizontal stripes, whose exquisitely stiffened shirt points imprisoned his beardless chin. A number of the pastel-gowned ladies present were decidedly pretty, some few were already accomplished coquettes, and one or two could sustain a light conversation without strain, but he found himself regarding them, if not in a paternal, then in an avuncular fashion at best. This was an unsettling notion to one who heretofore had glided unconcernedly through whatever social occasions presented themselves, mindlessly enjoying the give-and-take of social intercourse. It was probably more than time that he developed some discrimination, but if the restless dissatisfaction he was experiencing tonight persisted, he'd have to take care not to turn into one of those curmudgeonly types who eschewed all society.

Peter averted his eyes from the striped waistcoat, whose owner was now holding forth on a curricle race he had won that afternoon, and espied a familiar dark red head standing out in a group of chattering females in the next room. His boredom vanished and he experienced the now familiar jolt of pleasure that the sight of Serena invariably afforded him. He hadn't known she would be present tonight or he'd not have let himself be maneuvered into a corner where he would have to avoid wounding any sensibilities or arousing curiosity by his sudden departure. He was already working on the next problem of how to extricate Serena from her phalanx of dowagers without causing raised eyebrows all round as he made his way out of his own circle, aided by a generous expenditure of apologetic smiles and pantomime to the effect that he needed some relief from the heat.

That, at least, was no lie, he thought a moment later, running a finger inside the collar of his shirt where it was sticking to his neck. As he approached the other room at a leisurely stroll, he wondered if Serena might have had the same idea, for she was now heading briskly toward the back of the house, using her fan as she went. And I'll wager she did not trouble herself overmuch to cloak her retreat in a swirl of polite verbiage either, he speculated with amusement as he paused to bow to some of the ladies and exchange a few civil phrases to cloak his own pursuit.

Peter caught up with Serena in some sort of small conservatory, where, if the temperature was not actually much cooler, there were fewer candles burning to add to the illusion of heat. She had accepted a glass of negus from a circulating waiter and was standing staring out into the darkness between two potted palms along a glassed-in wall. His luck was in, for that straight back presented to the room had earned her a few minutes of solitude that he had no compunctions about invading.

"Hiding, Serena?"

She had stiffened at his approach, but relaxed again upon recognizing his voice. "Yes," she answered baldly, not bothering to turn her head more than a few degrees in acknowledgement of his presence.

And was the fact that she obviously did not feel compelled to expend sweet civility on him a sign of progress or the reverse? he pondered, wishing he could be sure it was the former. "Bored?" he asked with a smile of understanding that evoked a twitch of soft lips in return.

"Yes," she admitted with a small sigh, turning her head to face him fully. "I am so tired of repetitious small talk. I am as pleased as any of her future subjects must be that Princess Charlotte has married her German prince at last—though I must say that Leopold is my idea of a perfect stick, with that ridiculous formality of his. It is certainly appropriate that Marlborough House has been made available to them here, and nice that Claremont Park has been bought also, but I am really not interested in the details of her highness's silver wedding gown or the wreath of diamond roses she wore in her hair. Everywhere one goes, the royal wedding and unkind speculation about Mr. Brummell's financial troubles have been the main topics of conversation for weeks. And to think I might have been sailing into the Aegean by now, heading for the Acropolis." She hunched her shoulders and fell silent after this tirade, once more contemplating the shadowed garden area beyond the glass.

Serena had succeeded in surprising him yet again. That faraway expression he had noted once or twice when she was under siege by one or another of the town's gazetted fortune-hunters had really been just that—she had been off on some private mental journey, as she was at this moment.

"So the lady has the wanderlust? Have you done any foreign traveling—with your husband perhaps?"

She shook her head. "I've never been out of England except armchair traveling with a book. How I envy you your past opportunities to see something of the world, Lord Phillips. Oh, not with a weapon in your hand or facing danger, of course, but even under the conditions of war, you must have seen many beautiful and fascinating places and met different kinds of people."

"Yes, even in wartime, for instance, one can thrill to the grandeur of the rugged Pyrenees while cursing the difficulties encountered in traversing them with supply trains in freezing weather. Past Bayonne there was a prosperous area almost untouched by the war that we marched through on the way to take ships for America after the French surrender in May of fourteen. There were miles of silent pine forests; in fact, the inhabitants don't use candles in that district. They collect the sap from the fir trees in dishes and burn wicks in the turpentine for light. You'd have stared to see shepherds not too far away walking on stilts that were six or eight feet high in order to keep track of their sheep through the low growth around those parts."

Serena listened raptly as her friend's brother went on to describe other places seen on his journey to America, from the green and mountainous St. Michael's in the Azores to the dangerous reefs and clear waters of Bermuda with its scorching sunshine and huge caves whose beautiful interiors resembled magnificent cathedrals.

"You have seen and experienced so much," she said, her expression becoming wistful. "Tell me, when you were in America, did you get to visit their capital, Washington City?"

Peter laughed. " 'Visit' isn't quite the word I would have chosen, but yes, I was in Washington."

"What was it like? Is it a handsome city?"

"I suppose it might be one day, though why anyone would wish to live in that dreadful climate, hot and dank, with legions of ferocious insects, passes my understanding. It is a planned city, laid out for the Americans by a French engineer named L'Enfant, with wide avenues and a regular pattern of streets and squares, though many are still unpaved. The building their lawmakers meet in was quite handsome, built of some white stone, but I did not think much of their president's house. Admiral Cockburn ordered both burned after the Americans shot the general's horse when he first went into the city with a flag of truce to demand payment. There were fierce thunderstorms and even a hurricane that last day, so I don't believe much damage was actually done to the Capitol building. We were such a small force and so far from our ships and supplies at St. Benedict that we could not linger in the area and allow the Americans to regroup and mount a counterattack or trap us there."

The couple had remained standing by the glass wall in the conservatory while Peter attempted to satisfy his companion's insatiable curiosity with descriptions of foreign lands, but the relative privacy of this isolated situation was shattered suddenly by a jovial voice calling out, "Ah, there you are, Lady Whitlaw. Don't you know that beautiful women should never be permitted to hide in dark corners? There is someone here who wishes to be presented to you."

Serena had been so entranced that the interruption caught her completely unaware. Startled eyes swung to the short, rotund figure of Sir Edmund Haler, whose perspiring moon face was even more highly colored than usual above a wilting collar as he minced over to the couple near the palm trees. She was slow to notice the smiling man a half-step behind Sir Edmund.

"Lady Whitlaw, I have the honor to present Lord Whitlaw."

Sir Edmund's cackle at his supposed pleasantry impinged vaguely on Peter's awareness, but his covert attention was focused on the silent woman at his side, and he put a surreptitious hand under her elbow as all color fled her cheeks and it seemed that she might faint dead away. She regained control almost immediately, however, and he felt her stiffen with resolution. Her shoulders went back, her chin went up, and steady eyes, vacant of any expression, fixed themselves on the smiling countenance of the tall, well-set-up man in his early thirties who was bowing low over the hand she had extended with a slowness that bespoke reluctance in Peter's mind.

"How do you do, Lord Whitlaw?"

"At last we meet, my dear cousin. I have looked forward to this moment with great anticipation, but even your reputation for loveliness had not prepared me for the stunning reality of your beauty."

The gleaming smile that accompanied this effusion had no doubt claimed many women as willing victims, Peter judged, but it seemed Serena was not to be listed among their number. There was not the slightest softening of the marble perfection of her features as she replied coolly, "You are too kind, sir."

A short pause followed, broken by the earl, who protested with a light laugh, "Please, Cousin Serena, surely there can be no formality between two people so closely connected. I trust that you will soon come to think of me as Adrian."

Two exquisite eyebrows arced upward in real or pretended surprise. "But, sir, we never even chanced to meet during that period when a connection might be supposed to have existed."

"Alas, my military duties prevented our meeting until now, but I have sold out of the army. You must look upon me as a most willing champion. My cousin's widow must always have a close claim upon my protection and counsel."

Serena bowed and said again, "You are too kind. May I present Lord Phillips to you?"

The gentlemen exchanged measuring looks and polite

bows, but any inclination they might have felt to exchange any remarks beyond a brief greeting was aborted by Serena, who tucked her hand under Peter's arm and smiled dazzlingly for his sole benefit. She said with infectious gaiety, "Peter, we have remained away chattering so long my family will wonder if I have been kidnapped. I insist that you come and make my apologies with me. Will you excuse us please, gentlemen?"

Peter allowed himself to be drawn out of the conservatory. His blandly attentive demeanor concealed astonishment at the events of the last five minutes, nor did he comment on the fact that Serena's brightness fell away from her like a discarded cape as soon as she had put the width of the room between herself and the men whose eyes were boring into her back. Though consumed with curiosity, he had learned enough about the now expressionless woman beside him in the last few weeks to be reasonably certain that she would deny that this unexpected meeting with her husband's heir had given her a nasty shock. Therefore, he contented himself with issuing a gentle warning as they neared a group of women that included Mrs. Boynton.

"If you cannot produce at least a token smile, the ladies will all be speculating whether we have quarreled or deciding I must have been boring you to tears."

That got her attention. The green eyes were empty no longer as they flashed from the group in their path to her escort's encouraging face. She produced the requisite smile and said with a slight pressure on the arm under her fingers, "Thank you."

"No, it is I who must thank you."

She looked a silent question.

"For the promotion. To 'Peter.' " He enjoyed the blush that spread over her cheekbones even though well aware that it was put there less by embarrassment than annoyance at his perspicacity.

6

The new Lord Whitlaw lost no time in calling upon his cousin's widow. Serena received him with a chill civility that caused her mother, who was present at the interview, to take her severely to task when the visitor finally left, well after the time limit for a first call. The earl had been all affability and eagerness, seemingly undismayed by the necessity of supporting a disproportionate share of the conversation with a hostess who had nothing to offer beyond the most basic commonplaces of social exchange, and these in tones devoid alike of life and interest.

"I must say, Serena," Mrs. Boynton began the second the door closed behind their noble visitor, "that never did I expect to be put to the blush by a *lack* of articulation on your part. The veriest moonling could have given a better account of herself just now. Whatever must Lord Whitlaw be thinking of you?"

"Hopefully, he is now concluding that I am so dull and stupid that the game's not worth the candle," replied her unrepentant daughter, thrusting aside the piece of needlework behind which she had barricaded herself during the earl's visit. Her fingers began an impatient tapping rhythm on the table beside her chair.

"What a distinctly odd thing to say. I should think you would be pleased to find the new head of your husband's family so well-disposed toward you. It could have been rather awkward, you know, what with your inheriting all of Whitlaw's personal fortune instead of his rightful heir. Serena, please stop that incessant drumming. My nerves won't stand it."

The finger-tapping stopped and Serena transferred her

frowning gaze to her mother's face. "Not for a single instant do I believe that the present earl was less than deeply chagrined to discover himself the possessor of a title and estates without sufficient resources to maintain his position in proper style. Nor do I believe that he is well-disposed toward me personally, despite his fawning performance just now. I would have had more respect for him had he held me at arm's length, allowing me no more than the formal courtesy demanded by our connection."

"Well, I am strongly of the opinion that you should be grateful that Whitlaw has seen fit to project an attitude of family solidarity. It will be much more comfortable for you to be seen to be on good terms with him. For my part, I thought him quite charming and conversable, with a breadth of experience that must make him an agreeable addition to our little circle."

Serena raised her eyes to heaven in a mute plea for patience and managed to bite back the retort hovering on her tongue.

Mrs. Boynton, taking silence for encouragement, went on in a musing vein. "And he is so very handsome too, so straight and tall, and his bearing so soldierly. Did you notice, Serena, that despite the military side whiskers, there is a strong family resemblance to your late husband?"

"I noticed," Serena replied grimly, and bethought herself of some tasks she must instantly perform in another part of the house, thus effecting an escape before she could sink herself still further in her mother's estimation by giving voice to her candid opinion of the personal qualities of both earls of Whitlaw, past and present.

Lord Whitlaw called three times in the next ten days, either impervious to or at least undaunted by the lack of encouragement displayed by his late cousin's widow. Perhaps to make up for her daughter's want of enthusiasm, Mrs. Boynton was at pains to be cordial in her welcome, and Verity, once she had overcome her initial mistrust of a stranger, responded to his charming overtures with shy pleasure. Serena seethed in silence on these occasions, begrudging every pale civility that fell from her lips but careful not to betray the least hint of her deep-seated antagonism. It would have been a relief to give way to her feelings and depress his nauseating pretensions to affection in no uncertain terms, but prudence and caution held her back when good manners would have failed. Though she would have greeted with indignant denials any accusations that there was a thread of fear mixed in among her other reactions to Lord Whitlaw, she admitted an unusual need to keep her own counsel and display no reaction to his overtures except supreme indifference. The man who could pursue a blatantly false course when he must have seen it would avail him nothing was capable of seizing and twisting any circumstances or any weakness in his opponents to serve his own selfish ends. Though it did not become her to say so, and she had no intention of losing any advantage gained by her intuitive knowledge, she had become convinced at their first meeting that the new earl had deliberately arranged it, having already decided to acquire his cousin's fortune by marrying his widow.

It would have made no difference to his intention had I been the original pig-faced lady, she thought one day as she acknowledged an elaborate compliment with an unsmiling inclination of her head. He might have spared himself the trouble of fabricating his graceful remarks had he been aware that his handsome face, far from being a recommendation, doomed his cause at the outset by its striking similarity to his dead cousin's. It might be helpful if one of the previous earl's cronies dropped a word in his ear about the nature of that marriage, but perhaps that was indulging optimism too far. In the circles in which the fourth earl had traveled, keeping mistresses was very likely no reflection on the success or failure of a marriage. Serena gritted her teeth and prepared to endure the siege with as much stoicism as she could muster.

The earl's pointed attentions would have been easier to bear had they remained a private annoyance, but they threatened to become a public embarrassment as well. Serena's commitment to chaperoning her young sister made it a simple matter for him to dog her heels, at least until she prevailed upon Verity to withhold details of her social schedule when questioned by Lord Whitlaw in a seemingly innocuous manner. The innocent Verity had been unaware of the purpose behind his flattering interest in her affairs.

It was naturally impossible to avoid the man entirely, and Serena's sense of foreboding increased as a function of time. It required the strictest self-discipline to keep a rein on her volatile temper when he popped up at nearly every social event she attended, appropriating her company with a smiling assurance that made her long to slap his handsome face. By reminding herself at regular intervals that the most persistent man in creation could not prevail against an unswerving determination to deny his advances, she was able to maintain her attitude of civil indifference, but the toll on her disposition was mounting.

The next Wednesday Serena excused herself from joining her mother and Verity at Almack's. The Talbots had invited her to accompany them to a ball being given by a renowned political hostess, and they planned to call for her in their carriage, leaving Serena's free for the use of her family. When Natasha had delivered the invitation, she had accepted eagerly, expressing the hope that the conversation among a set of persons closely associated with government circles would be more far-ranging and significant than the usual inanities continually reiterated on what she had come to regard as a social treadmill. Unexpressed even to her dear friend was the additional hope that the interruption in her pattern of social engagements would earn her an evening free from the tensions aroused by Lord Whitlaw's unwelcome attentions.

"Persecution" was the word that leapt to the front of her mind when, little more than an hour after her arrival, Serena turned to make a laughing rejoinder to a scandalous remark uttered by Mr. Charles Talbot and met the confident smile of the fifth earl as he approached the group of which she was a part. A sizzle of fury and frustration zinged through her veins, and her lips closed on whatever she had been about to say, which thought became swamped in the surcease of violent mental agitation created by the unexpected appearance of her late husband's heir.

"I say, Lady Whitlaw, is anything amiss?" Mr. Talbot had followed the direction of her glance and now brought curious blue eyes back to Serena's rigid features.

"No, nothing." She forced a tight smile and addressed the earl. "Good evening, my lord. I believe you are acquainted with Mr. and Mrs. Cameron Talbot, but perhaps you have not yet met Mr. Charles Talbot?" By the time introductions and greetings had been exchanged all around, Serena had herself well in hand and was able to say with a fair assumption of casualness, "I had not thought to see your lordship tonight, you have become such a devotee of Almack's of late."

"And so I am in general, my dear cousin, but I found the place sadly lacking in attraction this evening and was consequently persuaded by my friend Torrington to look in on this ball. Since it has all the attraction Almack's lacked, I count myself singularly well-rewarded for my submissiveness to my friend's will."

"Indeed."

Natasha threw herself into the breach created by Serena's damping rejoinder with an inconsequential comment on the music being provided for the guests, and Cam asked the earl a question about the last months of his military service. Serena scarcely listened to the ensuing discussion. Her efforts were two-pronged: to maintain a pleasant demeanor while planning how to avoid being cornered by Lord Whitlaw. She had hit upon nothing more original than a sudden headache by the time the orchestra struck up again. Though she had not once glanced into the earl's face, she could sense that he was about to ask her to dance, when a cheerful voice at her elbow said:

"This waltz is mine, I believe, Serena."

Serena turned wordlessly into the arms of Peter Phillips, hoping her eagerness would be interpreted as pleasure rather than relief. That gentleman shed the light of his attractive smile on the group she was leaving, mur-

muring a quick greeting and apology as he swept his partner onto the floor.

Like his sister, Lord Phillips was an inspired dancer, and for several moments the pair circled the room to the lilting music without attempting any conversation. Serena's taut control relaxed gradually and she began to enjoy the sensation of moving in harmony with her partner.

"Ah, that's better," Lord Phillips said approvingly. "You might unclench your teeth now also."

There was a surprised flash in the green eyes that met his for an instant before dropping to the level of his chin. "I don't know what you mean."

"Now, now," he chided, "do not go all stiff on me again just when we have all the tabbies seated along the wall commenting on our brilliant performance and what a handsome couple we make. We mustn't disappoint our public."

Serena gasped as he swung her around in a series of showy turns, then grinned up at him tormentingly as she found her feet and entered into the spirit of his gaiety. "What boundless conceit," she scoffed as Natasha swept by in the arms of her husband, both faces alight with laughter as they did so, "and unjustified conceit too if you suppose that anyone will spare us a glance when your sister is on the floor. She and Cam are a truly beautiful couple."

Peter smiled at the vivid face upturned to his. "Yes, they are beautifully matched in every way, or perhaps I should rather say that they complement each other beautifully. Natasha's warmth has enriched Cam's existence, and his steadiness serves to keep her impulsive nature tethered in reality. Each feels incomplete without the other, which, when one comes to think of it, is a perfect description of marriage."

"You are not so naive, surely, as to believe that description applies to most marriages," Serena protested.

"No," agreed Peter, misliking the derision he heard in her voice, "but it is certainly not impossible of achievement when one begins with love and respect."

"Not impossible, perhaps, but not, I think, easily achieved."

"How much that is really worthwhile in this life is easily achieved? Not a great deal, I would venture to say."

Serena did not address herself to his rhetorical question. In any case, the topic of marriage was something she preferred not to discuss, certainly not with an unattached gentleman whose views could scarcely be deemed of much value.

After a short interval of whirling about the room in silence, Peter began again. "Having recently informed me that you are bored with the topic of Mr. Brummell's financial troubles, I presume that you would not care to comment on his precipitate flight to France to escape his creditors. Tell me instead what there is about the Earl of Whitlaw that makes you dislike him so intensely."

Serena nearly stumbled, but caught herself in time. "You are mistaken, sir," she declared icily. "I have no reason to dislike Whitlaw."

"No, that is what I thought—no personal reason, at least—if, as I apprehend, you met him for the first time at the Richardsons' dance. The fact remains, however, that you do dislike him quite violently. Why?"

"You are being offensive, sir. I have just told you I do not dislike Lord Whitlaw. Are you calling me a liar?"

"Well, yes, I'm afraid I must be," he replied with suspicious meekness, "though I assure you it was not my original intention. It was worth it, though, to see your magnificent eyes spark green fire. I can see that you are a believer in the policy of attack as the best defense, but do you not yet know that you do not need to defend yourself from me? I would never do anything to hurt you, Serena."

"You are the most vexatious man I have ever met," cried the sorely tried widow. "And to think that I was actually grateful to you for rescuing me . . ." She broke off, appalled at this revelation, and tried to undo the damage. "That is, I did not mean *rescue* precisely, but—"

"Never mind," he said soothingly. "It is unnecessary

to pile lie upon lie. I perfectly understand what you meant, my dear."

"I am not your dear!"

"No, not yet. I'll grant that I was being presumptuous, if you will not deny what is already between us."

"There is nothing between us, nothing at all!" Serena heard the hint of panic in her own voice and made a supreme effort to control her emotional response to Peter's baiting tactics. She forced her features into an arrangement of stony calm and met his glance squarely.

"There has been truth and candor between us from the first moment we met, Serena, and liking too. You do yourself less than justice by denying it. It is the act of a coward, and unworthy of you."

"I fear you are speaking in conundrums."

"Then I'll speak more plainly. I was a witness to your shock and distress on first meeting the present Earl of Whitlaw. I noticed the reluctance with which you accepted him as a dancing partner on two other occasions, and from ten feet away I could feel your annoyance—to put no higher—when he joined your conversation a few moments ago. Oh, it would not be apparent to most people," he assured her when her eyes dilated in alarm, "but I happen to know you rather well, Serena, though you choose not to acknowledge this."

When she maintained a stubborn silence, he said, selecting his words carefully, "It would be perfectly understandable that you should resent another man's assumption of your husband's honors, the fact that his cousin is alive when your husband is dead."

The stupefaction that crossed her face momentarily told him his carefully worked-out theory was in error. His eyes narrowed as he stared down into a lovely cold mask. "If not for that reason, then why do you dislike the new earl?"

"Because he is the spitting image of his predecessor, and it makes my skin crawl to be near him!"

The look of satisfaction on his partner's face was an indication that he had been unsuccessful in hiding his shock at her bitter words, but Peter had not been able to formulate a coherent question from the inchoate mass of sensation induced by this response when the music ended and Serena excused herself abruptly, leaving him staring blankly after her.

He realized he was standing stock-still in the middle of the floor and made his way toward the archway that led to the supper room. His pace quickened as he spotted a drift of wood-violet gauze until he caught up with Natasha and Cam as they approached a table groaning with foodstuffs.

"Excuse me, Cam, but I must speak with Tasha for a moment," he said, taking his sister's elbow and steering her away from the table. "For heaven's sake, what kind of marriage did Serena have?" he demanded a few seconds later as he seated her quickly at a small table in a corner of the room.

"What makes you think Serena has discussed her marriage with me?" Natasha hedged, blinking in surprise at the unexpected question.

Peter ran a hand over his hair from front to back before gripping the back of his neck and twisting his head from side to side to ease the tension in his neck muscles. "Dammit, Tasha, she just told me her skin crawls when Whitlaw comes near her, because he looks like her dead husband. What am I to make of that?"

"Well, I gather that the match was arranged by her family, though she did not imply there was any kind of coercion to gain her acceptance. She mentioned that it had not been a successful marriage, and that is all I can tell you, my dear brother. If you wish to know more, you must ask Serena."

Peter made a wry grimace. "A lot of good that would do me. She would not have said what she did tonight had I not pushed her to the wall to find out why she dislikes Whitlaw."

"Does she do so? I thought there was a bit of an atmosphere tonight when the earl joined us. Serena acted so . . . lifeless, which is very unlike her indeed. What is your interest in all this?"

Peter grinned at his sister's too-innocent expression.

"When there is anything to tell, you shall be the first to know," he promised.

"No *quid pro quo*, I see. How typically masculine."

"What is typically masculine?" asked Cam, approaching the table carrying a plate heaped with colorful tidbits. "Is it safe to join you now? Have all the family secrets been divulged?"

"Are your feelings wounded, darling?" Natasha looked up at him teasingly as he rubbed a gentle knuckle down her cheek. "Peter has been cross-questioning me about Serena's marriage, but he refuses to tell me why he is so interested."

"And quite right too." Cam deposited the plate in front of his wife. "You cannot expect a man to go around prattling about his emotions, certainly not until he is absolutely sure of what it is he really feels."

"And that is another thing that is typically masculine. Men always form an alliance against women's natural curiosity." Natasha's lips pursed in a delectable pout, then parted as her eyes alighted on the piled plate before her. "Goodness, Cam, I'll never be able to eat all this food."

"You won't have to, sweetheart. As soon as I fill another one with a few dainty morsels, we'll trade. Coming, Peter?"

As her grinning brother rose with a mocking bow to accompany his old friend to the refreshment table, Natasha sighed with resignation and muttered, "Two more masculine tactics: diversionary moves and strategic retreats."

"And one very feminine one," Peter tossed over his shoulder, "known as having the last word."

"Which you have just deprived me of." Natasha's dark eyes gleamed with amusement as she monitored the progress of the two men. She would be accused of bias, of course, but in her estimation they were the finest-looking men in this distinguished company. The chiseled perfection of Cam's features was without parallel in this or any gathering. It was always pure pleasure to gaze upon him. It must be acknowledged that the Earl of Whitlaw had a good athletic build and a profile suitable for a Greek coin, but he could not match Peter's air of breeding, that certain something in his easy bearing that proclaimed him a man at peace with himself. Peter's features might not be in the classical mold, but his smile was much more compelling and his intensely blue eyes more attractive with their dark lashes than the earl's blue-gray ones in their paler setting. Any woman possessing an ounce of discrimination would prefer Peter to Whitlaw, she decided with sisterly complacence.

Which brought her thoughts around to Serena. Natasha had not been displeased to learn that her friend disliked her husband's cousin. Honesty compelled her to admit that Serena had shown little sign of favoring Peter either, though she had detected a slight warming in her attitude recently. It was not much to build on, however, and despite Peter's reticence on the subject, his sister was nearly convinced that he was in love with the young widow. He had not requested any assistance, but Natasha stood ready to plead his cause whenever the opportunity arose. Knowing what she did of Serena's antipathy toward marriage, she could not be entirely sanguine about the outcome, even though her fondness rejected the idea that a woman honored by her brother's affection could fail to return it in full measure.

As she watched Cam and Peter return to their table with a waiter who carried a tray bearing food and glasses of sparkling champagne, Natasha's face was a study of loving concern. It was an odd sensation and an even odder situation. Except for his war injuries, which, although irritatingly slow to heal, had not had a lasting detrimental effect on his life, Peter, seven years her senior, had never needed her concern before. She had worried about his safety during his years in the army, but that had been almost an impersonal thing. Her fertile brain could conjure up multiple hazards of warfare, but she had never actually seen danger threaten Peter before. She had seen the way Peter looked at Serena when he thought himself safe from observation, however, and she felt her own experiences in the early days of falling in

love with Cam gave her a clearer picture of danger than
her smiling brother seemed to entertain.

"Why so solemn, Tasha?" Peter asked, handing her a
glass from the waiter's tray.

"Who, I? Solemn?" Suddenly Natasha was filled with
a reckless sense of confidence in her brother's ability to
crash through Serena's defenses. She raised her glass
high. "To success," she offered, drinking deep.

7

As the waltz music wound down, Serena's overriding desire was to escape, something she accomplished with more haste than grace by muttering a scarcely intelligible "Please excuse me" and walking swiftly away from Lord Phillips. She was guiltily aware that she'd left him looking conspicuous in the middle of the dance floor, but Peter's plight barely registered as she beat a fast retreat to the room where the ladies had left their wraps on arrival. It was his own fault in any case. If he had not pressed her and badgered her to reveal what was none of his affair, he would not now be deprived of that annoying air of imperturbability that he customarily wore like a cloak.

By the time she reached the chamber reserved for the ladies' use, Serena had all but forgotten that the original cause of her present distress was the unexpected appearance of Lord Whitlaw. She had looked forward to spending a pleasant evening in the Talbots' company, and now it was all spoiled. Her disappointment and resentment focused exclusively on the person of Peter Phillips. What right had he, a mere acquaintance, to question her as if *she* were his sister?

Serena rearranged her features into a polite acknowledgment as she swerved to avoid walking into a woman coming out of the cloakroom. There was no one within except the maid, whose assistance she waved away with an impersonal smile. She dropped onto a chair and eased out of her sandals, flexing and rubbing her toes for the attendant's benefit while her mind reverted to her problems.

Before this revealing evening she would have said that, apart from being where she did not wish to be and doing what she least wished to be doing this spring—a source of irritation that the knowledge that she was performing a duty to her family should have assuaged but didn't—she had only one irksome problem in her life in the person of the Earl of Whitlaw. A few moments ago her problems had doubled, if she had interpreted Peter Phillips' words correctly. Goodness knew she had no desire to see him as another suitor, and she might be mistaken—that had been a heated exchange on the dance floor. Of a certainty, she had lost command of her self-possession and said things she now wished unsaid; the same might be true of her antagonist. It would be comforting to believe that that strangely intimate conversation had been an aberration in their cool friendship, the impact of which would fade with the cooling of their tempers.

The problem with this rationalization was that Serena was well aware that she was the only one who had lost her temper, which she now deeply regretted, though the provocation had been great. Her eyes narrowed in concentration as she summoned up a mental picture of the elegant, assured Lord Phillips during their waltz. In the beginning he had been his usual urbane, slightly flippant self, teasing, poking, and prodding at her intellect as he was wont to do for no reason that she had ever been able to discern save a malicious entertainment he seemed to derive from her response to his tactics. Generally it pleased her to deny him the satisfaction of seeing her descend from her social form to give reign to her sharp tongue, but tonight he had caught her in a weakened state and eventually had elicited an admission of her detestation of Lord Whitlaw that she would give her eyeteeth to retract.

It was not that she feared he would bruit it about the town. Peter was not of the same ilk as Charles Talbot, who evidently enjoyed a well-deserved reputation for a scathing wit and a tendency to spread scandalous *on-dits*. Natasha's peculiar brother seemed to reserve any unkind impulses for herself alone, which was one reason tonight's confrontation had thrown her off her balance.

As she bent over her foot, Serena's fingers paused in their massaging action. She was recalling the uncharacteristic intensity of Peter's compelling blue eyes as he declared that she had no need of defenses against him. The irony of that reflection twisted her mouth into a grimace. If, as his later words seemed to indicate, he thought there was some romantic nonsense growing between them, then she was going to require more defenses than a medieval castle against that insidious persistence that she had identified—and mistrusted—in his character from the beginning of their acquaintance.

Not that he, any more than Whitlaw, was going to succeed in claiming her as a matrimonial prize, Serena vowed. Her teeth were clenched as she retied the strings of her sandals. As always with Serena, fear was barely recognized before being converted to anger. Her anger with Whitlaw for disrupting the pattern of her days was a pale thing in comparison to the fury that surged through her veins as she dwelt on the treachery of Peter Phillips. He had wormed his way into her confidence by insisting on selecting a horse for her even though she had not wished to be beholden to him, and he had then taken advantage of her natural gratitude to get upon first-name terms, which again was something she had not desired. What was even worse, he had slipped under her guard with his amusingly astringent manner and his uncanny knack of being on the spot just when she needed rescuing. She had begun to regard him as a friend, the one person apart from Natasha with whom she felt completely at ease during this strange Season. And he had betrayed her trust. He hadn't really wanted to be her friend at all. Like the other men who buzzed around her like bees, he had either marriage or a less-regular connection in mind. Lord Phillips, though, was worse than the others. At least they had not offered a deceptive hand in friendship.

At this point in her ruminations Serena looked up to find herself no longer in sole possession of the cloakroom. Two young women had entered, conversing in confidential tones. They looked startled when she arose from her chair and headed for the door with a civil nod.

Serena's features were set in a mask of cool composure that belied the state of her mind when she reentered the ballroom. The first person she encountered a step inside the entrance was the Earl of Whitlaw, whose white teeth gleamed in a satisfied smile as he begged the pleasure of her company at supper. Two hours earlier she would have been hard put to dissemble her irritation, but a fresh disaster had served to lessen the impact of the old one. She accepted his arm with a prim little smile and resigned herself to an uncomfortable half-hour of deflecting the earl's personal remarks and attempts to get up a flirtation.

As it turned out, she managed quite well. His presence, though no more agreeable than ever, had lost some of its power to intimidate, probably through repetition, she decided at the end of the ordeal. She had hit on the trick of getting him to recount some of his experiences on the Continent during the last two years. Even Lord Whitlaw couldn't turn a pointed inquiry about the architecture of Paris and Vienna into a campaign of flirtation. By making her questions specific and listening with wide-eyed attention to his replies, she was able to control the conversation, and by sitting carefully back from the table, she was able to evade his discreet efforts to touch her hand or arm. For a few moments he actually forgot his purpose while launched on a story that featured some dashing quasi-military intelligence-gathering on his part during the period after Napoleon had escaped from Elba. In her turn, Serena forgot her company, and her face lighted with interest in his tale.

She sensed when his attention shifted from his own words to her person and casually began preparations for leaving the table, blotting her lips on her serviette and pushing her plate a fraction of an inch away. "I see Mrs. Talbot in the doorway, my lord. She must be wondering what has become of me. Shall we go?"

Since Serena rose on her words, the earl had little choice but to comply hurriedly, but he contrived to halt her progress by stopping in front of her with his back to the doorway. "May I have the honor of escorting you home tonight, cousin?"

"Thank you, sir, but I am a member of the Talbot party this evening."

"I'll just have a word with Talbot. I'll wager he'll be grateful to be saved the extra trip."

"But *I* would not be grateful to be thought an inconsiderate and ungrateful guest, sir. I came with the Talbots and I shall return with them. Thank you for the supper."

As Serena stepped around the large frozen figure of Lord Whitlaw to join Natasha, she took away with her an image of a visage taut with barely controlled irritation that accompanied his stiff bow. The debonair mask has slipped this time, she noted with a satisfaction untinged by any remnant of her earlier apprehension. It had been sheer cowardice that had kept her tolerating his encroaching behavior these past weeks, but no more! Even if he and his late cousin were identical under the skin as well as being physical look-alikes, she had no cause to concern herself with this Earl of Whitlaw's character, because she would never be maneuvered into a position where she was under his domination, she vowed. Hers had been a hard lesson but one well-learned.

The man Serena left in the supper room was still staring after her when a drawling voice at his side recalled him to the present.

"The lady is not easily persuadable, I fear."

Lord Whitlaw started slightly and frowned at the thin, impeccably attired man with sharp features in a gaunt-cheeked face that testified to years of dissipation. "Torrington! I did not hear you approach. No, she's a damned independent madam, but beneath that bland missish manner she projects, I have just discovered hidden fire and perhaps even a modicum of intellect. This project has suddenly become infinitely more promising."

"Far be it from me to cast a rub in your way," said the aging exquisite beside him, opening a gold-and-enamel snuffbox with a practiced flip of one thumbnail. He paused to extract a pinch of the aromatic mixture, which he proceeded to inhale into one nostril. Not until he had repeated this process with the other nostril did he continue. "As I was saying, I would not for the world under-

estimate your talents where the fair sex is concerned, but
does it strike you that the lady shows a certain lack of
. . . er . . . enthusiasm for your company?"

"Accredited beauties like my new cousin feel they owe
it to their consequence to keep a man dangling for a time
before they accept him. She'll come around."

"Ah? I bow to your superior knowledge of such delicate matters," replied Lord Torrington, dusting a few
grains of snuff from his black sleeve with his handkerchief. "Since I have rather a lot at stake myself, I naturally extend my best wishes for a successful conclusion to
your . . . er . . . 'project,' I believe, was your word."

"Don't worry, you'll get your money back as soon as
the knot is tied." Lord Whitlaw's lips thinned to an
unpleasant line.

"Dear me, did I sound as though I were worried, dear
boy? Perish the thought. Believe me, I entertain no
doubts whatsoever that I shall be repaid in full." Lord
Torrington's already thin mouth stretched into a humourless
approximation of a smile as he bowed and faded into the
background to allow the passage of a new group of guests
into the supper room.

Lord Whitlaw spun on his heel and headed back to the
ballroom, where he devoted himself to jealously watching his quarry as she circulated about the edges of the
dance floor with the Talbots, who presented her to various acquaintances from time to time. From his several
vantage points over the next hour, he confirmed that her
manner seemed to be more animated than when in his
company, and judging from the reactions of those persons with whom she spoke, her conversation proved more
entertaining than he had ever found it. Despite his confident assertions to Torrington earlier, the earl began to
suspect that the widow's demeanor toward himself was
deliberately calculated to disaffect him, possibly with the
object of averting an offer of marriage. He should have
guessed that no one with that spectacular coloring could
possess so colorless a personality, except that it had not
occurred to him that his attentions would be so unwelcome. He could claim with no fear of contradiction that

his advances had been almost universally welcomed by females of all types and stations for better than a dozen years. It was all of a piece with his miserable luck that when he finally decided to get leg-shackled, he must needs court a disagreeable creature with a freakish turn to her nature. Now that he came to think of it, he'd noticed that she gave short shrift to all the men who clustered around her, even that Phillips fellow, who had the advantage of being her bosom friend's brother.

With this realization, Lord Whitlaw was tempted to abandon the whole scheme and look elsewhere for a suitable wife, but he'd invested a lot of time in that redheaded icicle, and she met his basic financial requirements better than some virginal heiress with anxious parents to appease. Besides, right from the start he'd been intrigued by the idea of taking over his dead cousin's woman as well as his position. And it was the only way to get the money Julian had denied him during his lifetime and after his death.

At that moment the fifth earl's glance met that of the fourth earl's widow as she looked up from her conversation. Under his stare the vivacity he'd noted an instant before was replaced by that curiously lifeless indifference he'd come to associate with her, and any indecision about whether or not to retire from the lists was resolved then and there. By heaven, here was a female just begging to be mastered. If he couldn't gain her consent by the usual means, then he'd see what less-conventional methods could achieve.

Lord Whitlaw gave his cousin-in-law a mocking salute and took himself off to the cardroom, where he spent an unusually profitable hour playing whist, which he was pleased to see as an omen of future success in his quest.

The next morning Serena simulated an enthusiasm she was far from feeling in response to her mother's inquiries about her party. As expected, Mrs. Boynton and Verity had enjoyed a typical evening at Almack's, unvaried by any new elements or acquaintances.

It was one of the mornings Serena had set aside for exercising with Natasha, but she went off to the Talbot house with less than her usual pleasure. The chance of meeting Peter Phillips during these sessions was slight, but her desire to avoid him was marked enough to produce a tension in her body that resisted her efforts at relaxation. During the first half of the practice hour she found it a more difficult task than usual to stretch out her muscles. It required dogged persistence and fixed concentration on isolated parts of her body to attain a state approaching her normal limberness by the time Miss Tottenham rose from the piano bench.

As was her custom, Natasha plied the accompanist with tea and delicacies from the kitchen. Miss Tottenham was looking a bit less emaciated these days but her nervous fluttery manner had not abated even when she began to feel comfortable enough in the large house in Portman Square to inquire for periodic reports on Justin's progress. Today she regaled Natasha and Serena with stories of the indignities she endured at the hands of some of the persons who engaged her services as a music teacher.

"Arrivistes, that's what they are," she pronounced between dainty mouthfuls of plum cake. "Their manners bespeak their lack of gentility despite their haughty airs and rich furnishings."

When Miss Tottenham had gone, Natasha persuaded her friend to stay for another cup of tea, though Serena's state of mind was such that she would have preferred to forgo the customary *tête-à-tête* lest the conversation should somehow come around to the person of Lord Phillips. Natasha forestalled the plea of another engagement hovering on the tip of her tongue by mentioning that Nurse was going to bring Justin down for a visit. Since serious conversation could never flourish when the active infant was present, Serena sat back and prepared to enjoy herself.

"You seemed to be doing a lot of muttering under your breath during the exercise routine today," Natasha observed with smiling sympathy. "Is the London pace starting to wear you down?"

"It must be," Serena admitted, taking a sip of her tea. "I was a bit tired this morning and found it difficult to get really involved at first, but once I've finished exercising, I feel more invigorated. What about you? Do you never feel tired or out-of-sorts during the Season?"

"I'm scarcely ever tired, but then, I don't go the pace the way you must with a girl in her first Season to chaperone. It never ceases to amaze me how these girls manage to racket around till the wee hours of the morning night after night without becoming ill or at least losing their looks from exhaustion."

"I am persuaded none but the most robust or most dedicated of them do go through it unscathed. Every now and again Verity must have a day of complete quiet with no evening activity scheduled, so that she may catch up on her rest and soothe down her nerves. I cannot recall ever getting to that stage during my own come-out, but then, my constitution is stronger than Verity's."

"It must be the single-minded dedication to catching a husband that keeps them going," Natasha said with a grin. "What about Verity? Is there any sign of a growing attachment in that quarter?"

"Andrew Silverdale is becoming rather particular in his attentions, and there are one or two others that she seems to favor, at least as dancing partners, but I have seen no evidence of anything warmer on her part. Now that she has gotten over her initial timidity and made friends, she is enjoying the experience in her own quiet way, but I do not believe Verity will ever be a really *ton*-ish sort of person. That is why it's vital that she marry the right sort of man, one who won't expect her to shine as a society hostess."

"It's vital that all females marry the right sort of man, whatever sort that might be. Speaking of which, would I be correct in assuming that you have recently acquired a serious suitor?"

Serena froze, her mind so full of Peter Phillips' perfidy that she did not at first realize that Natasha must be speaking of the earl. "Whitlaw? I fear you are indeed correct, worse luck."

"You do not like him? He is certainly handsome enough to make most girls swoon."

"I don't trust handsome men," Serena snapped.

"I hope you will except Cam from that categorical denunciation," Natasha replied cheerfully. There was a teasing glint in her dark eyes, and a smile tugged at her lips as Serena blushed and stammered.

"Of . . . of course. I was speaking generally. In general, very handsome men tend to be odiously vain and smugly certain that every female must fall at their feet in adoration."

"Much like very beautiful women," Natasha put in mildly. "Not Cam, though. It always embarrassed him that females couldn't keep from staring at him in admiration, myself included." She chuckled. "I do believe he was used to regard his face as a cross to bear. I have saved him from all that by removing him from circulation, though women still stare, of course, and try to practice their arts of fascination on him, particularly Lady Frobisher," she concluded dryly.

"You . . . Do you never worry that one day he will succumb to . . . ? *No*, forgive me, it was monstrous of me to voice such a speculation. Please do not regard it."

Natasha ignored her friend's crimson-cheeked distress and addressed herself to the issue she had raised. "I am very secure in Cam's love, thrilled by it, warmed and surrounded by it." Her voice was soft, the dark eyes serious as she went on. "No one can know or control the future, but in marriage more than any other relationship there must be complete trust or you don't have anything at all."

"Sometimes one's trust is betrayed."

"True, and it must be a devastating experience, but humans aren't perfect beings; we're all flawed and need forgiveness at times, especially marriage partners, because they can wound each other more than anyone else by the very nature of marriage. It's the other side of the coin: the joys of marriage are also greater than all others."

"Well, it's not for me, thank you. It sounds much too uncomfortable, and if I were ever so idiotic as to fall in love, it would not be with anyone like Lord Whitlaw. He sees marriage to me as a way to gain his cousin's fortune along with his title and honors."

"Not a flattering prospect, admittedly, but I think you underrate yourself, Serena, and you should not. If the opposite of vanity is a sin, then you are a sinner indeed. Do you not know how beautiful you are with your regal bearing and striking coloring? Do you never look in your mirror? I have observed the reactions of a number of gentlemen on seeing you for the first time. They halt, they stare, then invariably they straighten up and throw their shoulders back before approaching you. It may be that you underestimate Lord Whitlaw too. You might at least credit the man with an honest admiration."

"Lord Whitlaw," Serena retorted, "would have courted me with exactly the same false flattery had I been hump-backed and spotted. He reminds me of a snake, beautiful in his way, coiled gracefully, just waiting to strike when the victim is in position."

Natasha laughed at the analogy but protested, "You are too severe, but I see there is no reasoning with you on the subject of Lord Whitlaw. I must confess that I did not take to him myself when I met him in Brussels last year. One rather suspects that he cherishes an inflated idea of the effect of that undeniably prepossessing profile and physique on the female of the species."

"Well, here is one female who is immune to his so-called charms."

Serena plunked her cup down in its saucer with a crisp little noise, and her rounded chin firmed in a way Natasha could only describe as militant. She had been hoping to put in a favorable word for her brother once she had ascertained whether her friend favored Lord Whitlaw's suit, but somehow the moment and Serena's mood did not seem auspicious for such sisterly intervention. She wisely decided against meddling, and at that moment Nurse appeared with a bright-eyed chortling baby, which effectively turned both women's thoughts to a happier subject.

8

Now was not the moment for heroics or applying pressure, Lord Phillips decided on the morning after his explosive contretemps with Serena, which he reviewed in light of the information Natasha had supplied, scant though it was, about her friend's marriage. He might have done considerable damage to their tenuous friendship by pressing her when she was already somewhat distraught to the point where she lost her temper and revealed things she had wished to keep private. It was a foregone conclusion that she was now angry, and her anger would be directed at him. Much though it chafed him to let the grass grow under his feet, he had best play least-in-sight for a time, until her resentment faded.

It would be comforting to believe that a temporary pique summed up the situation, but in his heart he feared this was the lesser aspect of his problem. He had begun to make some progress with Serena of late. Against her will, she found him amusing and had come to feel fairly comfortable in his company. There had been a mild welcome in her eyes at times, even when his appearance was not a timely rescue from Lord Whitlaw's advances. He had destroyed that ease by abandoning his careful strategy in the heat of the moment and allowing her a glimpse of his feelings. She had panicked. He had seen it in her eyes and heard it in her voice.

It had been obvious all along that Serena was quite different from most women in that she did not seek or seem to welcome masculine admiration. Everything about her fascinated him, from the glory of her rich russet hair and magnificent eyes to the hint of bravado with which she met the world, at least the masculine half, but this touch-me-not quality had intrigued and challenged him from the start. It had also baffled his seeking intelligence until now.

He could make no claims to a perfect understanding of the complex individual that was Serena Allenby—if he were so blessed by fortune as to gain her hand, that would be the happy quest of a lifetime—but the revelation that her marriage "had not been a success," vague though the description was, provided a flare of intense light by which to examine and interpret her behavior. For want of an apparent cause, he had previously attributed her lack of response to male admiration to her recently widowed state. It had seemed reasonable to postulate a lingering grief and a concomitant, perhaps not even understood avoidance of emotion. One couldn't be hurt if one avoided forming attachments. Without actually putting his passing thoughts into a systematic framework, he had instinctively bent his efforts toward gaining her confidence in him as a person whose company she could enjoy without fearing that emotional demands would be made on her. Meanwhile, his own feelings had to be kept out of sight lest he frighten her away before she was ready to accept them. Until last night he had managed to sink the impatient lover in the role of friend, taking comfort in signs of definite progress.

Accusing eyes in the mirror stared back at him above the lather his valet was applying to his face. There was no escaping the fact that he'd brought his own laborious efforts to naught during that waltz. What had possessed him to press her in that inquisitorial manner? He tilted his chin up in response to his man's direction, thus removing the image of a fool from his sight. The fact that he'd been nettled by her cynical comments on marriage was no excuse, nor was his legitimate desire to learn what there was between Serena and her husband's heir that she should react so strongly to the man. If there was any truth in him at all, he'd better admit that he'd simply lost his head and tried first to force an acknowledgment out of her that there existed some degree of attachment between themselves, and then, not content with receiving the reply he least wanted but should have expected, he'd compounded his error by relentlessly pinning her down until her temper flared and she divulged both her aversion to Whitlaw and its shocking cause.

The eyes in the mirror were somber now as he took the damp towel from his valet and completed the task of removing the traces of soap from his neck and ears before tackling the ticklish chore of arranging his neckcloth in the precise folds he favored. To his man Marsden, hovering in the background with several spare neckcloths draped over his arm in the rare event that he ruined his first attempt, the frown on his master's face would seem to be one of concentration, but Peter's thoughts were not on his busy fingers at the moment.

Unless he could come to a better understanding of Serena's marriage, last night's fiasco could be much more serious than a temporary setback. "Not a successful marriage" could cover a vast amount of territory. He'd not been curious before, preferring like the ostrich to remain ignorant of something he did not wish to acknowledge, but now he felt a burning need to know everything so that he might reassess his own strategy. After all, it was one thing to take matters slowly in courting a woman whose grief had not yet healed, and quite another to have to deal with the prejudices of a confirmed manhater. Was this the case? Could Serena's behavior be interpreted in that light?

As he lowered his chin and dropped his jaw to press in the proper creases, Peter wore an air of abstraction which lingered as he accepted Marsden's assistance in shrugging into a coat of burgundy superfine that looked as if it had been molded on his form while still providing a modicum of free movement within. It never did to lose sight of comfort entirely, though Cam jokingly accused him of being a dandy who cared for nothing save the cut of his clothes. Had he been present this morning, Cam would have been astonished at the lack of attention to the details of his appearance being paid by his fastidious brother-in-law as he accepted a ruby tie pin from his valet and slipped on his gold signet ring.

Lord Phillips was considering where to begin his search for information. Natasha had already warned him not to ask her any more questions, and Serena would be unwilling to tell him the time of day until her temper had cooled. She would be doubly on guard in the future against any personal revelations. Verity had never spoken of her sister's marriage, and he did not quite like using the child in such a way. That would seem to reduce the possibilities to masculine sources. Cam, who had been out of the country during most of Serena's marriage, was an unlikely conduit of information, but his cousin Charles was a fixture in London and seemed to be the type who knew everything that happened and where the bodies were buried, not to mention the skeletons.

Further subjecting Mr. Charles Talbot to mental analysis, Peter decided his chances of accidentally meeting this gentleman would be enhanced by a stroll though White's rather than a look-in at Jackson's Boxing Saloon or a ride in the park. He accepted his hat and ebony walking stick from Marsden, picked up his gloves, and prepared to set out in pursuit of knowledge.

The sound of a carriage pulling up outside the house gave him pause halfway down the stairs. Having no desire to do the pretty to any of Natasha's callers at present, he stayed out of sight above the landing, ready to sprint back upstairs should the visitors be admitted. His prudence was rewarded a moment later when Serena was escorted from a room on the ground level to her waiting carriage by Dawson. He'd forgotten it was an exercise morning. Feeling thankful to have escaped a frosty greeting from his uncompromising beloved, he waited another minute after Dawson returned to the nether regions before leaving the house.

It took two days of casual patrolling before Peter ran his quarry to earth in the dining room at White's. Having spotted Talbot's light brown head bent over a solitary meal, he supplied himself with a prop in the form of a newspaper and wandered into the dining room, glancing idly around. He was hailed by Cam's cousin, who lifted his glass and invited, "Join me, Phillips, unless you are meeting someone?"

"Thank you. The friend I was expecting sent word he could not make it after all," Peter replied, trusting that Talbot would not ask the name of his nonexistent friend. "What looks good?" he asked, glancing at the other's plate as he seated himself across the table.

"The veal chop is not completely inedible," Mr. Talbot said. He signaled to the waiter. "The same for Lord Phillips, and bring another bottle of the burgundy."

While they waited for Peter's meal to arrive, they spoke of inconsequential things in the manner of persons whose knowledge of each other comes mostly at second hand.

"How is your arm coming along?" Mr. Talbot asked, his eyes lingering for a time on the fading but still discernible scar on Lord Phillips' cheek. "Natasha was concerned that it was slow to heal."

"It was, but I would say now that I have about ninety percent of the movement and strength back, though I was sparring at Jackson's the other day, and my right is definitely not what it was used to be."

"Then if you should ever feel the urge to swing at me, I beg you will use your right hand."

Peter grinned in appreciation of this pleasantry and took a sip from his wineglass.

They spoke desultorily of some of the reform bills being debated in Parliament. Talbot did most of the talking while Peter caught up on his meal. He was listening with only part of his attention as he scrambled around in his brain for a way to introduce the topic of Serena's marriage in a casual manner that would not arouse the other man's curiosity. Charles Talbot was the last person in the world to whom anyone would choose to make a present of his deepest feelings. He stared down at his veal chop in frowning concentration as he slowly sliced off a piece.

"I fear you are having difficulty with that chop. Accept my apologies if I steered you wrong in recommending it."

"Oh, no, no, it is perfectly acceptable," Peter protested, quickly helping himself to another forkful. He caught the other's eyes roaming his face in an assessing manner and raised his brows in question.

"Was I staring? Forgive the impertinence, but I could not help trying to discern some . . ."

"Family resemblance to my sister? Don't apologize. I'm used to that look. Serena—Lady Whitlaw—subjected me to the same scrutiny when we met, and concluded one of us must be a changeling."

"Ah, the fair Juno, the elsusive Lady Whitlaw. Unlike you, I am not among the fortunate few privileged to use her Christian name."

"No doubt because you do not have the good fortune to be her dear friend's brother. If you seek that privilege, I would advise you to beg Natasha to intercede for you."

"Tempting though the lady's fortune and beauty undoubtedly are, I have regretfully concluded that she is too big to make an aesthetically pleasing match for one of my moderate inches, and aesthetics being all-important in my life, I must concentrate my efforts on more diminutive heiresses. Lady Whitlaw's statuesque figure requires a big hulk . . . er, that is to say, a man of heroic stature, like yourself, for instance, to properly complement her appeal."

"Or Lord Whitlaw perhaps?" Peter suggested, refusing to take offense at the calculated slip of the tongue. "I noticed they made a striking couple on the dance floor."

"Surely you jest? After seeing them together only once, it was perfectly plain to my poor intelligence that it would not do at all. She fairly bristles with antagonism when Whitlaw comes near. Can you possibly have failed to notice?" Skepticism looked out of one pair of bright blue eyes, to be met by bland surprise in an equally bright pair.

"I can't say that I have noted a particular aversion to Lord Whitlaw. Serena strikes me as universally unreceptive to masculine charms."

"Not surprising, really." Charles paused to take a drink from his glass while Peter tried to curb his eagerness. He permitted himself another encouraging lift of his brows, but held his tongue. After a tense hiatus, the other obliged by going on. "Whitlaw, and I refer to the late unlamented fourth earl, was, to put it succinctly, an inveterate woman-chaser. Most parents would have locked up their daughters in his vicinity, but Boynton found the price offered sufficient to quiet any scruples he might have possessed about handing his daughter over to a man who was rarely sober after noontime and kept a stable of mistresses to boot."

"What about Serena? Did she know nothing of this?"

Talbot shrugged. "Who would have told her? You know how sheltered such girls are. It's my guess she was flattered to be singled out by a wealthy titled man, older and more articulate than the beardless chubs who danced around her in fawning adoration. If you think she and the present earl make a handsome couple, well, the fourth earl was every bit as dashing in his day, before the drink really got to him."

"How did he die?"

"A hunting accident while drunk as a lord, no pun intended. And now the lovely widow is rolling in lovely money, which proves there is some justice in the world, does it not? Or do I mean irony?"

"If he left her his private fortune, might that not be an indication that the marriage was a success?"

"It might, except for two things: one, it was well-known that Whitlaw hated his cousin like poison—he'd never have left him a groat beyond the entail—and two, the happy couple were scarcely ever seen together after the honeymoon. To the best of my knowledge, Lady Whitlaw never left Herefordshire after her marriage. Certainly she did not reappear in London again until this spring. Whitlaw went back to his old haunts, if you take my meaning."

"I see. In view of what you have told me, I would have to agree that Serena's unencouraging attitude toward men is not surprising. Doubtless she now plans to enjoy her fortune and her freedom, and who can blame her?"

Charles Talbot listened to this casual statement with a

knowing look on his face. "Well, now, something tells me this issue is no longer so clear-cut as it once was. A fascinating picture is beginning to form in my mind of an immovable object about to encounter an irresistible force. Which will prevail, I wonder?"

"I'm afraid you've lost me," Peter said apologetically, polishing off the last of his chop, though it cost an effort. He could certainly understand Cam's lack of affinity for his cousin. The fellow had the nature of a buzzing insect, constantly plaguing his victim for the pleasure of seeing him squirm.

"Oh, I should hate to think so poorly of your powers of comprehension as to have to explain which applies to whom, but I am persuaded I need not. I wonder whom I shall back?" Charles mused.

"You find your fellow creatures an unfailing source of amusement, do you?" Peter asked in level tones.

"Not unfailing, my dear fellow—that would be too much to hope for. You know, I should make you pay for this meal. You've gotten your money's worth in information. Now do not, I beg of you, persist in maintaining that look of imbecilic incomprehension. I am well aware that I in my innocence issued the invitation and I am prepared to pay the toll."

"I do not recall introducing any topic of conversation," replied Peter, still with an air of one seeking enlightenment.

"Very true, but if memory serves, it was you who introduced the lady's name into the conversation, and very cleverly done too. I'd give a lot to know how long you've been stalking me, but I do see that that is another question you would consider indelicate." He sighed. "I really do hope you did not strike it lucky on the very first try."

Peter smiled but made no answer, and Charles finally turned the subject to an impersonal topic. No more was said of Serena that day. Oddly enough, when Charles Talbot abandoned his petty verbal swordplay he could speak to a variety of present-day issues like a sensible man, even displaying an analytical turn of mind that seemed at variance with his butterfly image. Peter was

forced to alter and expand his original estimation of
Cam's cousin.

The interview with Charles Talbot had provided the
information Peter sought, but at a price he had hoped to
avoid. It would be idle to suppose that someone of
Charles's news-gathering proclivity would allow the incident to fade into decent oblivion. He could only hope
that his clumsy approach would not result in Serena's
name being entered in the betting book at White's. No
respectable woman would welcome that kind of notoriety.

There was no satisfaction in having obtained evidence
that Serena's husband had been a chronic philanderer
and an inebriate. Her continued unresponsiveness to masculine blandishments could now be seen as the result of a
determined policy of avoidance, even renunciation. If the
panic-driven denial she had made of any closeness between themselves was a fair indication, the hard-won
gains he had prided himself on achieving over a period of
weeks had been nullified in the course of one climactic
dance.

Peter's unhappy suspicions on this head received ample confirmation over the next sennight. Serena's manner
to him when they met in company was remote to the
point of stiffness. She excused herself from dancing with
him at Almack's and refused an invitation to ride in the
park on the grounds of having too little free time to ride
at present. When he encountered her two days later
riding with another admirer, she returned his mild greeting with a defiant stare rather than the shamed blushes
befitting someone caught out in a social lie. He was being
punished with a vengeance for the crime of aspiring to
her confidence.

For reasons of policy, Peter would not have displayed
any annoyance at her graceless behavior, but he actually
experienced none. It was natural to him to make every
allowance for her fear that the independent role she had
designed for her future should be threatened. The surety
that he more than Whitlaw threatened that security kept
him from committing acts of recklessness out of discour-
agement. Also he deemed his makeup more suited to a

waiting game than Serena's, despite her praiseworthy but unavailing attempts to match her nature to her name.

Matters were still in the same unsatisfactory state one fine late-spring morning more than a week after the quarrel on the dance floor, when Peter, finding himself on Piccadilly near St. James's Church, wandered into Hatchard's book shop for a browse round. He was glancing through an edition of paintings of Venice and Rome when a soft "Oh, dear!" in familiar tones alerted him. He started around the end of the row of shelves as a pleasant masculine voice offered, "Allow me to reach the book for you, ma'am. This one?"

Peter entered the adjacent row of shelves in time to see an unknown young man hold out a volume to Verity Boynton with a smiling comment. "It strikes me as a poor practice to place a book as popular as *Waverley* nearly out of reach."

"Y-yes, th-thank you, sir. Oh, dear . . ." This last exclamation came as the books already resting in the girl's arms slid to the floor despite her juggling attempts to shift them while accepting the book the young man still extended to her. Both figures instinctively bent down, sinking to their knees to retrieve the fallen books, and in so doing bumped knees.

"I do b-beg your pardon, sir. So clumsy of me."

Peter could see that Verity's cheeks were the color of the pink sash around the waist of her sprigged-muslin dress as she sprang back from the contact, but the man remained composed as he held out an imperative hand and assisted her to her feet.

"It was entirely my fault, ma'am. Please stay there while I gather up these books for you." He smiled kindly at the embarrassed girl before proceeding to retrieve the scattered volumes. Peter had taken a step forward initially to assist in this chore, but something in the attitude of the pair involved kept him still after that one step. The gentleman's back was partially turned but Verity was nearly facing his way and must have seen him had her attention not been so concentrated on the figure of the slim stranger. When the latter stood up again, holding

out the books toward the waiting girl, his gaze was as
rapt as hers had been.

"Here you are, ma'am. No harm done."

"No. Thank you so much, sir. I must apologize for
being so very clumsy and inconveniencing you."

"Not at all." The man's voice was most decided. "It
could never be anything but a privilege to be of assistance to you." His fervent words rang with sincerity and
seemed to startle both parties, for there was an instant of
charged silence before the gentleman doffed his hat and
said on a more restrained note, "May I introduce myself,
ma'am? My name is Nigel Selcort."

"I am Verity Boynton," she managed, barely above a
whisper.

"Verity," he repeated, caressing the syllables. "What's
in a name? Could any appellation be more charming or
more perfectly suited to its owner? You—"

"So this is where you've gotten to, Verity," said another voice with a far-less-worshipful intonation.

Serena's appearance at the other end of the aisle acted
on her sister and Mr. Selcort like a dash of water on a
sleepwalker. They jerked back in unison and turned dazed
faces in her direction as she followed her voice down the
aisle toward the unmoving pair.

"May I know the name of your friend, Verity?" Serena's words were noncommittal, but the emerald glance
flashing between the two was sharp.

"He . . . this is Mr. Selcort," her sister began.

"I have just been presenting my friend Selcort to your
sister, Serena." Lord Phillips spoke up, having drawn
nearer to the enlarged party unperceived by any of its
members.

Three heads turned his way and three pairs of eyes
focused on him with a variety of expressions that nearly
caused him to lose his countenance. Serena looked affronted, Verity's large eyes were eloquent of gratitude,
and Mr. Selcort's were astonished. His lips parted, then
pressed together again, his attitude one of watchfulness.

"With your permission, I'll finish what I started," Peter went on with a smiling bow in Serena's direction. "Lady Whitlaw, may I present Mr. Selcort?"

The gentleman bowed over Serena's hand and made the proper responses, his intelligent gray eyes meeting hers with impersonal courtesy. She performed her part equally well, asking with a little smile, "Do you live in London, Mr. Selcort?"

"No, ma'am, I am here on a visit to some friends."

"I see. I hope your stay in town will prove enjoyable. Verity, my dear, I fear we must be going. It grows late and we are expected home for luncheon."

"Yes, of course."

Serena's eyes fell on the books in her sister's arms. "Goodness, do you intend to purchase all those?"

"Oh, no. I was trying to decide on which to select for Perry when I spotted *Waverley.* I'll put them back."

"Allow me do it for you, Miss Boynton," begged Mr. Selcort, making a move to relieve her of her burden.

It was Serena who said, "Thank you, Mr. Selcort, you are very kind," as the young girl, much paler now, turned the books over to him mutely, her glance falling away almost immediately from the intensity of his.

Peter thought he detected a plea for help in the farewell look Verity directed at him as she murmured an echo to her sister's "Good morning, gentlemen," when they moved away, leaving the two men standing in the aisle. His own inclusion in the collective "gentlemen" was the closest Serena had come to speaking to him, nor had she glanced at him after that first annoyed look.

He closed his mind to his personal problems and turned to study the young man at his side, approving on the whole of what he saw. Air and address were deferentially pleasing in a young man of three- or four-and-twenty and allied to an added touch of quiet confidence. His person was attractive without being in any way remarkable. He was dressed with neatness and propriety and no pretensions to the fashionable. His blue coat was of good cloth and well-cut but did not hug his loose-limbed form. His linen was spotless, his waistcoat plain, and his cravat of moderate height and complexity. A single fob hung below his waistcoat and he wore no jewelry except a small pearl tie pin. Under a wavy mane of gold-streaked fair hair cut shorter than the prevailing fashion his face was long and thin-cheeked, his nose straight and rather long, his chin, below a sensitively cut mouth, almost aggressively square. It was those clear, narrow gray eyes beneath straight brows that gave his countenance its distinctive look of intelligence.

Those narrow eyes were now turning toward Peter, a question in their depths.

"I agree that it is time to find out exactly what it is I've done," Peter said, a quizzical smile playing about his mouth.

The smile was not returned. "Why did you do it?" asked Mr. Selcort gravely.

"To be honest, I'm not entirely certain whether I sponsored you to help your cause or to annoy Serena, but I must admit I expected more of gratitude and less of censure on your part." His tone invited explanation.

"Perhaps I had best tell you right off that I am in orders and am not quite comfortable with anything that smacks of deception."

"A minister," Peter groaned. "That tears it. Serena would never sit still for a mere parson courting her sister."

Mr. Selcort drew himself up to his considerable height. His eyes were almost on a level with the other's as he replied with a challenging tilt to his chin, "The ministry is an honorable calling that requires no apology to anyone."

"I couldn't agree with you more, but unless you are the possessor of a splendid living and an independent income, you aren't going to be regarded as a serious contender for the hand of Verity Boynton."

A dark flush spread over Mr. Selcort's pronounced cheekbones and he uttered with difficulty, "I have just this instant met Miss Boynton."

"That's right," Peter agreed with cheerful brutality, "and if I was mistaken in believing you completely bowled out by her, then there's no problem at all and no reason to prolong this conversation either."

The ensuing silence lasted for a full minute while the

younger man wrestled with his pride and the other watched him not unsympathetically. At last Mr. Selcort said on a sigh, "You were not mistaken, sir. She is the loveliest girl I've ever seen, and the sweetest."

"You may be right, though it's beyond me how you can be so sure in less than five minutes. However, I digress. I take it you are indicating a desire to improve your acquaintance with Miss Boynton even though I warn you her family will not look favorably on your suit. Is that a fair statement?"

The pause was shorter this time. "I am not entirely dependent on the stipend from the living that will shortly come to me. My family is well-respected in Dorset, but we are neither wealthy nor ennobled. Are you?"

"Am I what?"

"Wealthy or ennobled?"

"At the risk of further exacerbating that stiff pride of yours, I'll have to admit to both, I'm afraid, but I was also in the military for almost ten years and have friends in all walks of life. Now, unless you intend to buy all those books you are clutching to your chest, I suggest that you put them back on the shelves so that I can take you to my club for lunch, where we shall have to compound the original deception by inventing a tale to account for our friendship. What is it?" he asked as a strange expression crossed the young man's face. "Another attack of scruples?"

"I've just realized that I don't even know your name."

Peter gave a hoot of laughter, quickly muted in respect for their surroundings. "If Serena hadn't been so intent on sending me to Coventry just now, she might have dropped my name and discovered the truth from your blank look. We'll take that as a good omen, shall we?"

9

"Mama," said Serena, lowering her embroidery frame to her lap, "have you noticed anything . . . odd about Verity lately?"

"Mmmmn, what did you say, my dear?" Mrs. Boynton looked up from the pile of bills she was studying, an abstracted frown gradually smoothing away from her still-pretty face as she focused myopic blue eyes on her elder daughter.

The ladies were established in the small ground-floor apartment at the rear of the house that served as a morning room. Serena was nestled in the corner of the rose-colored sofa, a selection of bright embroidery silks spilling out of the tapestry work bag on the cushion beside her, while Mrs. Boynton sat at a tulipwood desk near the window.

"I asked if you'd noticed anything strange in Verity's behavior of late."

"In what way strange?" Mrs. Boynton's eyes slid again to the bill in her hand. "I cannot credit the cost of those three bonnets just delivered from Madame Irene, quite ordinary straw for the warmer weather and with nothing extravagant about the trimmings to elevate the price. Would you check the addition, Serena?"

"Yes, later. Will you attend to me for a moment, please, Mama?"

"I am attending, dearest. You evidently think Verity is acting oddly, and I asked you in what way."

"For a few days last week she seemed quite animated, almost eager to fulfill our social obligations, which you will grant is unusual even though she has overcome her shyness to a great extent. But lately she has not been in spirits. Quite the reverse, I would say. On two occasions this week she has pleaded a headache so that we have left parties early, and it seems to me she has been a trifle mopish about the house too. Do you think she could be sickening for something?"

"Have you asked her if anything is wrong?"

"Yes, of course I have."

"And what did she reply?" prompted Mrs. Boynton when her daughter's subsequent pause had gone on too long.

"At first she denied anything was amiss, but when I pressed her about her lack of spirits, she allowed as how she was missing her music more than she had anticipated. She has been used to spend several hours each day at the pianoforte."

"Yes, dear, I know. And did you believe her?"

Serena, noting her mother's amused little smile, said a touch defensively, "Well, I have hired a piano for the remainder of our lease. It arrives tomorrow. I don't know why I did not think of it in the beginning. Music will be a welcome addition to our Sunday-night suppers as well as affording pleasure to Verity."

"Yes, dear."

The smile still lingered in Mrs. Boynton's eyes as she turned back to her bills, and her daughter demanded, "If you do not believe Verity's mopishness is related to her music, then to what *do* you attribute it?"

"I cannot be certain at this stage, but I would say she displays all the classic symptoms of a girl in love: evasiveness, languishing airs, a sudden access of interest when a caller is announced, instantly followed by disappointment when the wrong person is shown in, a tendency to dissolve into tears over the least little thing, and pathetic attempts to appear happy and normal when others comment on her behavior."

"Are you sure of this? I do not recall anything of the sort."

Mrs. Boynton's large eyes rested on her daughter's startled, slightly challenging countenance. "Well, you never suffered from this particular complaint, but my sisters did. I did myself, come to that," she added with a reminiscent little smile that was lost on Serena, who had been doing some rapid thinking while her mother spoke. Now she announced:

"If you are indeed correct, then I believe I know who the man is."

"That is the thing that had me stymied, for I cannot think she has demonstrated a decided preference for any of her admirers. Who is it?"

"None of her admirers, at least no one known to us. Lord Phillips presented a friend to her in Hatchard's last week, and I thought at the time that there was something odd about the way they looked at each other, an intentness that made one feel *de trop* somehow."

"Who is he? What is his name?"

"Selcort, Nigel Selcort, but I have no idea who his family might be. Have you ever heard of them? I believe he said he is from Dorset."

"The only Selcorts I ever heard of were a dreadful group of mushrooms from Yorkshire." Mrs. Boynton shuddered delicately. "What is he like?"

"Oh, quite ordinary. He is young, about three- or four-and-twenty, I should say, tall and thin, with pleasant but undistinguished features, a bit more serious-minded, from his appearance, than most of her court."

"Has she met him since?"

"I am nearly certain she has not, which would account for most of that behavior you described. I have rather kept an eye out for him myself because of that strange impression I received the day we met him. Where is Verity today?"

"Lunching with the Silverdales. Until you mentioned Mr. Selcort's name, I was coming around to your view that Andrew might do very well for Verity, since Lord Phillips' interest in her is clearly of a brotherly nature."

Serena shot her mother a rapier look designed to detect any hidden meaning, but Mrs. Boynton's expression remained innocent until a sudden flash of comprehension caused her to raise her head. "I wonder . . . Verity mentioned this morning that Lord Phillips would be coming to supper this Sunday *with a friend*. She was very casual about it, but I remember thinking that this would be the first time Lord Phillips has joined us, which is not to be wondered at, since we have kept these occasions as informal get-togethers for Verity's particular friends, and they are considerably younger than he for the most part."

"What would you care to wager against Lord Phillips' friend being named Selcort?"

"Not a great deal, but why do you look so displeased, dearest? How else are young people to advance their acquaintance with those to whom they take a fancy, if not through the good offices of friends?"

"Why have we not met this Nigel Selcort at Almack's? Why has Lord Phillips not brought him to call before this? The only answer must be that he is totally ineligible, that's why."

"Nonsense, my dear. Any friend of Lord Phillips' must be perfectly acceptable, after all."

"There is a world of difference, Mama, between socially acceptable and matrimonially eligible. You may depend upon it, this Mr. Selcort will turn out to be impossible."

"I am persuaded that you take too serious a view of the matter, Serena," her parent had protested, but by the time the last happy, replete guest had departed on Sunday evening, Mrs. Boynton was inclined to accept that her elder daughter's instincts had not been at fault.

She found Mr. Nigel Selcort much as Serena described him. There was much to like and nothing to object to in appearance and address. His attire was distinguished by none of the quirks of fashion popular among the other young men in Verity's set, and he wore his unremarkable garments with the unconscious air of one supremely at ease with his own presence. She also noted that seriousness of manner described by Serena, but was not personally in a position to put forth an opinion on the range of his conversational skills at the end of the evening. On discovering within one minute of their initial meeting that Mr. Selcort was in orders and on the brink of taking

up his first position in the church, Mrs. Boynton had
skillfully passed him along to the Silverdale sisters while
she sought to master her disappointment and chagrin.
She had exchanged a speaking look with Serena before
herding everyone into the dining room, where a tempting
array of mostly cold foods was set out all ready for the
guests to select for themselves.

The keynote on these occasions was informality, with
each participant free to find the company and place that
best suited him or her while the food was actually being
consumed. Before the arrival of the pianoforte, the young
people had generally amused themselves after eating with
some sort of charades or round games. Mrs. Boynton
was grateful that the instrument's availability lent itself to
a change of program this time. A faint hope that Serena
had been mistaken in her identification of Mr. Selcort as
the man for whom her sister was pining had been squashed
when Verity and her new admirer somehow managed to
overset her relatives' attempts to steer them in opposite
directions and had ended by effectively dining *tête-à-tête*
in an alcove made by the clever rearrangement of chairs
as the others milled around them unnoticed. If Mrs.
Boynton's fears had needed confirmation, she had only
to glance at Andrew Silverdale's glowering face as his
eyes continually sought out Verity and her supper partner. The poor boy was obviously eaten up by jealousy. It
was Andrew who led the chorus of requests that Verity
play for her guests, and Mrs. Boynton and Serena were
delighted to take advantage of the situation to detach her
from Lord Phillips' friend.

Shy though she undoubtedly was in all other aspects of
her life, Verity had the soul of an artist when it came to
her music. There was no maidenly shrinking to contend
with; she played willingly, at first some of her own favorite compositions and then requests from her friends. It
was an easy matter to go from there to vocal and choral
selections, which took the party happily to the signal for
departure.

This came rather early on the night in question, in the
person of the son of the house, whose unexpected arrival

in the bosom of his family occurred during a rollicking rendition of "He Who Would an Alehouse Keep" sung by the entire company. Serena, who could not carry a tune to save her life, chanced to look up as the door to the hall opened. She rose precipitately from her seat, such an expression of glad welcome on her face as Lord Phillips, keeping his usual unobtrusive watch on her movements, had never seen before. For an instant he was thoroughly disconcerted to see her hurl herself at the tall man who appeared in the doorway and embraced her with enthusiasm, but when the two drew apart, the family resemblance was marked enough to put his fears to rest.

Mr. Peregrine Boynton stood some five or six inches above his sister's considerable height and had the shoulders of an ox, though his large frame still bore the leanness of extreme youth. In coloring he was more allied to Verity, with blue eyes and a head of strawberry-blond curls any girl would envy, but Peter thought his features a masculine version of Serena's, with an even more decided chin.

"Perry!"

Verity's little cry and the abrupt cessation of the accompaniment brought the song to a ragged halt and all eyes to the handsome couple just inside the doorway. The young giant blushed fiery red but he laughed good-naturedly too and bent to catch up his other sister into a bear hug before releasing her to cross the room to his stunned but ecstatic mother.

The next few moments were a hubbub of introductions and farewells as the guests tactfully took their leave *en masse* after extending a friendly welcome to the son of the house, who, in the midst of all the confusion, seemed to blend a good portion of his elder sister's poise with a disarming touch of the younger's diffidence.

In describing the scene to his sister the next day, Lord Phillips chuckled and predicted that Mr. Peregrine Boynton would set a lot of maidens' hearts fluttering in a couple of years' time. "And I can name three hearts that were no doubt a bit agitated within a very few minutes of his arrival.''

"What do you mean, Peter? What three hearts?" asked Natasha, at a loss to understand the amusement in her brother's eyes.

"His mother's and sisters', you goose. Think," he urged when she still looked all at sea. "What does the unscheduled arrival of a student during term usually connote?"

The light dawned. "Do you mean he's been suspended? Oh, dear, poor Mrs. Boynton. She truly believes Oxford is honored to have her brilliant son enrolled there."

"A doting mama, I collect?"

"Heavens, yes. The sun rises and sets in Peregrine's shoes. Her daughters are lesser mortals compared with the godlike creature that is her son."

"From what I saw last night, all of them dote on him, even Serena."

"Do not look so jealous. I dote on you, do I not?" Natasha's grin of pure mischief widened when he looked revolted at the thought.

"Heaven forbid." He pinched her chin and would have left the room, but his sister said hastily:

"Stay a moment, Peter. I need to talk with you about this dinner party next week. You haven't forgotten?"

"I had, actually, but I'll be there, never fear. Who is invited?"

"Cam's uncle, Sir Humphrey, and Charles, and a few colleagues from the ministry. I've asked the Boynton ladies to leaven the political mixture a bit. Does Peregrine's arrival mean I shall have to include him, do you think? He's awfully young, and the only really young lady coming is his sister."

"Oh, I shouldn't think that will be necessary. The boy won't wish to be dragged off to dull dinner parties the minute he gets to town."

"Thank you so much! I'll have you know, brother dear, that my parties are not considered dull. My guests are carefully chosen for their conversational brilliance."

"Verity Boynton?" His eyebrows escalated, and Natasha admitted:

"Well, yes, I know she's inclined to be tongue-tied in company, but I can scarcely omit her when her mother and sister are invited. And that is why I need your advice. I'd thought Verity might partner Charles originally, but he considers her vapid, and I'm afraid she might feel a trifle uncomfortable if he should give way to his strange sense of humor if she bores him."

"Scare her witless, you mean, with his viper's tongue. It would be tantamount to throwing a goldfish into a tank with a shark."

"Can you suggest someone more suitable? You know her friends better than I do. Serena mentioned that Andrew Silverdale is one of them. Shall I ask him?"

"No," Peter said, drawing out the word as if pondering a difficult decision. "I believe my old friend Nigel Selcort might be more to her taste, and he has the added advantage of possessing a brain and a tongue."

Natasha wrinkled her forehead in puzzlement. "I do not believe I've ever heard you speak of Mr. Selcort. An old friend, did you say? A military man?"

"No, actually he's a minister."

"A *minister*?"

Peter had been edging toward the door as he spoke. Now he tossed a nonchalant "See you tonight" in the direction of his dumbfounded sister and took himself off before any more questions might be forthcoming.

Meanwhile the ripples from Peregrine's arrival had died down and the household in Beak Street had closed protectively around the newcomer once it was clear that his academic suspension had been for a minor peccadillo involving a donkey race in some hallowed precinct and was in effect only for the rest of the current term.

"I don't know what we shall do with you, Perry," Serena commented the next morning as all three ladies sat nursing their coffee while the beloved male creature discussed an elaborate breakfast sufficient for a platoon of soldiers. "We are horridly social, I'm afraid, and frankly I shouldn't think we could afford to feed you for long," she added, eyeing the two-pound slab of ham her brother had just added to his plate after demolishing six eggs.

"You would not wish me to go into a decline," he pleaded with a grin as he reached for the mustard.

"Oh, no, we wouldn't wish that," she agreed before her mother said, ignoring the byplay:

"We shall have to procure a voucher for Almack's for Peregrine."

"Oh, no, you don't, Mama. Recollect that I'm only nineteen, far too young to be hanging out for a wife. You wouldn't wish to throw me to the husband hunters just yet, would you?"

"Well, I—"

"Of course not. You are a woman of deep compassion. Besides, I haven't got a formal rig," he finished triumphantly.

Verity giggled, and his elder sister concealed a smile.

"That's easily mended," said Mrs. Boynton. "Your first stop shall be at the tailor's this morning. Weston will make you up a coat. Your father always said no one got the details as right as Weston."

"My first stop will be at the stables to assure myself that Jeb's arrangements for the horses are adequate. We got in fairly late last night."

"Now, that is something you may do without formal rig, Perry," Serena said before her mother could protest, "ride with me in the mornings."

"Well, I don't mind that. You always were a bruising rider," her brother conceded magnanimously.

"And that way Serena will be able to refuse all those riding invitations from gentlemen who bore her with their compliments," Verity said with demure mischief.

"Wait until you see Dancer, Perry." Serena turned her shoulder on her sister's teasing. "She's the most beautiful chestnut filly, complete to a shade—beautiful conformation and perfect manners now that she is used to the city noises and traffic."

"Where did you get her?"

"Lord Phillips found her for me at Tattersall's."

"Is this Lord Phillips one of your suitors?"

"Of course not; he's merely my friend's brother," Serena replied impatiently.

It was perhaps fortunate that she did not see the significant look Verity directed at Perry while explaining, "Lord Phillips was the only man here last night who could nearly look you in the eye."

"Ah, I have him now. Older than the others. He must ride nearly fifteen stone."

"All this talk about horses is getting away from the point, which is how Peregrine will occupy himself in town," Mrs. Boynton said when she could edge a word in.

"Now, Mama, don't have me on your mind. I shall do fine. There's plenty to occupy me in London. And no voucher for Almack's please. I have no intention of dancing attendance on a gaggle of man-hunting females. Tell you what," he added to forestall his parent's incipient objection, "once I get myself rigged out, I'll escort you and the girls to the occasional party or play, though *not* the opera, mind, but for the most part I plan to work out at Jackson's and just see something of the city while I'm here. No need to fear I'll be bored."

And with that vague description of his intentions his relatives had to be content, for he excused himself to see about his horses after patting his mother's arm in a gesture of mingled appeasement and affection.

Peregrine's departure left a huge gap in the atmosphere of the dining room, and not simply because of his size and the aura of vitality he took with him. His arrival the previous evening had derailed for a time all consideration of the potentially dangerous attraction that seemed to be developing between Verity and Lord Phillips' friend. No words on the subject had passed between Mrs. Boynton and Serena; indeed there had as yet been no opportunity for comments, but now, as the door closed behind Peregrine, it was clear from the look exchanged between them that their minds were once more recalled to that awkward situation. A swift glance over her coffee cup at her dreamy-eyed sister convinced Serena that Verity's thoughts were also on the person of Mr. Selcort.

Never one to evade an issue, she replaced her cup in its saucer and addressed the younger girl. "Forgive my

bluntness, Verity, but I think it infinitely advisable to
drop a hint in your ear at the outset." She hesitated and
regarded the stiffening figure of her sister with sympathy
but said firmly, "Do not allow yourself to become fond
of Mr. Selcort, my dear. He is a very pleasant young man
but hopelessly ineligible. You do see that, do you not?"

If she hoped by spelling it out clearly to wring a denial
of involvement from her generally compliant sister, she
had never been more mistaken, however, for although all
color fled Verity's face at the frontal attack, she drew
herself up straighter in her chair and replied with quiet
composure, "No, I do not see that Mr. Selcort is ineligible. I have only met him twice and have no knowledge of
his circumstances except that he is about to take over an
excellent living not far from his family's home in Dorset.
That scarcely makes him ineligible to aspire to the hand
of a nearly dowerless female of no extraordinary beauty
or accomplishment."

"You have the background and breeding to aim for a
much higher station in life, Verity. Andrew Silverdale is
already in love with you and can offer a fine position in
society and a secure future."

"*You* opted for position and security, Serena. Did it
make you happy?"

"Have you the least idea of what your life would be as
a pastor's wife? You would be forever at the beck and
call of everyone in the parrish, and your every action,
even the way you dress, would be critically observed and
reported on. A minister's wife cannot call her soul her
own."

"Since I have not been asked to become the wife of a
minister, this conversation is not only premature but
pointless," Verity retorted, rising quickly from her chair.
"If you will excuse me, Mama, I have to attend to some
personal chores this morning."

Taking her mother's dazed nod for permission, Verity
left the room, ignoring her sister's "*Wait!*"

Serena's glance returned from the closing door to find
her mother's eyes fixed accusingly on her.

"Well, you certainly made a mull of that. Did you

have to be so dogmatic and bossy? Could you not have been more tactful in your approach?"

"How would tact have served us better? You heard her. She is so besotted with this nobody after two meetings that she is ready to rear on her hind legs and fight the world. I must say I was absolutely flabbergasted to see her show such spirit. I did not think she had it in her, and I admire her for it, but it won't do, Mama. Verity would be crushed by the life she would lead as a pastor's wife. Andrew Silverdale will cosset her and see that she does not overtax her strength. Oh, it is all wrong! She must be made to see reason!" Serena half-rose as if to go after her sister.

"Now, don't you enact me a Cheltenham tragedy too. One is quite sufficient, I assure you. At least this scene served to put us on notice. Sit down, there's a good girl, and let us consider this matter unemotionally. Call for more coffee, Serena. This has gone cold."

Serena did as her mother bade, containing her impatience as best she could until they were alone once more with a fresh pot of coffee. She had not liked to interrupt her parent's brooding cogitation and had curtailed her nervous finger drumming, at a look from that lady.

"Well?" she asked anxiously when she had refilled both cups. "Have you thought of anything we can do to bring her to her senses?"

"As I see it, we shan't have to do anything if we are careful," Mrs. Boynton said calmly. "Verity may have tumbled into love with this young man in a twinkling, but who's to say he is in the same case? I shouldn't think he has the entrée to Almack's, and he knew no one here last night except Lord Phillips. If you were to drop a hint in *his* ear, where it will do the most good, we may be able to prevent their ever meeting again. There has to be some communication for a romance to flourish or it withers away from lack of sustenance. I will inform Richford that we are not at home to Mr. Selcort should he have the temerity to call here."

Serena was not best pleased to have the task of begging a favor from Lord Phillips thrust upon her, but she could not but agree with her mother's reasoning, and with her further caution.

"I think, my dear, that though we shall probably be able to choke off this infatuation, we had best be prepared to accept that Verity will not be amenable to offers from Andrew Silverdale or any others of her suitors for the immediate present. I had so hoped to have her settled this year too. I cannot help wishing that wretched young man at Jericho!"

10

Mrs. Boynton's hopes to exile Mr. Selcort from their vicinity received a rude jolt a few days later when he turned up as a guest at the Talbots' dinner party. Discretion had prevented Serena from mentioning him to Natasha during their exercise sessions, and on the two occasions when she had been in company with Lord Phillips in the interim, she had not been able to arrange the privacy necessary to such a delicate errand as her mother desired. Truth to tell, she had made no real effort to gain his ear on either occasion since, though her desperate anger at him for stepping outside of his role as a comfortable friend had not lasted beyond a few days, the feeling of awkwardness that moment had given birth to threatened to become permanent, at least on her side. She had noted with more than a trace of resentment that Peter's demeanor toward her remained exactly what it had been prior to that one revealing moment. She would have been happy to dismiss the incident as overreaction or outright misunderstanding on her part, but her instinct was too strong, so the strain remained.

Life had become rather complicated of late, and Serena was struggling to keep from sinking into the dismals. In addition to the estrangement with Peter Phillips and the need to be constantly on her toes to evade Lord Whitlaw's attentions, her former happy relations with her sister had suffered considerably since their set-to over Mr. Selcort. Verity had not actually rebuffed her sister's efforts at mending matters, but she had refused to reopen the discussion, saying simply that they would have to agree to disagree on that subject. She did not sulk or quarrel, but neither did she confide any of her feelings to her sister. Serena's marriage had put the younger girl out of the habit of sharing her thoughts with her sister, and even their current proximity this spring had not served to reestablish the old pattern. It was impossible to force her confidence, and Serena felt she had lost something of value.

Natasha's friendship was the one saving grace of this disappointing London Season. Serena had regarded this dinner party as a respite from looking over her shoulder for dangers, as it were, so she received a decided shock when the first person she set eyes on as their party was shown into the drawing room was the tall thin figure of Mr. Nigel Selcort unfolding himself from a chair. Verity's little intake of breath was perfectly apparent to her sister, as was the slight check to Mrs. Boynton's step.

Serena's eyes flew to her smiling hostess with a question in the green depths, but she was reassured by the latter's ease and subsequent surprise during the introductions when it became evident that Mr. Selcort was already known to her friends. Obviously Natasha had been neatly manipulated, and one did not need more than one guess as to the identity of the manipulator. Serena acknowledged Lord Phillips with a tight-lipped nod and moved on to smile warmly at her host.

Cam and Natasha made a most appealing pair, with his spectacular good looks and her exotic vibrancy. She was especially radiant tonight in a shimmering gown of an opalescent pearl shade that seemed to float about her supple figure. With it she wore an exquisite necklace of rubies and diamonds that elicited a spontaneous gasp of admiration from Mrs. Boynton. The matching earrings hung nearly to her shoulders and caught the light with each movement of her head. Raven-dark hair was pulled back from her heart-shaped face and arranged in a complicated series of braids and loops that enhanced her delicate profile and served as a dramatic setting for ruby-and-diamond hair ornaments.

"You look absolutely magnificent tonight, Natasha," Serena remarked within Lord Phillips' hearing.

"It is amazing, is it not, how nearly regal even a little

dab of a female can appear when she's wearing a fortune in jewels," the lady's loving brother said with a teasing look that earned him an admonitory rap on the knuckles from his victim's fan before she moved away to greet another guest.

"Yes, fie on you, Lord Phillips," Mrs. Boynton scolded, overhearing this ungallant remark. "Your sister is a most attractive young woman, whatever she wears."

"I never denied it, ma'am, but regality is another matter. Now, your daughter, I make no doubt, would look like a young queen were she wearing naught but a flour sack."

Serena, in a beautifully draped gown of gold silk tissue that set off her perfectly proportioned form to advantage, stared straight ahead and concentrated on fighting off the blush that was threatening her composure, but she was forced to look at him when he addressed her directly.

"Do you dislike jewelry, Serena? I do not believe I have ever seen you wear any jewels except those pearls."

Her fingers went to her necklace in a reflexive gesture. "My parents gave me these when I made my come-out. I have no other jewelry except for a few trinkets. As for any so-called regal airs, you must blame my martinet of a governess, who made me walk around with books on my head for hours at a time. If I dropped one, my knuckles were rapped a good deal harder than yours just now."

"Poor little girl," he mocked, but there was a caressing note in his voice that caused a ripple along her nerves. She was inordinately relieved when someone claimed his attention at this point.

Serena's feelings hardened against Lord Phillips the next instant, when she spotted Verity and Mr. Selcort chatting together, oblivious of the hubbub around them. Her mother managed to insinuate herself between the two before Serena could approach, for all the difference such puny efforts would make. She was unsurprised when Mr. Selcort led Verity in to dinner and Peter Phillips came to collect her. This was what came of tiptoeing around the subject of her odious brother to spare Natasha's feelings. Blinded by her own partiality, Natasha probably thought any female must count herself fortunate to be distinguished by Lord Phillips' notice. That this was exactly so among the vast majority of the nubile young women who populated the drawing rooms and dance floors of London this Season was a phenomenon that passed Serena's understanding. She resigned herself to another ruined evening but was pleasantly surprised to discover that the Foreign Office man on her right was a most congenial dinner partner who could converse rationally on subjects as diverse as the Holy Alliance dreamed up by Alexander of Russia, and Mr. Samuel Romilly's latest efforts to get Parliament to remove the death penalty as punishment for the theft of a few shillings' value.

In due course it became necessary to switch her attention to Lord Phillips, but she did not turn in his direction until commanded by his voice in her ear.

"As a point of interest, might I know if I have committed some new transgression to earn your disapprobation?"

Serena started slightly and widened her eyes as if she had forgotten he was there, though she had been aware of the proximity of his physical presence throughout her conversation with her other neighbor. "I beg pardon?"

"As far as I know, there is nothing wrong with your hearing," Peter replied evenly, keeping exasperation at bay.

"Talking in conundrums again, sir?" The infelicitous nature of this inadvertent reference to their last real conversation caused her to drop her eyes and compress her lips briefly at the challenge in electric-blue eyes before she mastered her facial muscles and forced herself to return his look calmly.

"I see you do not need to be reminded that I am always willing to be quite plain with you."

"Then you will not cavil at a little plain speaking from me. Natasha has told me that you played matchmaker for her and Cam. I could wish you had been satisfied with one resounding success to your credit." Her eyes followed his, which flicked involuntarily to Verity and Mr. Selcort, seated across the table but within their range of vision. Even through the maze of branches of a convoluted silver-and-glass epergne in the center of the table it was apparent that the two were utterly absorbed in each other. "Exactly," said Serena.

"That meeting in Hatchard's was a complete accident."

"Do you deny, then, that you brought Mr. Selcort to Beak Street for the express purpose of fostering what you knew to be a disastrous connection?"

"Couched in those terms, most definitely."

"What terms would you employ to describe your action?"

"Oh, climb down from your high ropes, Serena," Peter retorted, nettled despite himself. "Like you, I have eyes in my head and could see the attraction between them at that first meeting. When Verity invited me to Sunday supper I knew that she was hoping I'd ask to bring Selcort along. You may believe I would not have obliged her had he been totally ineligible, but that is certainly not the case. He was not born without a shirt. His family is reasonably well-off and he will have an independent income as well as his stipend."

"A mere minister from an insignificant country family? He's a nobody!" Serena cut in, her eyes sparking green fire.

Peter regarded her thoughtfully. "I had not realized you were quite such a snob."

"I am not a snob, and calling hard names won't change anything. Verity's birth entitles her to look as high as she pleases for a husband. The Boyntons and the Goodhues are both old and respected families."

"She is equally entitled to choose the man with whom she will spend her life on some more rational basis than social prominence, for which—"

"She's besotted with the man! What's rational about that?"

"For which," he persisted, "I can only applaud her discrimination. Nigel Selcort is a young man of high principles and excellent understanding. His character is strong and upstanding, and he's worth a dozen Andrew Silverdales. Verity is to be commended on her appreciation of real quality."

"Of course you would say that—he is a friend of yours."

Peter hesitated as he stared at the lovely, angry woman at his side, and then burned his bridges. "I prefer to have no lies between us, Serena. I met Selcort for the first time in Hatchard's," he admitted, mentally bracing for the expected storm as astonishment and sheer fury chased across her mobile features in turn.

"Why, you . . . you despicable . . ." Words failed her as narrow-cut nostrils flared and her eyes blazed emerald in a white face. "I'd know how to get satisfaction from you if I were a man," she hissed through gritted teeth.

"Or even if you were a woman," he said more softly yet. The words were no sooner said than regretted. He felt her shocked recoil and hastened to apologize. "That really was a despicable thing to say. Please forgive me."

Serena's only reply was to turn her shoulder on him. A quick look around the table reassured him that their acrimonious exchange had been conducted in low-enough tones to go unremarked, though his sister was looking at him now in some concern. He managed a small quirk of his lips in Natasha's direction before returning his eyes to his plate. Fortunately his other partner was still engrossed with the man to her left. He sipped his wine slowly, all appetite having deserted him. A sideways glance revealed that Serena's fingers trembled as she pushed the chicken collops around on her plate with her fork.

That had been very ill-done of him, it went without saying, but the quarrel had blown up so quickly that he had forgotten where they were. He sighed silently. It seemed he and Serena were fated to reserve their most intimate exchanges for the most public of occasions. He wondered if she felt any portion of the frustration that coursed through his veins at these abortive discussions. He had forced the previous one on her, but this time she had been the instigator. And that was not the only difference. This time, he vowed, as his eyes roamed around the table over his wineglass, noting Mrs. Boynton's animated expression as she was being well-entertained by Sir Humphrey Talbot, and the engrossed young lovebirds in their own private world, this time he would not play the coward, waiting tamely until it should be Serena's pleasure to readmit him to the ranks of her friends. It was more than time the two of them cleared away the obstacles between them and brought their real sentiments out into the open. If he had no chance with her, it would be best to find out once and for all. It was driving him mad to be around her frequently and yet be unable to communicate directly and honestly.

As he reached this momentous decision, Peter chanced to look up and meet the mocking gaze of Charles Talbot almost directly across the table. The latter raised his glass and directed a smile somewhere between Peter and Serena, as though still unsure whether to place his money on the unmovable object or the irresistible force.

That there would be no opportunity to be private with Serena again that evening was a foregone conclusion. When the gentlemen joined the ladies in the drawing room after a highly political session with the port, she was installed between the garrulous wives of two of Cam's colleagues, whose interminable conversation seemed to hold her enthralled until tea was served. By that time Charles Talbot had maneuvered himself onto a settee beside her, where he proceeded to divert her successfully, judging by the occasional peals of laughter that erupted from her. She refused to acknowledge Peter's existence by so much as a glance even at parting, though she was compelled to extend a reluctant hand to him to avoid calling attention to herself.

Peter had still not gotten within hailing distance of the lovely and intransigent widow several days later when he happened to be driving his curricle on Oxford Street in time to witness the aftermath of a minor accident on the westbound side of the street. A light traveling carriage and a tilbury had evidently locked wheels, for the middle-aged coachman was busy calming his nervous pair while a sportily clad young man, evidently the driver of the tilbury, attempted to separate the two vehicles. A small knot of curious bystanders was gathered at the scene, but their attention seemed to be focused more on something going on next to the curbside than the efforts of the respective drivers. Peter would have driven on past the accident scene had not his quick eye spotted among the crowd a gleaming dark red head kneeling over a figure on the cobblestones. At the same instant, Mr. Nigel Selcort, at his side, called out:

"Wait! That is Verity . . . Miss Boynton over there."

Peter drew up and thrust the reins and whip into his passenger's hands before that young man could protest, with a curt command to "Hold 'em."

He hurried across the street, taking in the essentials as he went. Serena, unmindful of the thin white dress she was wearing on a rare warm day of this unusually wet summer, was squatting beside a child who appeared to be unconscious. She had evidently requisitioned the handkerchiefs of a couple of spectators, for she was binding up a head wound as he approached. A swift glance assured him that Verity, though pale and obviously concerned, was in no danger of succumbing to vapors as she stood quietly by, holding her sister's reticule and her own.

"What happened?" he asked, making his way to Serena's side. "Is the boy badly injured?"

"Oh, it's you." She barely looked up from her task. "I do not believe anything is broken, though there are several abrasions on his right arm and leg and a cut on his head, as well as a bump. He's beginning to come around now."

Pity stirred in Peter's breast as he gazed down at the wretched scrap of humanity. The child's thin shirt and dirty, worn nankeens would have been scarcely adequate to cover him decently before the accident, but now they were more disgusting by virtue of bloodstains and ragged tears. A little color was creeping back into the wan, dirt-streaked face, and a pair of dazed brown eyes opened suddenly to stare in confused fascination at the beautiful face hovering over him. The confusion cleared rapidly as other faces, more avid than concerned, impinged on the child's awareness.

"I didn't do noffink!" he declared wildly, making a disjointed attempt to scramble up that was easily prevented by Serena's firm hands.

Fortunately, no one save Peter noticed that Verity's small, sandal-clad foot unobtrusively nudged a large orange behind a heap of sticks and dirt at the edge of the road before she moved slightly forward, dropping the skirt she had been holding a fastidious inch above the cobblestones.

"No, don't move yet until I secure this bandage. Where do you live, boy? We'll have you home in a trice." Serena glanced up at her silent sister. "Has Samuel got the carriage free yet, Verity?"

"*No!*" Peter expostulated. "He probably lives in some back slum, judging by his appearance."

"I have no intention of letting him out of my sight until I can return him to his mother's care," Serena replied defiantly, before addressing the frightened child once more. "There, do you think you can sit up now?"

Verity took an obedient step toward the carriage, but Peter laid a staying hand on her arm, though his eyes never moved from the pair on the street as he said with steely softness, "You are not going to take your sister into a slum area, Serena."

She looked up at that, her face set in stubborn lines. "My carriage was in some degree responsible for this child's injury, and I intend to see him safely home. If you wish to be of service, you may escort Verity home for me. I shall be perfectly fine with Samuel, my coachman."

At this point various persons among the whispering knot of onlookers raised their voices with suggestions as to what ought to be done, ranging from turning the young hemp over to a magistrate—this from a motherly-looking matron—to driving the boy straight to the nearest hospital.

Ignoring all contributions of advice, Peter swooped forward and scooped up the child into his arms before Serena could assist him to his feet. "I have Selcort with me," he explained. "He can take Verity home in my curricle while I go with you."

Two pairs of eyes clashed in a battle of wills. He had no difficulty in following her thoughts as she hesitated, unwilling to leave her sister in Mr. Selcort's exclusive company. "Unless you'd care to entrust the boy to us. I promise you we will see he gets safely home."

At this suggestion, the child, who had already indicated his vocal displeasure at being captured by a grim-faced stranger, began to cry in earnest, and Serena surrendered to the exigencies of the situation. "Very well, Verity may go with Mr. Selcort," she conceded grudgingly. "Samuel seems to have settled the horses, and the other driver has moved his vehicle over to the side and is headed this way. Quickly, before he reaches us with more protestations of innocence, hand the boy up to me; then you may take Verity over to your curricle, which I trust will proceed directly to Beak Street."

Peter disciplined a smile at this wry comment, knowing as well as she that the lovebirds would be less than human if they refrained from taking advantage of the fortuitous chance to enjoy a private *tête-à-tête*. "The last time I checked, there was no impropriety in driving in an open carriage with a respectable young man," he assured her cheerfully, handing the piteously crying child up into the carriage before escorting Verity across the street, where he left her to make the necessary explanations to Mr. Selcort.

When Peter returned to Serena's carriage a moment later, she had succeeded in quieting the youngster's sobs. "He says his name is Tom Wheatley and he lives in the Seven Dials section. Do you know where that is?" she asked from the interior.

He nodded. "Just as I expected." After giving the coachman directions, Peter climbed aboard and they headed toward Charing Cross Road. "Are you sure his wounds don't need to be stitched or anything?" he asked with a dubious look at the tattered and bloody remnants of the boy's shirt sleeve as he half-lay across the opposite seat, supported in Serena's arms.

"There is a bump on the back of his head and a cut that bled a lot but isn't serious. The abrasions look a lot worse than they are, though I am persuaded they are quite painful and will have to be cleaned and anointed with basilicum salve. Should we stop and procure some from an apothecary?"

It was decided to do this in the event that Tom's mother was not prepared to care for her son's injuries. When Peter returned with a selection of medical supplies, the child moaned slightly as the carriage started up again with a lurching movement.

"What hurts most, Tom?" Serena asked anxiously.

"After that topper, I've got a queer morley, and me mam won't 'alf kill me for ruinin' me mish," the boy replied, sniveling again.

"What did he say? I don't understand." Serena raised a puzzled glance to Lord Phillips' amused countenance.

"Well, I don't claim to be an expert on thieves' cant, but I think he means that his head hurts after the blow and he's afraid his mother will beat him for ruining his shirt."

"*Thieves' cant*! But he is only eight years old!"

"No doubt, but unless I'm badly mistaken, your sister destroyed the evidence of his crime."

Serena stared. "Verity did *what*? Oh, you are joking me!"

"Not at all. Do you recall that your little protégé, on regaining consciousness, protested his innocence unaccused? Well, there was a perfect orange in the street near where he fell. Ah, yes, note the interest," Peter remarked as the child stiffened in Serena's arms. "Anyway, Verity, in an admirable display of *sangfroid*, pushed the evidence out of sight with her foot."

While Serena digested this doubly startling information, Samuel pounded on the carriage roof with the handle of his whip to indicate he needed more precise directions, and Peter roused their injured passenger to guide them to his home.

Serena was unprepared for the degree of squalor obtaining in the neighborhood that had spawned little Tom with his sullen cat's wariness and frightened eyes. That the streets in a slum area would be mean, narrow, and filthy, and the houses dilapidated, was certainly to be expected, at least by the intellect. It was the foul smell of the place and the presence of some of the inhabitants out on the steps and in the streets, driven outdoors no doubt by the uncomfortable temperatures within on such a hot day, that came close to unnerving her, determined though she was to remain phlegmatic. She had often seen beggars near the theaters, but almost any one of the poorly dressed denizens of Seven Dials could have exchanged places with the professionals who worked Covent Garden. Ragged children played in the streets while their elders congregated on the steps of their dwellings, singly or in gossiping groups. A number were drinking out of a bewildering variety of containers, and some individuals of both sexes were sprawled against the steps in a drunken stupor. The most frightening aspect of all to Serena was the atmosphere of collective apathy that pervaded the area. Even those people who weren't drunk had blank eyes that looked at their world without hope or even interest. She shivered despite the heat in the stuffy carriage. She clutched Tom tighter in a spurt of reluctance to return him to such depressing surroundings, but at that moment the boy broke away to point out his street.

"Will you lend me some money, Peter?" she whispered as the carriage came to a stop in front of a three-story brick house no less run-down than its neighbors, though there were no loiterers on the steps, she saw with relief. "Verity still has my reticule, and I would like to leave something for food and to replace Tom's shirt."

"Better not, unless we make reasonably certain it won't go for drink. You may send a footman tomorrow with supplies if you wish to aid them."

Seeing the wisdom of this course, Serena subsided. It was not without trepidation that she followed the limping child up two flights of rickety stairs to an airless apartment, but the sight of Mrs. Wheatley was marginally reassuring. She was a small, wiry-looking woman with hard eyes of a darker brown than Tom's, but she was passably clean of person, and the room they entered, while poorly furnished, was neat. There were a couple of flower prints tacked up on a wall in a brave attempt to beautify the place, and a much-darned but clean cloth covered a table that held a couple of china items, perhaps fairings.

Taking in these propitious signs also, Lord Phillips left

some money with Mrs. Wheatley after they had explained their errand and given her the medical supplies they had purchased en route. After one intent look at her son's scraped flesh, she had ignored him while the accident was explained to her to the best of their ability. Peter had come on the scene late, and even Serena in the closed carriage had not really witnessed what had happened. Tom, when appealed to by her, proved either deliberately obtuse or evasive in his brief description of the affair, and he showed a lamentable tendency to whine when his parent questioned his presence in a district so remote from home. She soon abandoned her efforts in order to thank her son's rescuers, but from the sharp glance she directed at her offspring, Master Tom was scheduled for a severe scold when the visitors departed, if not the beating he had feared. His eyes had lighted up at sight of the largess the swell had given his mother, and she, noting the response, had warned him swiftly to keep his mummer clapped shut when his father and brother came home if he knew what was good for him. Serena could only hope this was an indication that the money would go for essentials.

A pensive but not uncomfortable silence reigned in the carriage later as it headed back toward Beak Street. It was evident that Serena was still dwelling on the situation they had just left, and Peter was content to watch her unobtrusively and wait for her reaction. At length she said on a sigh, "It must be well nigh impossible to remain respectable under the sordid conditions prevailing in such areas. One's faith and stamina, even the will to continue existence, must be continually challenged."

"Grinding poverty is a continuing curse on mankind," he agreed.

"Are there many areas like this?"

"Seven Dials is one of the worst slums, but there are many districts nearly as bad. London's population is more than a million, and a significant portion of that population does little better than subsist. Conditions will get worse in the immediate future."

She lifted troubled questioning eyes to his and he

elaborated. "The abrupt ending of the orders for woolen cloth for soldiers' uniforms and armaments and ammunition with which to wage war is among the first results of peace. As the manufactories in the north release their workers, these people and their families by the thousands will flood into the cities looking for employment. The landless poor have no other option. A couple of hundred thousand returning soldiers over the next year or two will add to the problem. There are hard times ahead."

"What can be done about it?"

"In the long run it will be necessary to develop new markets for our manufactured goods, but the rest of Europe is equally poor right at present. Shortsightedness has ever been the affliction of governments. Increasing the burden of poor relief on the parishes isn't going to alleviate the problem significantly. People need work to do if they are to keep their self-respect. Otherwise, half the population will be maintaining the other half in jails and workhouses. Crime is already on the increase everywhere."

"Are you saying that there isn't much an individual can do," Serena asked dispiritedly, "except to provide employment when possible and give the occasional donation to persons or societies that try to aid the poor?"

"If you do not scruple to risk alienating your friends in a good cause," Peter suggested, "some of these societies are quite eager for personal assistance, and sources of revenue are never despised, you know."

"Yes, if we are to stay much longer in town, I am resolved to become more involved in this work."

"Had you planned to leave soon?"

With this sharp question the temporary rapport between them dissolved instantly. Serena replied with a touch of asperity, "I had hoped to have Verity safely riveted by this time, so that I might be off on my travels. And it might have happened, too, had not some busyhead, who shall be nameless for the sake of civility, not interfered so inexcusably."

"Fustian, Serena. You know that for a lie. Had Selcort not appeared on the scene, Verity still would have refused your candidate. She's not so desperate to marry at seventeen that she'd accept an Andrew Silverdale."

"And what, pray, is so wrong with Andrew Silverdale? He would make an unexceptionable husband for a girl like Verity."

"He's a slowtop, for one thing, but the only consideration that should concern those who have her interests at heart is that she doesn't love him."

Serena waved away the second objection and addressed herself to the first. "I am excessively attached to my sister, but Verity isn't precisely needle-witted herself, so why should she object to a husband whose understanding is certainly adequate, though he makes no pretensions to being a scholar?"

"I think you are not very well-acquainted with your sister," Peter replied still more inexcusably. "Her interests may not be scholarly, but there is nothing deficient about her understanding. Verity may not be as quick-thinking or acting as you are, but she has a good deal of common sense. Nor is she the helpless creature you seem to consider her. Today, for example, she behaved with quiet good sense, displaying no tendency to fly to pieces in an emergency, which I assure you is what many a flighty social butterfly would do in the same circumstances. And it was owing entirely to her discreet action in hiding that orange that no more of a rumpus was kicked up by that motley crowd of spectators. Had they the least evidence that the boy had been engaged in thievery, we would have found ourselves in the basket with regard to delivering him to his home undeterred."

Serena would be ashamed of herself later, but Peter's ardent championship of her sister, combined with an implied criticism of her own regard for Verity's worth, stung her badly, and she hit out in blind retaliation. "I am astonished that, given your fervent admiration for my little sister, you have not offered for her yourself. At least you are a better catch than a poor country parson."

She had striven for a tone of disinterested amusement, but her glance faltered under his burning regard, and she turned to look out the window, thankful to see the car-

Dorothy Mack

riage turning into Great Pulteney Street. She would shortly be home.

"That was unworthy of you, Serena, and you well know the reason. As far as Selcort and Verity are concerned, if the attachment proves to be lasting, you will have to countenance the match eventually."

"If the attachment persists, it will be all your doing!" she flared, bent on developing a newly discovered talent for making bad worse. "You have provided each and every opportunity for ripening what should have been an exceedingly short acquaintance. Even today it is thanks to your intervention that they are no doubt tooling around the town in an open carriage at this moment, billing and cooing for everyone to see."

"Would you rather they were cozily ensconced in this closed carriage while we tooled around the town with the curricle, you in your dirt- and blood-stained dress, quarreling for everyone to see?"

"That is not what I meant!"

"I know what you meant," he said wearily. "We are nearly at your door. Might we postpone this childish exchange while I ask you to ride with me tomorrow? We can resume our quarrel then if you wish."

In her state of whipped-up anger, Serena was totally immune to the charm of Peter's smile. "I am already engaged to ride tomorrow," she said shortly as the carriage halted in front of her house. "Do not trouble to get out. Samuel will take you wherever you wish to go."

To her annoyance, he insisted on accompanying her to her door. She would not give him the satisfaction of further protesting, however, merely saying a brief good-bye before closing the door firmly behind her.

Peter replaced his hat on his crisp light brown locks and waved the carriage on. He needed exercise, even a tame walk, to help him deal with the megrims left by another frustrating set-to with the loveliest and most aggravating woman in all of London.

11

Verity's heart gave a definite skip as she verified that the man across the street in Lord Phillips' curricle was indeed Mr. Selcort, but after the first involuntary look, she kept her eyes on the little drama being enacted in front of her. She was only a bit player on this stage, Serena having been the star of the rescue scene and now being forced to share the leading role with Lord Phillips, who had engaged her in a duel of wills. Verity's lips remained closed, but she willed success to Lord Phillips with all her might, knowing she had the most to gain or lose by the outcome of the struggle between two frighteningly strong-minded individuals.

Scarcely a minute later, she was crossing Oxford Street with eyes demurely downcast and her hand on Lord Phillips' arm. A sudden squeezing of her fingers brought her eyes around to meet the amused gaze of her champion.

"Aren't you even going to thank me?" he asked, adopting a wounded expression that made her lips quirk, though she blushed too.

"Of . . . of course. It was exceedingly kind of you."

"Then do not waste your time," he advised her in an undertone as they came abreast of a slightly miffed Mr. Selcort, who had been hard put to contain his curiosity and impatience as he was constrained to sit in the curricle out of earshot of the scene taking place across the road.

"Ah, Selcort, thank you, dear fellow, for taking care of my horses. Now, if you would add to your goodness by escorting Miss Boynton to her home, Lady Whitlaw and I shall be eternally grateful to you." Verity was forced to look away and bite her lip at such an outra-

geous remark, an action that caused her to miss Mr.
Selcort's reply, but since Lord Phillips handed her up
into the curricle immediately, she assumed the commission had been accepted willingly.

More than willingly, in fact. Mr. Selcort turned a glowing look on his slightly embarrassed passenger. "I have
only a hazy notion of what has been happening across the
road, but may I say, without in any way wishing harm to
anyone, that I regard this incident as a great piece of luck
for me."

Laboring under all the disadvantages that could beset a
well-brought-up young lady of naturally modest temperament in such circumstances, Verity was at a loss for a
response that would offer encouragement without being
thought forward, and she could only stammer, "You . . .
you are too kind, sir."

"I hope you will believe that my words had nothing to
do with kindness or civility; they came straight from my
heart." He had the pair of matched grays well in hand by
now and was able to position his head to study the
charming profile presented to him, at least that portion
that was not concealed by the wide brim of her stylish
bonnet. This did not tell him much, nor did her gloved
hands clasped together in her lap as she stared straight
ahead, and he said urgently, "Miss Boynton—Verity—
look at me."

This command brought into viewing range a pair of
blue-green eyes with a painful question in their depths.
"You do believe me, do you not?"

"Well . . . I . . . This is only our fourth meeting."

"I believe I knew at that first meeting," he said simply.

"But you never called." And now there was a faint
hint of accusation in the soft voice. "All of our encounters have been quite accidental."

Mr. Selcort returned his attention to the horses for a
moment while he considered his answer, finally deciding
the unvarnished truth was necessary in their situation. "I
have called at Beak Street three times and have been
turned away by your butler on each occasion. Either the
ladies were not receiving that day or the ladies were not

at home." He kept all inflection from his voice but looked a question, which was answered in part by the rush of pink that warmed Verity's cheeks.

She hung her head but attempted no reply. Impossible to inform a man who had not yet unequivocally declared his intentions that his hypothetical suit was not looked upon with favor by her family.

Mr. Selcort must have recognized her dilemma, because he said at once, "It is not to be wondered at that your family would prefer a more brilliant match for you. I am not of your world and—"

"Do not say so!"

"Stay, my dear one. I must say it and you must understand that this is indeed true in more than one sense. My life's work has already been charted, and it is presumptuous of me to dream that someone like you would be willing to share it. Therefore, though it grieves me to press you, I must ask you to tell me if you have any doubts at all. My situation is difficult and we cannot count on fortuitous meetings in the future."

"I have no doubts."

This time there was no hesitation, nor, when he searched the flower face turned to his, was there any sign of shrinking. For a long enchanted moment of wordless communication, the world and its problems ceased to exist for them as their eyes exchanged a solemn pledge of devotion.

All too soon reality intruded on the lovers' moving idyll, in the form of a near-accident as a high-perch phaeton swept past the curricle, its driver delivering himself of a terse suggestion that people of problematical driving ability should confine their activities in future to empty fields.

Forcibly recalled to his surroundings, Mr. Selcort, his expression sheepish, was relieved to find his passenger's nerves unaffected by the experience as he once again exerted control over the lively pair.

"Verity, my dear one, there is so much to say and so little time. Will you give me a few more minutes before I deliver you to your door? I'd suggest the park, but we would be caught up in the crush and very likely forced to acknowledge half your acquaintance. Should you object to driving around some of the quieter streets for a while longer?"

Verity had no fault to find with this program. The words "so little time" had struck a chill deep into her heart and she was of a mood to seize any excuse to prolong their meeting.

"It is more than probable that we shall have to wait to marry, perhaps even until you come of age, though I trust it won't come to that," he added when a little gasp of dismay escaped her lips.

"Oh, Nigel, I am persuaded Mama will relent when she sees that I do not mean to have anyone else, no matter how brilliant the match. Not that I ever had any expectation or any desire to make a brilliant match, you understand. Serena did, and it brought her nothing but unhappiness."

"Then perhaps your sister will stand our friend?" he ventured.

"I . . . I fear not. Serena seems to have the ridiculous notion that I am incapable of living a modest existence and must be eternally cosseted and pampered. I never have been, you know," she explained with a sweetly earnest look that made him ache to pull up the horses and enfold her in his arms. "For the past two years since my father died, I have taken much of the responsibility for running the house from my mother's shoulders and have been well-trained in matters of domestic economy. Serena says a pastor's wife is at the beck and call of the parish and is liable to have her every action scrutinized, but I don't think I should mind that very much if I can be a help to you, though one thing I should hate is not to have any time at all for my music or . . . or my children," she finished in a rush, determined to confess all weaknesses.

He paid her the compliment of squarely addressing her concerns. "Perhaps more is demanded of a pastor's wife than of other ladies in similar circumstances, though I would argue that there are at least as many calls upon the time and talents of women in that stratum of society to which you belong. Certainly the great hostesses have much organizational business with which to occupy themselves, as well as scores of retainers for whose lives they are in large measure responsible. I believe I can promise you sufficient leisure for music and family concerns, but there is no gainsaying that the pastor and his family live their lives under the scrutiny of their flock. Verity, my love, I am utterly convinced that you, with your sweet nature and kindness to everyone, will make an exemplary wife for a pastor, and I consider myself the most fortunate man alive." Mr. Selcort's voice rang with passionate sincerity. Verity gazed in wonder into his serious eyes and made a silent vow to prove herself worthy of such faith.

In the wake of such supremely gratifying sentiments, it was small wonder that the pair in Lord Phillips' curricle quite lost sight of their surroundings and the relentless passage of time, engrossed as they were in relating to each other all the significant details of their past lives and future dreams. Verity was the first to come to a realization that they had spent rather more than a few stolen minutes driving aimlessly up and down the residential streets of the West End. Noting all of a sudden that they were in Grosvenor Square and still wending in a westerly direction, she exclaimed:

"Nigel, how long has it been since we left Oxford Street? I would not for the world wish to give Serena an opportunity to charge me with taking advantage of the situation."

"I don't believe we've been gone above twenty minutes or so," her betrothed replied soothingly, though if pressed, he would have had to admit his estimate might be on the optimistic side. He turned the curricle back toward Regent Street and said in some surprise, "Do you know, I still have only a general idea of what the situation actually was. What happened?"

"We were coming home from a visit to the British Museum—Serena likes that sort of thing—when our carriage was involved in an accident. From my side, I hap-

pened to see a child dart into the street up ahead of us.
The next thing we knew, another carriage had swerved
into us, I assume in an effort to avoid the boy. Fortunately, the child wasn't badly hurt, though he was unconscious for a time. Serena bound up a cut on his head, and
we were going to take him home as soon as the carriages
were separated; but Lord Phillips objected strenuously,
saying the child was so poorly dressed he must come
from a back slum, and it would be dangerous for us to go
there. Serena was determined to go anyway, so she asked
Lord Phillips to escort me home." A gleam of mischief
appeared in her aquamarine eyes for a second. "Serena's
face was a picture when Lord Phillips told her you were
in the curricle and could see me home while he went with
her and the boy. She was most unwilling to permit this,
so Lord Phillips offered his and your services to conduct
the boy home instead. By then the child was creating a
noisy scene because he was afraid of Lord Phillips, so
Serena, who is absurdly tenderhearted where children
are concerned, capitulated, and here I am."

"And with such a marvelous result. It seems we owe
our good fortune to a crying child. Life takes some
strange turns."

"Yes. Hideous to think we might never have met if
you had not gone into Hatchard's that day with Lord
Phillips," Verity said innocently. "You never came to
any of the balls or parties before then."

A tinge of color crept into Mr. Selcort's lean cheeks.
"Verity, my love, I'm afraid I was a party to a crucial
deception that day, which has preyed on my conscience
ever since. Not the doing, really, because that seemed so
natural and harmless, but the fact that by concealing it
later, there would never exist perfect truth between us. I
have been determined to clear the matter up at the first
opportunity."

"What matter? What deception?"

"I did not go to Hatchard's with Lord Phillips; in fact,
we had never met. He overheard our meeting and witnessed your sister's arrival and simply jumped into the
breach, so to speak, pretending to be a friend of mine."

Verity's lovely eyes had grown large with surprise during her betrothed's confession, and now she exclaimed, "Why would he do such a thing?" before blushing furiously as a reason occurred to her. "That . . . that was excessively kind of him," she managed.

There was a decided twinkle in Mr. Selcort's narrow eyes as he enjoyed his love's pretty confusion. "Actually, Phillips told me at the time that he wasn't sure whether he did it to help us or to annoy your sister. I believe his subsequent actions in providing opportunities for us to meet were performed in a pure spirit of friendship toward us, however, perhaps even at some personal cost."

He looked a question, and she did not pretend to misunderstand. "Yes, Serena has been pointedly cool to Lord Phillips recently, and I truly feel for his wounded sensibility because, though he has not confided in me, I have sometimes wondered if he might be in love with her."

It was Verity's turn to pose a mute question. Mr. Selcort paused to consider it. "He hasn't confided in me either, but I have noticed something, some nuance in his manner when he looks at her if he thinks himself unobserved, and I confess that same thought has crossed my mind. Does she not care for him at all?"

"I . . . I do not think so, but I scarcely understand Serena these days." She raised troubled eyes to his. "Before her marriage, my sister was the most vibrant, joyful person I knew, always sparkling with anticipation, and she was such fun to be with. She was subdued when she came home for Papa's funeral, and then her husband died. One would not expect her to be exuberant these days, but it is more than that. She still radiates energy, but often a tense sort of energy, as if she were in a cage and struggling to break out. At other times she seems to do everything in a mechanical way, as if her mind and spirit were far removed from the scene. She did not wish to come to London this Season. She had dreamed of traveling to Greece and Rome, but Mama persuaded her to come and support her through the ordeal. I believe it is Serena who pays our living expenses here."

Mr. Selcort had listened to Verity's painful attempt to explain her sister to him, or perhaps to herself, with as much concentration as he could spare from guiding the grays. Now he asked, "You do not think she may still be grieving for her husband?"

"Oh, no. In fact, I am persuaded she actually disliked her husband. I feel a wretch to speak of things of such a private nature, but she has all but put the sentiment into words herself, though she never voluntarily mentions Lord Whitlaw. Sometimes I cannot help feeling that she dislikes all men now."

"We are nearly at your door, my love." Seeing a flash of apprehension darken his beloved's sea-colored eyes, Mr. Selcort said jokingly to lighten her thoughts, "If your redoubtable sister seems disposed to take you to task for not going straight home, you must throw all the blame on me. Tell her the horses ran away with us, which is very nearly true."

"I'll do no such thing," declared Verity, showing spirit on her lover's behalf. "You are a fine driver, and I'll not have Serena think otherwise. Sooner or later everything must come out in any case, and if I cannot muster the resolution to fight for my happiness, I don't deserve it."

"That's my girl," said Mr. Selcort, enchanted by the sight of his gentle fiancée bristling in his defense. "It is likely that their errand will have taken some little time to accomplish, and unless I miss my guess, Lord Phillips will not be backward in seizing an opportunity to enjoy as much of your sister's company as possible."

Mr. Selcort's guess had sounded eminently reasonable at the time, but alas, the lovers' luck had run out. Verity had no sooner set her foot on the bottom step, after learning from Richford that Lady Whitlaw had not yet returned, when carriage wheels sounded outside. She fought down a craven impulse to fly upstairs, remaining where she stood as the butler returned to the front door for the second time in as many minutes.

Serena greeted Richford briefly, then espied her sister on the stairs. "So you are back," she said. "Just."

"Yes." The fingers with which she untied the pink

satin ribbons of her straw bonnet might have been steadier, but Verity exhibited a new confidence that produced a corresponding narrowing of her sister's eyes. "Did you return the boy to his mother?"

"Yes."

Verity held her ground, but her heart plummeted toward the region of her stomach as Serena came forward. Temper glittered in green eyes, and the lovely mouth was pressed shut while she wrenched off a charming bonnet and gave her head a shake, one hand impatiently brushing back a stray wisp of hair. The barely controlled energy radiating from every line of her sister's statuesque figure put Verity forcibly in mind of a cat getting set for attack, tail carried high and bushy. "Here you are." She held out Serena's reticule, which she still carried, noticing as her sister's hand came out in automatic compliance that she was minus one glove and her hand was streaked with dirt.

"I wish to talk to you," Serena said abruptly. "Come to my room after I've removed the dirt." She grimaced at her hand and ran up the stairs.

Verity was relieved to see a decided improvement in her sister's appearance when she knocked on her door twenty minutes later. All evidence of the accident and its aftermath had been removed from her person, her hair was freshly arranged, and she looked cool and attractive in a crisp peach-colored cotton gown that should have clashed with her hair but didn't. Serena's manner had undergone a change for the better too. The temper had died out of her eyes and the smile with which she greeted her sister, though brief, was genuine as she waved her to the only upholstered chair in the room while she perched herself on her dressing-table bench with her back to the mirror.

"Verity, my dear," she began in her direct way, "I know you do not want to discuss Mr. Selcort, but I really think we must— "

"Oh, no," Verity broke in, "it was only when I did not know how he felt about me that it seemed pointless to become involved in a discussion. I don't mind now."

The ensuing silence clanged with alarm signals for Serena as her eyes fastened on her sister's face, faintly smiling and calm. "Does that mean that now you *do* know how he feels about you?"

"Yes. He loves me and wishes to marry me. I feel exactly the same." Verity's eyes held more understanding than apprehension as they followed her sister's agitated movements as Serena surged up from the bench on a loudly expelled breath and began stalking about the small room.

"This is exactly what I feared would happen! Oh, I could *strangle* that man with my bare hands!"

"Strangle Nigel! Really, Serena, you go too far!"

"What?" Serena whirled to face her indignant sister. "Of course I did not mean Nigel," she said impatiently, "so you need not poker up in that ridiculous fashion. I was referring to that devil Peter Phillips! This is all his doing." She pinned Verity with an accusing stare. "Were you aware that he and Mr. Selcort were not even acquainted before that regrettable day in the bookstore? And he had the unmitigated effrontery to parade him about society in the guise of an old friend!" She was about to embark on yet another tour of the room after flinging this rhetorical question, when something in her sister's face stopped her short. "You *did* know!"

"Nigel told me today," Verity admitted, "but, Serena, are you not being too harsh on Lord Phillips? He was merely doing a kindness, a very great kindness for Nigel and me." She pleaded for her benefactor, aware of suppressing part of the truth but sinking any pangs of guilt in a spirit of reciprocity as she continued, "Besides, Lord Phillips is irrelevant to our discussion. Nigel and I would have loved each other with no intervention on his part."

"You would never have *seen* each other again but for that fiend's intervention! *Irrelevant!*" She threw up her hands.

"But I think we would have," Verity said softly. "Oh, not right away, perhaps, but I believe it was meant that Nigel and I should meet."

Serena slapped a palm to her forehead and cast her

eyes upward. "Deliver me, I beg, from such mawkish twaddle!"

Verity lapsed into a silence that was not broken until Serena, having exhausted herself in her pacing, mastered her spleen and returned to her seat. Her face wore the expression of a patient nanny reasoning with a young charge as she leaned forward and tried a new tack. "If you believe Mama will consent to see you married to a mere reverend, you are very much mistaken."

"I know it is not what she or you wished for me, but if I don't object to living modestly, why should Mama and you?"

"At the moment you are in the full flush of infatuation . . . all right, first love," she amended, forestalling Verity's obvious objection, "but I assure you, that sort of feeling of the world well-lost for love does not last. We do not want you to regret settling for the humdrum life of a pastor's wife in the years to come."

"I think you cannot know me very well, Serena," Verity began, and hesitated at the startled flicker in her sister's eyes. "I do not find life in the country humdrum. I enjoy managing a household, and take pleasure in the routine of daily tasks and the rhythm of the seasons. I don't expect everyone I meet to be remarkable for intellectual or artistic prowess or fascinating conversation. I am not like you. I am quite ordinary myself and am content in the company of ordinary persons. It is enough for me that an extraordinarily fine man loves me and wishes me to be his wife. In fact, I feel exceedingly blessed that this should be so, and I am prepared to wait until you and Mama come to understand and accept that I do know what is best for me."

Throughout much of this speech Serena studied her sister's sweetly serious countenance as if it were a text written in a language she could not quite grasp; then she shifted her frowning gaze to the toe of her sandal. She raised her eyes as Verity stood up, but her glance slid away from that of the younger girl until Verity indicated her intention to seek out their parent.

"Do not bring this subject up with Mama yet, Verity. There is no point in upsetting her just yet."

It was Verity's turn to examine her sister's face. She opened her lips, then closed them again, contenting herself with a nod of acquiescence before leaving the room.

Serena sat unmoving for a long time after the image of her sister wearing an unfamiliar look of maturity as she closed the door faded from her memory. She had listened to what Verity had to say and been impressed against her will by the lack of childish pleading and the quiet confidence with which she presented her case. So much her mind had grasped despite the fact that she had been thrown off her mental stride at the outset by hearing Verity, in almost the same words Peter Phillips had used, state flatly that Serena did not really know her little sister.

Two of them in the space of an hour. And neither had been decently hesitant or tentative about expressing such a damning opinion. Who should better understand Verity than the sister, not five years her senior, who had loved her and watched over her from babyhood? She was not denying that Verity had emerged into young womanhood during the two years since she'd last been home, but the *essential* Verity, the personality and nature of her sister, hadn't changed beyond a lifetime's intimate knowledge. Because she was unwilling to see her only sister make an irrevocable mistake, even if it meant losing some of her confidence while Verity was in the throes of an emotional impulse that was almost guaranteed to be ephemeral, was she to be branded as lacking in understanding? Verity could be excused on the grounds of her irrational emotional state, but by what right or privilege did a mere acquaintance like Peter Phillips set himself up as a judge of her sister's nature or her own knowledge of that sister?

Serena's frown deepened and her sense of outrage grew as she recalled that a simple charge of lack of understanding had not been the worst of Lord Phillips' insults this afternoon. He had all but accused her of setting her face against a marriage with Mr. Selcort for worldly reasons unconcerned with Verity's well-being and happiness. That he could even entertain such an opinion for a moment proved how little his professions of friendship were worth. One could not think so badly of anyone one sincerely esteemed. Actually, she should be happy to have discovered his lack of real regard for her. He would no longer be a threat to her contentment with the life she had chosen.

Having neatly disposed of her own little problem, Serena turned her mind back to Verity, but in this realm she could come to no satisfying conclusions. That Verity believed herself to have formed a lasting attachment to Mr. Selcort was now confirmed, and they could no doubt expect a formal request for her hand shortly. Naturally, Mama would refuse on Verity's behalf, but it would not end there. What would come to an end was all hope of seeing her happily bestowed elsewhere in the immediate future. Verity's was not a frivolous nature, and she would not readily transfer her affections to a more suitable candidate. It might take some time before she could be brought to accept that she was ill-equipped to endure a lifetime of pinching and scraping and doing without the little elegancies of life. Trying to look on the bright side, Serena considered there was one situation she need no longer dread. Verity had proved far too independent and resolute to fear that Mama might maneuver her into the kind of bargain she herself had accepted. If Mama's resources were less adequate next year, she would just have to assume more of the burden for her sister's second Season.

Meanwhile, there was no real reason to linger in London. There might be time to arrange some sort of European trip before winter set in. Serena wondered fleetingly why the thought of solitary travel was not quite so appealing as it had been last winter, and concluded that the trials and fatigues of this hectic Season had taken a natural toll on her enthusiasm. Certainly it was difficult to muster up much enthusiasm for any activity these days.

The entrance of Betsy, audibly wondering why her mistress had not summoned her to help her dress for

dinner, roused Serena from pursuing yet another unsatisfactory line of thought. She looked up with a wan smile
and spent the next half-hour briskly denying all suggestions of illness or lethargy put forth by her solicitous but
too-curious abigail.

12

Serena was still struggling in the grip of an uncharacteristic lassitude the next morning when she joined her brother for a prebreakfast ride in the park. She had little to contribute as they trotted through the streets en route, replying to his observations in an absentminded fashion that even a young man as self-absorbed as Peregrine could scarcely fail to remark.

"What time did you get to bed last night? You're still half-asleep. Is the pace of the wicked city too much for you, old girl?" he asked with a teasing grin.

Serena was conscious of a warm rush of affection as she stared into her brother's green-blue eyes alight with mischief. "Old, am I? The day is not yet approaching when these old bones are unable to keep up with the children of the family."

"Is that so?" Perry was more than ready to accept his sister's tacit challenge, and the two riders exploded into the park through the Stanhope Gate, going neck-or-nothing toward the Row, heedless alike of the admiration such a striking pair garnered in some quarters and the few disapproving looks their uninhibited antics earned them in others.

For a few minutes Serena reveled in the power and speed beneath her, enjoying the sensation of damp air rushing past her face and the rhythmic pounding of Dancer's hooves echoing throughout her body as she urged the game filly to stay abreast of Perry's stronger mount. It was with palpable reluctance that they eventually curtailed their wild race, forced into a decorous trot by the unwelcome presence of other riders on the path. The

face Serena turned to her laughing brother was alive with
satisfaction and fading excitement.

"That was marvelous, Perry! Isn't Dancer a jewel? She
gave Ebony a run for his money and enjoyed herself
mightily in the doing." She leaned over to bestow an
approving pat on the chestnut's neck as she spoke, and
laughed as the filly tossed her head coquettishly.

"Lord Phillips found you a good 'un, right enough. I
wouldn't mind owning that big bay of his, either. Now,
there's a magnificent animal!"

"Oh, have you seen Fiero?"

"Yes. I met Lord Phillips riding here one day, and he
invited me to go to Jackson's with him. Introduced me to
the great man himself, which was jolly decent of him,
because I'm a far cry from his league at present. He's got
the most lethal left hand I've ever seen outside of the
professional ring, and if his right was more deadly before
he took that bullet, I can only feel sorry for anyone slow
enough to have encountered its full strength in those
days."

"Boxing, ugh!" Serena wrinkled her delightful nose
that was the feminine counterpart of the young giant's
beside her and contrived to look superior, but Perry was
not to be drawn.

"One naturally doesn't expect females to appreciate
the Fancy," he returned with masculine tolerance, "but I
can tell you I mean to improve my style, and Jackson's is
the place to do it, especially if the champion himself
takes an interest in one. I've not got much science as yet,
but my reach and strength are natural advantages, and
I'm determined to improve my footwork. Your other
suitor is a good boxer too, but Lord Phillips' footwork is
much better than Whitlaw's."

"Where did you meet Lord Whitlaw?"

"He came to the house one morning when you were at
Mrs. Talbot's. Seemed disappointed to miss you. He's a
great gun. Took me to the Fives' Court one night to
watch some matches."

"Surely Lord Whitlaw is much older than your friends,
Perry?" Serena strove to keep any hint of censure from

her voice, but the idea of a friendship developing between her young brother and the worldly Whitlaw disturbed her where she had been unconcerned over his acquaintance with Lord Phillips.

"In general, yes, but Whitlaw isn't the least bit stuffy like most of the men who dangle after you. He likes a bit of action and fun and knows his way around town better than most."

Perry's casual words sowed a tiny seed of disquiet in Serena's mind, but she recognized the futility of trying to forbid the association. By the time they reached Perry's age, young men were well-skilled in eluding any attempts on the part of their womenfolk to control their activities. It was not in her nature to see a problem without making a push to solve it, however, and she said, choosing her words carefully, "I trust you are aware that there are places in town whose specialty is separating unwary people from their money by practices that verge on the criminal?"

"Lord, yes, I'm not so green as to patronize gaming hells where the tables are rigged; in fact, I find playing cards for hours on end tedious dull sport at best." Perry's handsome features rearranged themselves into a carefree smile as he gazed into his sister's serious face. "You and Mama needn't have me on your minds at all. There are much better ways to spend one's time in London."

It was on the tip of her tongue to ask for examples, but Serena refrained. If he answered at all, it would no doubt be to offer some patently harmless prevarications such as visiting the mechanical museums or Astley's Amphitheatre. It would be no more than she deserved for trying to pin him down, but she could not be quite easy in her mind about Perry's sojourn in town. The few moments of exquisite pleasure during their gallop had chased away her blue devils temporarily, but by the time Perry had left her at the house on Beak Street and gone off to return the horses to the stables, the formless malaise had crept back, dampening her natural optimism and nibbling away at her store of energy.

The next few days passed uneventfully enough on the

surface. The days it didn't rain, Serena rode with Perry
before breakfast. One morning was spent exercising with
Natasha and then playing with Justin, who had just cele-
brated his first birthday and crowned the occasion by
determined but as yet unsuccessful attempts to walk un-
aided. They entertained callers one morning and she
bore the familiar exchange of civil inanities with exemplary patience, but the next day at that hour she ruth-
lessly carried Verity off to the shops. Even a tiresome
round of small errands was preferable to another session
of boredom in a confined space.

Wednesday evening was set aside for Almack's, of
course. Since Mr. Selcort did not possess the social cre-
dentials to procure a voucher, they were safe from meeting him in those hallowed precincts. On the other hand,
Serena had long since ceased to regard these ritualized
balls with the expectant delight of her first Season. Mrs.
Boynton had begged off from attending, complaining of
a raspy throat, and Serena took advantage of her status
as chaperone to decline all invitations to dance, burying
herself amongst a knot of dowagers sitting along one of
the walls. This transparent maneuver discouraged the
more fainthearted of her admirers but did not deter the
two she most wished to avoid.

She greeted Lord Phillips with cool reserve when he
approached, and declined his request that she give him
the pleasure of a dance, stating flatly that she would not
be dancing that evening. Undaunted, he produced a lazy
smile that included the avidly listening dowagers and
professed himself well-satisfied to take a rest in such
pleasant company. One of the matrons, who good-
naturedly offered to slide down a seat so that he might sit
by dear Lady Whitlaw, earned an especially sweet smile
all for herself.

For the duration of the next set, Serena sat nearly
silent as Lord Phillips proceeded to entertain upwards of
a half-dozen of society's highest sticklers with gentle,
undemanding conversation interspersed with amusing and
self-deprecating stories of his difficulties in fitting himself
back into the life of the city after nearly ten years in the

military. Annoyed though Serena certainly was, she was compelled to admire a masterly performance as the dowagers succumbed to his infectious charm, nodding their turbaned heads in understanding from time to time or tittering behind their fans at some piece of audacious flattery aimed at one or another of their company. Her temper was not sweetened by his accomplishment, since she remained convinced its sole purpose was to annoy her and show up her own graceless behavior in comparison. It was doubly galling, when he took his leave at the end of the set, to listen to his praises sung by her companions and be forced to agree with smiling annoyance that his manners and address were superior to those of the vast majority of his generation, who frequently ignored their elders in a careless fashion that reflected sadly on their upbringing. He came in for additional plaudits when one of the ladies pointed out that upon leaving them he had presented himself to a quiet, plain young lady who had been sitting forlornly in the middle of another group of matrons during the previous set. When next glimpsed whirling around the room in Lord Phillips' arms, the girl wore such a look of glowing pleasure as to render her almost pretty.

In sharp contrast to Peter's polished style, Lord Whitlaw, who had seemingly arrived just before the doors closed at eleven, came directly across the room to Serena after standing within the entrance for a few moments scanning the room with frowning intentness. He insinuated his large frame between her and her nearest neighbor, with his back firmly to this lady, and smiled with charm as he asked his cousin-in-law to dance. When Serena repeated her standard excuse for denying the invitation, most of the charm left his expression, though his lips remained smiling.

"I have come here tonight for the sole purpose of dancing with you," he said, trying for a wheedling tone. "Surely you could not be so cruel, fair cousin, as to cast down my hopes?"

"Life is full of little disappointments, sir," Serena countered lightly, conscious of a dozen ears on the stretch behind his broad back, "but take heart. There are a number of lovely and charming young ladies present who would be honored to partner you."

"There is only one person with whom I wish to dance," he replied, ignoring his clear cue to take a gracious leave.

"It is not in my power to grant your request, sir," she said stiffly, refusing to express a conventional regret. "I have already denied myself to other gentlemen tonight. It would be most unseemly in me to reverse that decision now."

"There are some requests it is well within your power to grant, however. I will call upon you tomorrow if I may."

His eyes demanded a response, and Serena murmured that they would be receiving morning callers on the morrow.

"I shall be seeking a private interview with you," Lord Whitlaw said deliberately.

Impotent fury flooded through Serena at the presumption and bad taste that could prompt such a statement in a public place before an interested audience of confirmed tattlemongers. "I cannot imagine that we have anything to say to each other that requires privacy, my lord," she said repressively, sending him a look of distilled dislike.

"Can you not? Perhaps a night's sleep will bring enlightenment." He laughed and bowed very low before taking himself off, leaving an enraged and embarrassed Serena to face the thinly disguised curiosity of her neighbors. Fortunately, this ordeal was considerably alleviated by Mrs. Arbuthnot, whose heart was kinder than most and who introduced a new topic of conversation before the earl was out of earshot.

Still, the rest of the ball was a severe trial. For one of her quick-flaring temper, she was getting rather a lot of practice in concealing her emotions lately, Serena reflected with wry amusement as she climbed wearily into her carriage at the end of a miserable evening. The need to damp down her anger had only spread the blaze beneath her surface calm, and this was transformed into an unshakable determination to deny Whitlaw his private interview. This much satisfaction she was resolved on to pay him back for the embarrassment he had just subjected her to. In the muddled state of mind induced by vague unhappiness and flaming rage, she failed to take into consideration the fact that he would not be deterred forever from coming to the point.

She had known from the beginning that Whitlaw planned to marry her. He was not stupid. Not even a monumental conceit could blind him to her consistent efforts to discourage his courtship within the bounds of civility. Eventually she would have to face an unpleasant scene when she refused his offer, but not tomorrow.

In the event, it was not Lord Whitlaw who made an offer of marriage the next day, but Mr. Selcort.

Serena had quitted the house immediately after breakfast on a trumped-up errand, bringing Betsy with her, as much for company as propriety. Despite the intermittent showers, they spent an enjoyable few hours wandering around the large emporiums and small shops. Betsy, with her clear-eyed view of the world and strong common sense, was good company, and the outspoken manner that resisted correction and was the very opposite of the servility expected of well-trained domestic servants had the value of taking Serena out of herself. It was a time-honored custom for abigails to inherit their mistresses' cast-off clothing, but most of Serena's things were too big to alter successfully for the rail-thin Betsy, so they did some shopping for the maid also. Always generous to those around her, Serena was in a reckless frame of mind that would have led her to agree to several times the expenditure that Betsy deemed proper.

They returned home in perfect charity with each other, and Serena had all but forgotten for the moment the reason behind the unscheduled shopping trip when she was summoned to her mother's room. A day or two after the accident on Oxford Street she had warned Mrs. Boynton of the likelihood of an imminent application by Mr. Selcort for Verity's hand, but Lord Whitlaw's announcement at Almack's had driven it from her mind, so it was with some surprise that she listened to her mother's tale.

Mrs. Boynton's dresser was doing her mistress's hair when Serena entered, but was instantly dismissed with a wave of that lady's hand and a hasty "That will be all for now, Murdock, thank you."

Serena, her hand still on the doorknob, stood back to allow passage to the dresser, who exited with reluctant steps and a speculative look on her austere features that didn't change when Serena bestowed a smiling nod on her as she closed the door.

"Where have you been gone to for hours and hours?" demanded Mrs. Boynton without preamble as she sprang up from the cane-back chair in front of the dressing table, her still-pretty face drawn up in tight lines as she rushed across the room toward her daughter. She did not wait for an answer but continued in faintly querulous accents. "I have had a dreadful morning. That unsuitable young man presented himself not fifteen minutes after you left, requesting a private audience with me." She paused dramatically, and her daughter said with a calm reasonableness that did nothing to soothe her parent's ruffled nerves:

"Well, I warned you that he would come seeking Verity's hand, so it surely could not have been a surprise."

"Of course it was a surprise!" The vehemence in her mother's tones caused Serena to blink. "We had made it so plain that we did not wish to encourage the connection that no one with an ounce of breeding or sensitivity could have failed to take the hint!"

"Except a man in love," came the dry interjection.

"Yes, well, I never expected him to actually have the audacity to confront me in my own house with a proposal he knew beyond doubting was completely unacceptable to Verity's family."

Obviously her mother's penchant for seeing things the way she wished them to be had ill-served her today. She had been emotionally unprepared for the difficult interview. Serena made soothing noises, a small frown between her brows. "Was Mr. Selcort uncivil or disrespectful to you, Mama? I would not have thought it of him."

"No, not uncivil precisely, though his manners are always too stiff for my taste. He always looks at one with that piercing stare as if he were preaching a sermon to a sinner." Mrs. Boynton hunched a shoulder pettishly, and it dawned on Serena that her parent felt uncomfortable in Mr. Selcort's presence, though she could not be sure whether it was the young man's serious demeanor or a more general reaction to his calling, prompted by some half-remembered experience in the past that was responsible.

"How did he take his rejection?"

"He *didn't*!" As her daughter's eyebrows climbed, Mrs. Boynton backtracked hastily. "Oh, he got out something about realizing all too well the difference between his station and Verity's, but then he went on to say that he believed the attachment between them was one that would stand the test of separation—that he could not relinquish his suit permanently until Verity signified a change of heart. He said that while Verity remained pledged to him in spirit, he would be prepared to wait until she came of age if necessary. He said a whole lot more too about hoping I would come to see that they were suited to each other, until I became so incensed I told him flatly that I would never give my consent to such an unequal match."

At this, Serena caught her lower lip between her teeth, silent but troubled.

"Why do you look like that? Would you have held out hope to that difficult young man?" demanded Mrs. Boynton. "If memory serves, you were equally adamant against this match." She was looking faintly belligerent and her voice held a defensive note.

Serena hastened to placate her. "No, no, Mama, I meant no criticism. It is just that I wish I were more convinced that we are acting for the best in refusing Mr. Selcort outright." She shrugged helplessly. "I thought so at first, but Verity is so quietly certain that she knows her own mind that I cannot help being impressed by her maturity."

"Would you see your sister throw away her life at seventeen?"

"No, certainly they must wait." On this point Serena was unshaken in her belief that her sister was too young to be allowed to make such a lasting decision. "Does Verity know that Mr. Selcort has declared himself?"

Her mother's eyes slid away and she made a slight gesture of resignation. "Oh, yes. I called her in afterward and tried to make her see reason, but she is every bit as obstinate in her own quiet way as you are. She insisted she would wait for Mr. Selcort forever if necessary. I don't know what I have ever done to deserve such treatment at the hands of my children, especially when I am feeling quite dreadfully unwell with this wretched sore throat."

Acquainted from childhood with her mother's propensity for embroidering on her grievances at great length, Serena invented a chore that would necessitate her immediate removal from the vicinity, recommending tea with honey for her mother's throat as she went. She was almost through the door when Mrs. Boynton called after her,

"Oh, by the by, Serena, Lord Whitlaw called this morning also. He seemed quite put out that you were not here to receive him, and stayed no more than a minute or two."

Safely on the other side of the door, Serena permitted herself a rather grim smile, knowing all the while that her sense of triumph was destined to be ephemeral. She could not hope to evade the man forever.

Two days later, at a private ball, Serena saw Lord Whitlaw bearing down on her as she melted away from a chattering group, intent on seeking out her sister, whom she had lost sight of for the last few minutes. Though Verity was noticeably subdued in spirit, her behavior since Mr. Selcort's unsuccessful application had been exemplary. Tonight, however, the rejected suitor had shown up in company with Peter Phillips. This first meeting between the pair since their hopes had been formally blighted might be fraught with emotion, and it would not do to create talk among the hawk-eyed matrons who missed none of the courtship byplay from their vantage points along the perimeter of the ballroom.

Serena tried to slip past Lord Whitlaw with only a nod, but he put out a hand to stop her. She jerked her arm away from his hand in an involuntary motion but, conscious of interested eyes on them, resisted the urge to stalk away. She raised her eyes to his in an inquiring fashion, keeping her muscles relaxed with an effort.

"Forgive my abruptness, cousin," said the earl, dropping his hand to his side, "but your mother is not here this evening and I thought you would wish to know that your sister and that young friend of Lord Phillips' have slipped away to a room at the back of the house. No doubt it is all very innocent, but a young girl's reputation is so fragile." He paused suggestively.

"She promised . . ." Serena's lips snapped shut, then opened after she drew a shaky breath. Her voice was under control as she asked quietly, "Where is this room, sir?"

"Come, I'll show you." He put his hand on her arm again to guide her, and this time Serena let it stay, her concern for Verity wiping every other thought from her mind.

"I feel like a mean snitch," Lord Whitlaw confessed as they exited the ballroom into a narrow passage that ran from the front to the back of the house, turning to the right toward the rear. "It is abominable to spoil a harmless *tête-à-tête*, but someone might discover them, and wagging tongues can be fatal."

"You were very right to come to me," Serena said, her voice warmed by the first flash of approval she had ever felt toward him.

"Here we are." They had paused at a door in the paneled passage, dimly lighted by a branching candle sconce on the wall opposite. He opened a door and stepped back for her to enter.

Serena's searching eyes discerned the emptiness of the room before she had taken two steps, and she whirled about in time to see Lord Whitlaw turn the key in the

lock of the door he had silently closed. Before her bemused brain could make sense of what was happening,
he pocketed the key and smiled at her as he advanced
into the room.

"Since you were unavailable when I called at your
home the other day, I thought we might have our little
talk here, my dear cousin."

13

Serena scarcely took in Lord Whitlaw's words. In the silence that followed, she removed her gaze from the pocket where the key had disappeared and fixed it on his face with painful intensity.

"Verity?" she whispered.

He shrugged. "Talking with a group of friends when last I saw her."

"Then you were lying about her going off with Mr. Selcort?"

"I prefer to think of it as employing a small stratagem made necessary by the depth of my feelings, surely forgivable in the circumstances. Everything may be forgiven a lover."

Freed from any immediate concern for her sister, Serena experienced a delayed jolt of anger along her nerves that was almost exhilarating in its effect. He had been determined to force an interview, refusing to recognize her efforts to discourage his courtship. Very well, he should have his interview. This man had made her stay in London a misery; she owed him no courtesy, no carefully conned phrases to spare his supposed feelings. Her chin went up and she held her ground as he continued to approach, stopping a scant few inches from her person in what she saw as an attempt at mastery that failed in its intent. Serena, uplifted by the ether of pure rage, was beyond intimidation. She stared up at the handsome face close to hers, at beautifully molded features beneath fine-grained skin already tanned despite a scarcity of sun this summer, at a wide smiling mouth revealing a row of perfect teeth, at light blue eyes that repelled her with their coldness.

"I don't see a lover," she said.

Serena knew by the slight spasm that crossed his features that he was disconcerted by her unfeminine directness, but his recovery was quick. "Ah, but given the opportunity, I will show you a lover!" he said fervently, wrapping his arms around her so swiftly she was powerless to prevent the indignity, though twin green flames burned in her white face. "Don't you know how your beauty excites a man's senses? I've wanted you from the moment I first clapped eyes on you. Marry me, Serena. You won't be disappointed."

"I don't believe a word of it! You know you have no feelings for me—it's your cousin's fortune you want. And you've known all along that I haven't the least intention in the world of marrying you."

During the delivery of this forthright speech, Serena had stood stiffly within the circle of the earl's arms, but as the impact of her words hit her captor, there was a lessening of pressure which she took instant advantage of by strongly throwing out both elbows against his arms and slipping out from under his loosened grip in an unexpected movement that won her freedom before he could exert his superior strength to prevent her escape. He did lunge forward in an attempt to grab her arm, but she prudently whisked herself behind the big desk that was positioned across a corner of the room.

"Do stop this ludicrous charade," she begged. "I promise you nothing on earth would prevail upon me to become your wife."

Lord Whitlaw had gone a dull red at her tone of amused contempt. There was nothing of the heartbroken lover about him, however. Chagrin, yes, but the rigid line of his jaw was an indication of clenched teeth within, and his arctic eyes could have frozen water. His nostrils were a bit pinched as he made a minute adjustment of the shirt cuff beneath his black sleeve, keeping his attention on his fingers.

"Oh, I feel sure I can prevail upon you to change your

mind. After all, we shall have sufficient time and privacy in which to reconsider your rash answer."

"If you are threatening to keep me locked in here with you, I should warn you that it will avail you nothing. My answer will be the same, however long it takes for someone to discover us here."

"When you assess the damage that will be done to your reputation should anyone try to enter this room, I am persuaded you will decide marriage to me will be preferable. Two sensible people such as we are can surely come to a mutually agreeable arrangement for dwelling together amicably without . . . er . . . crowding each other."

"Such exquisite consideration," mocked Serena lightly, "though perhaps not the most romantic speech ever recorded."

"Just say the word that will make me the happiest of men and it will be my very great pleasure to accede to your desire for romance." When she made an impatient gesture with her hand, he changed tactics once more, saying prosaically, "Since you require time to make your decision, we may as well be comfortable. Being a perfect gentleman, I cannot sit while a lady is standing, so may I suggest that you sit down?"

Without a word, Serena dropped onto the chair behind the desk, taking advantage of the cessation in hostilities to take stock of her surroundings for the first time. The room they were in was evidently a small study, and under other circumstances might be described as cozy, with its gleaming dark-paneled walls and attractive Aubusson carpet. There were only two other chairs in addition to the one she occupied behind the desk, large-scale wing-back chairs covered in a scenic print, the colors of which were indistinguishable in the inadequate light provided by a single wall sconce next to the door. A small round table with a piecrust rim stood between the chairs, placed facing the desk at a comfortable distance for conversation. Against the wall behind the chairs under a painting of a hunting scene stood a cabinet whose top held a tray containing a decanter and several glasses. The wall to

Serena's left was largely taken up by a pair of French doors that presumably opened out into a back garden, as did the ballroom. Her eyes slid quickly away from the doors to disguise her sudden hope that these might offer an avenue of escape. The draperies had not been pulled across this expanse of glass, a hopeful sign that the servants had not yet locked up for the night. The only other item in the room appeared to be a large globe, its stand placed in front of the pulled-back draperies at the end of the doors to receive the best light.

Her eyes returned from their quick survey, inevitably drawn to the elegant figure in the wing chair on the right. Lord Whitlaw was sitting sprawled at his ease, his ankles crossed in an extended position, his elbows held in at his waist while long fingers met under his chin in a travesty of a prayerful position. He was studying her coolly, and her spine stiffened in response as she returned the look with an expressionless mien.

"I must say you are a cool one," he commented with what sounded oddly like genuine admiration. "We shall make a good team."

Serena shook her head decisively. "No, we should not. You would do much better to set your cap for a more malleable heiress, one who will be so bowled out by your good looks that you'll be able to mold her into the sort of wife you wish—while her blind adoration lasts."

"You've got a viper's tongue, cousin, but I'm not complaining, mind you. I prefer women with spirit; they present more of a challenge."

"Thank you, but neither compliments nor insults will serve to change my decision."

"Perhaps not, but I think you would not wish to be the object of scandal just when you are trying to get your sister safely riveted. . . . What, no comeback?" he added when she pressed her lips together and made no reply.

"I am no green girl to fear gossiping tongues, and you cannot create much of a scandal out of two mature persons electing to sit out a number of dances in the privacy of a study. Besides, if the door is locked, no one is likely to discover us anyway."

"Time enough to unlock it when I hear voices in the passageway, but not," he added with soft menace, "time enough for you to unlock those window doors if that thought crossed your mind. And we won't be merely sitting and conversing when someone enters this room. We'll be engaged in a much more enjoyable activity on that convenient desktop."

Serena controlled the shudder of rage and fright that raced through her at his implication. Her voice revealed none of her feelings as she said quite distinctly, "Let me hasten to disabuse you of any idea you might have that I would passively submit to such an outrage. A screaming, clawing victim would not accord well with your tale of mutual passion."

"But at that point it would scarcely matter to your reputation, would it, my dear Serena? Women who lead men on and then cry rape do not escape the censure of society."

"You may believe me, my lord, when I say that I would greatly prefer the censure of society to marriage with such a loathsome creature as you!"

At the scorn in Serena's voice Lord Whitlaw's muscles tensed as if to spring, and hers tightened defensively in response, but a sound from the French doors brought both heads swinging around to witness the entrance of Lord Phillips from the garden.

"Is this a private conference or may I join in?" he asked, stepping all the way into the room and sweeping a mild gaze over the shocked faces confronting him.

"We would not be here if we did not wish to be private," Lord Whitlaw snapped. "Kindly go out the way you came."

"No, Peter, please stay!" Serena found her tongue at last. "He has locked the door. The key is in his breast pocket."

"I'll have that key, if you please," said Lord Phillips, holding out a hand. There was no emotion in his voice, but Serena caught her breath at the danger that stared out of his eyes.

The earl, however, was not disposed to accede to this

peremptory demand. "But I don't please, and somehow I do not think you would care to involve Serena in a public brawl." He had risen from his chair at the other's entrance, and the two men, both well over six feet of solid muscle, stood eye-to-eye in a primal challenge that struck terror into Serena's heart.

"She won't be here to be involved. Go out the way I came in, Serena. I have unlocked the closest window to this room in the ballroom to your right. You may watch for a chance to slip in behind the draperies, which are partially closed. Be quick, I hear voices in the hall." Peter never shifted his glance from the other man's furious face, but he was aware of her hesitation. "Go, Serena, now," he repeated placidly.

Reluctantly Serena obeyed him, gliding out from behind the desk and scooting through the open doors into the garden. At the last instant she could not prevent her concerned gaze from traveling to Lord Whitlaw, who stood transfixed with helpless rage. Peter held the crucial ground between him and his quarry. The hatred on his face acknowledged the fact that any fighting would delay him long enough to allow her to escape his trap.

"You may as well unlock the door. It will save awkward explanations," Peter suggested as the voices outside came closer.

The earl whirled on his heel and did just that, opening the door in the surprised face of his host for the evening. With a muttered excuse he strode out of the study past the two men in the doorway.

"Good evening, Sinderby," Lord Phillips said with an apologetic smile. "I hope very much that you will pardon the presumption that led Lord Whitlaw and me to appropriate your study for our little business talk." Aware of his host's eyes on the open doors behind him, Peter went on smoothly, "It was most agreeable to secure a little privacy and a breath of fresh air at the same time." He was holding a little pocketbook open in his hand, and his genial host, spotting it, said heartily:

"Not at all, my dear fellow. Delighted to be of service. Pray do not disturb yourself. Take all the time you like.

Rotherham and I shall go into the morning room instead."

Lord Sinderby bowed himself out, smiling widely, and Peter heaved a sigh of relief as the door clicked shut behind the pair. He was fairly sure they had seen nothing untoward in the incident. As he replaced the pocketbook and sauntered over to close the French doors, he wore a thoughtful expression that turned to consternation as he came face-to-face with Serena on the threshold.

"Have they gone?" she whispered.

"What are you doing here? I thought you were safely back in the ballroom."

"There is a congenial group chattering away right in front of the unlocked window. They haven't budged an inch, so I decided to come back in through this room instead of standing outside in the cold."

Noting the tremors she could not suppress, Peter pulled her into the room. He took the precaution of locking the doors behind her and closing the draperies before addressing himself to her current problem by hauling her into his arms.

She started to struggle at once. "Stop that," Peter ordered in very unloverlike tones. "You cannot go back into the ballroom until you stop shivering. I'm merely going to warm you up a bit." In proof of this statement, he began rubbing his hands up and down her back in quick impersonal strokes that certainly generated some heat—and even more friction. Serena stood it for a second or two, then stepped back determinedly.

"Thank you," she said, sending him a cool look. "I'll take over now. It is really only my bare arms that are cold." She proceeded to rub her arms alternately with her other hand, avoiding his eyes as she concentrated on her actions.

"Why did you come here alone with Whitlaw?" Peter asked after a charged instant of silence.

That brought indignant eyes up to meet his. "I didn't—that is to say, I did not do it intentionally. He told me Verity and Mr. Selcort were in here. How did you find us?" she asked in her turn after he had emitted an explosive sound of disgust, though whether at Lord

Whitlaw's treachery or her own stupidity, she could not
be sure.

"I saw you go down the corridor with him. When I
tried the door handle and found it locked, I had to find
another way in. Fortunately, there is nothing unusual
about this particular arrangement of rooms in a town
house. I was grateful not to have to break the glass to get
in."

He was looking very impatient, and Serena, who was
experiencing a reaction now that the potentially disastrous situation had been averted, fought against unaccus-
tomed tears of weakness crowding behind her eyelashes.
She opened her eyes wide to prevent them from spilling
over and said gruffly, staring over his shoulder, "I really
do thank you for coming to my rescue once again, Peter.
He said he would keep me here until I agreed to marry
him—which I would never have done, of course," she
added as fury darkened his face, "but there could have
been a frightful scandal if someone had tried to come
in." Her eyes avoided his as she blinked rapidly, still
chafing her arms for warmth.

"Don't cry, sweetheart; it didn't happen."

Not once in her nearly two-and-twenty years had Serena ever heard that tone of voice addressed to her. Her
right hand stilled its rubbing motion on her arm and
some force operating against her will lifted her eyes to
his face. The tenderness she'd heard in his voice was
reflected in his eyes, and a gentle smile curved his lips.
To her astonished shame, the tears trembling on her
lashes spilled over and trickled down her cheeks even as
she foolishly declared, "I never cry."

He chuckled softly, a bare breath of sound. The same
mysterious force held her utterly still as his hands took
hold of her upper arms and his head descended toward
hers. At first his lips were warm and gentle on hers in a
kiss so light she almost doubted its existence. Afterward,
Serena wondered with a sense of shamed embarrassment
if she had been the one to increase the pressure as
suddenly she found herself drowning in a whirlpool of
sensation as he wrapped strong arms around her and

fastened his mouth on hers with a seeking hunger that escalated her unease to full-scale panic in an instant. She struggled frantically and was lingeringly released by his hands and mouth, but those compelling eyes continued to hold hers as she stared up at him in white-faced horror.

"No . . . oh, no, *no!*"

"Yes . . . oh, yes, yes," he rebutted with tender mockery. "Didn't you know it was inevitable that this should happen?"

"Nothing has happened, nothing at all! Nothing has changed," she repeated her frantic denial and had the dubious satisfaction of seeing the tenderness in his face supplanted by impatience.

"You may deny it until the last trump, but it will still be a lie and you know it. However, this is no place for a personal discussion. We'll talk later."

"No, there is nothing to talk about, now or any other time!"

"And that is another lie. You are a coward, Serena, but we'll talk about that later too. You must get back to the ballroom before someone else comes along."

Serena, striving to regain her composure, was no longer listening to him. With a quickness that took him by surprise, she turned and bolted from the study, leaving the door open behind her. Peter took a step in pursuit, then halted. Better not to be seen in her company just at present. He could only hope she'd manage to reenter the ballroom without attracting undue attention. At the moment she bore all the appearance of a wild creature at bay. He frowned heavily and forced himself to remain in his paneled prison for another five minutes, trying at the same time to get his thoughts in some kind of order.

One vital question had been settled, he realized with quiet jubilation, dropping into one of the wing-back chairs to wait out his incarceration in comfort. He knew past doubting that Serena had responded to his ill-timed ardor just now. Not for long, and obviously against that iron will of hers, but for a brace of heartbeats she had melted against him and returned his kiss.

He spent the next few minutes spinning a delightful future with Serena at the center of his life. He couldn't wait to show Springbrook to her. She would love his home. Serena was essentially a lover of the outdoors, and spring came earliest to the soft country of Devon. Somehow he was certain she would also share his affinity for the wild empty moorland country which formed such a startling contrast to the lovely green villages and seaside towns of the area. They would ride together and explore every inch of Dartmoor.

They would travel too. Fortunately, his cousin Ruppert Carteret ran the estate admirably in his absence. He might consider his prosy deliberation something of a cross to be borne, but Ruppert was entirely reliable, and his presence at Springbrook would allow Peter to show Serena all the places she longed to see in the old and the new world. She was no delicate creature with nerves to be daunted by the discomforts of foreign travel. Serena would march shoulder-to-shoulder with the man she loved, tackling each obstacle with spirit and energy and the will to overcome. He suspected she might be capable of aggravating him to the point of retaliation—she was bossy and opinionated and too damned independent—but she would never bore him. Her mind was too active and questing for that.

Lost in rosy visions of the future, Peter had completely lost sight of the sordid events that had led up to his present contentment, and the five minutes he had allotted before returning to the party were long up when he finally reined in his imagination and bethought himself of practicalities. Despite her brief surrender, Serena had left vehemently denying the attachment between them. He had called her a coward, and in a contradictory way that was quite true. Though he'd long admired her physical pluck and valiant spirit, it had become increasingly apparent over the course of their acquaintance that she was unwilling, even afraid to love a man, and had formed a definite resolution to remain unmarried. He had committed himself to the patient pursuit and inching progress that his intelligence told him was the only possible course—

his role was to be the dripping water that wore away stone—while hoping desperately for a dramatic breach in her defenses. Tonight's emotional ordeal might have provided that breakthrough. The next step was to consolidate his gains and convince her of the benefits of love while she was in a vulnerable state. A successful campaign depended upon denying the defenders the opportunity to repair the breach.

He would leave nothing to chance, Peter mused, preparing to leave Lord Sinderby's deceptively ordinary study. He knew from Peregrine Boynton that Serena was in the habit of riding with her brother in Hyde Park in the early morning. Tomorrow she would find herself with an additional escort, and one, moreover, who intended to stick like glue until they had resolved their situation. His optimism was such that he did not waste a moment contemplating any resolution that did not give him the girl he loved.

14

Lord Phillips' jubilant optimism about the inevitability of a shared future with Serena was severely tested over the next sennight, as was his patience. The impulsive decision to accost her in the park was nullified by Mother Nature in the form of a steady downpour that continued for two days without cessation. Not even Serena with her unfeminine disregard for creature comforts in the pursuit of exercise would have ventured out in such conditions.

On the afternoon of the second day his restlessness demanded action of some sort, no matter how slight the promise of a successful outcome. The chance of snatching a few moments of private conversation in a room full of callers was negligible at best, but he presented himself in Beak Street nevertheless, to be turned back at the front door by Richford with the news that the ladies were from home. He tried again the following day, to find Mrs. Boynton and Verity entertaining visitors in the drawing room. Of Serena there was no sign, and when he at last succeeded in getting Verity's ear, his inquiries as to her sister's whereabouts brought the disturbing news that Serena was indisposed. When he questioned her further, it didn't take extraordinary perceptiveness on his part to discern that Verity's soft replies disclaiming any cause for concern about her sister's health were uttered in the embarrassed manner of one unused to telling social lies.

Serena was taking no chances at all of meeting him, he thought wrathfully, recalling that she had sent a note excusing herself from her standing arrangement to exercise with Natasha that morning. Glancing at his companion, he saw that Verity was looking anxious, and he smoothed all expression from his face. No need to take out his frustration on the inoffensive girl beside him. He smiled at her, and though she smiled back readily, he could see, beneath the surface relief that he was not going to cross-question her about her tiresome sister, that Verity was unhappy. Nigel had told him of his unsuccessful petition, of course, and he had intended to put in a good word for the young cleric with Serena at the earliest opportunity, but the scene in Lord Sinderby's study had wiped all thoughts of the disappointed pair from his mind.

Now he said kindly, "It distresses me to see you so unhappy, Verity. Is there no hope that your mother might be persuaded to reconsider her decision? I would be most willing to talk to her about Nigel to reassure her as to his character and prospects."

Verity's eyes widened in surprise, then darted to where her mother sat engrossed in conversation with Sir Humphrey Talbot and two of her women friends. She said, her ordinary soft tones muted still further, "You are very kind, sir, indeed you have been our true friend from the beginning, and I am so very grateful to you, but I fear nothing can alter the fact that Mama and Serena do not consider Nigel a suitable husband for me."

"He is not completely without expectations, you know. Perhaps your family have not perfectly understood that he will be quite comfortably circumstanced in time?"

"It is not merely that Nigel is not wealthy. Mama feels, they both feel, that I would miss not being in the first circles of society and would come to regret my decision eventually, but they are wrong. I don't care a rap for all that, and I could never regret marrying Nigel." Her voice, though soft, shook with the strength of her conviction.

"Nigel is a fortunate man indeed," Peter said, concealing a pang of something resembling envy as he spoke. He watched the faint color that had risen at his words recede from Verity's cheeks, leaving her paler than before.

"This need not be a final break, my dear child. You must not despair. You are both young yet, and much can happen in a year or two. Nigel's is not a capricious nature, nor, I imagine, is yours. These matters have a way of working out in time if you have faith and trust in each other." Peter felt awkward offering such scant comfort, but Verity looked at him with gratitude.

"Oh, yes, I know that eventually we shall marry, but the waiting will be difficult, especially since we shan't be able to see each other at all once Nigel leaves London, which he tells me will be fairly soon now." Despite her best efforts at control, her lips trembled and a sheen of unshed tears filmed her eyes. "We will not be able to say good-bye properly even if we should be so fortunate as to meet again before he goes away."

"Now, that is something I can and will alter." The smile that was so like his sister's appeared in Peter's eyes and he had the satisfaction of seeing hope creep back into Verity's disconsolate little face.

"C-could you?" she whispered, her hands clasped together in unconscious supplication, her sea-colored eyes huge and questioning.

"Nothing could be simpler," he replied promptly, with a confidence that wasn't entirely manufactured for her benefit, though he hoped she would not ask how he was going to arrange matters, for he hadn't a notion at the moment.

As it never occurred to Verity to question the ability of her champion to accomplish anything he set his mind to, she contented herself with offering her fervent though low-voiced thanks on behalf of herself and Mr. Selcort.

Peter said his farewells shortly thereafter, warm satisfaction at having restored Verity's spirits compensating, for the moment at least, for the simmering frustration that taunted him with regard to his own limping love affair. He plunged into devising a scheme that would enable the young lovers to say their good-byes in privacy, for Verity had been correct in her assumption that Mr. Selcort's time in London was fast drawing to a close. To this end he paid a visit to the premises of Messrs. Sharp and Bland of South Audley Street, the firm that had been entrusted by him with the construction of a new traveling carriage that was to incorporate every advancement in design to guarantee the most comfortable ride possible at the greatest speeds attainable under all road conditions. The results of this visit being highly encouraging, he proceeded to outline his plan to Mr. Selcort and received that gentleman's heartfelt thanks for making possible the farewell meeting with his beloved that he had cudgeled his brains in vain to try to arrange.

Though busy with his good works over the succeeding days, Peter was not so preoccupied that he did not haunt the places where Serena might be expected to appear, but on this score his luck remained out. She might as well have dropped off the face of the earth as far as he was concerned. By now he knew Serena well enough that he never questioned that it was a quite deliberate policy on her part to avoid him. So much for his hopes of striking while the iron was hot. He would catch up with her sooner or later, but not before she'd had ample time to repair the breach and refortify her defenses. He might love her to the point of desperation, but that redheaded termagant had the power to irritate him beyond measure, and what was worse, he suspected she knew this and enjoyed the knowledge. He who had always considered himself in full control of his life was now floundering in a limbo, the termination of which state depended entirely on another person. He foresaw a cat-and-dog existence with Serena, but even that did not signify—he felt no envy for the peace and tranquillity in which Verity and Nigel would most likely dwell together. As long as he had Serena's love, he could do without peace and tranquillity.

And that was the crux of the matter. He did not know Serena's well-guarded heart. The flush of optimism arising out of their last meeting had faded as the barren days stretched into a sennight. A niggling doubt that he might have read too much into her momentary surrender blossomed into full-scale internal conflict. He had not taken into account the fact that Serena had been married. It did not necessarily follow that she loved him just because her senses had been aroused for a brief passionate interval, and nothing less than her whole heart was acceptable to him. He knew she bore him no personal antipathy such as Whitlaw aroused in her breast, but was forced to the lowering conclusion that a disinterested observer would have difficulty discerning a difference based strictly upon Serena's actions, a thought that did little to bolster his spirits as the appointed time approached for the farewell meeting between Verity and Mr. Selcort.

Peter would have been greatly heartened had he been privileged to observe Serena in the bosom of her family during the period following the eventful evening at the Sinderbys'.

She had raced out of the study like some demented creature. It was more than she deserved to find the dim corridor empty, a piece of good fortune that accorded her a respite in which to compose herself before reentering the ballroom. After a nervous backward glance to confirm that Peter had not come in pursuit, she slowed her steps to a walk, pinched her cheeks painfully to restore the color that had drained out of her face when he had released her, and fixed her stiff lips into a semblance of a social smile.

Her entrance into the ballroom went unremarked, and though there was no question of enjoying herself, given the present state of her nerves, at least she was spared the upset of additional contact with either of the two men responsible for her present mental turmoil.

She was so intent upon seeming her normal self in the carriage on the way home that she kept up a steady stream of commonplaces, not even aware that Verity was quieter than usual, until, running out of innocuous topics, she ceased her feverish babble with the abruptness of someone who'd had a hand put over her mouth. They rode the rest of the way in a shared silence that neither noticed, each being lost in her own reverie.

Sleep was the furthest thing from Serena's mind when she was at last alone in her bedchamber that night. She had received a shock that must be dealt with before she could seek oblivion. She piled the pillows up behind her and sat among them, her arms embracing her raised knees as she grappled with the unwelcome knowledge that had come to her in Peter's arms, knowledge that had hit with the force of a hammer blow.

She had listened to Natasha extolling marital intimacy with a skepticism engendered by her own unhappy experience. Whitlaw had pursued his own pleasure with no thought for her sensibilities. Her pleasure or lack of it never had been an object with him, though at the same time he had conveyed the impression that there was something lacking in her, and for want of evidence to the contrary, she had accepted his judgment as valid and planned her life accordingly during her widowhood.

The few moments in Peter's embrace tonight had changed reality forever. Her instinctive denial to him that anything of moment had occurred had been a lie, recognized by her as such even as she had reiterated the lie in her panic. For she had enjoyed every heartbeat of that brief interval out of time, reveling in the exciting sensual flow coursing within her tingling body. She had wanted it to go on forever, thus the frantic denial, because nothing had really changed despite the shattering discovery that she was not essentially different from other women.

Releasing her knees and leaning back into her pillows, Serena considered her nature, bringing ruthless honesty to the task. A short period of frowning concentration was sufficient to convince her that she was temperamentally unsuited to the married state. She resented any curbs on her freedom of action, she liked having control of her own money, and was not prepared to relinquish this privilege, and though she would certainly regret having to forgo having children of her own, she could enjoy being an indulgent aunt to those Perry and Verity would doubtless produce. In addition, she knew herself to be too fond of getting her own way to be willing to submit to the will of another person without good cause or prolonged argument. The traditional acceptance of masculine domination had never seemed sufficient cause to her in the past, and this was unlikely to change simply because a man's kiss reduced her to a state of quivering pleasure. Unaware that her fingers were tracing back and forth across her parted lips, she decided that the major portion of her weakness during Peter's embrace was very likely attributable to the circumstance of its being the first time she had ever felt pleasure in the activity. She told herself sensibly that the reaction would lessen with repetition, and in any case was an ephemeral feeling that should not be allowed to influence her rational decision.

Having thus redefined the evening's events in logical terms and reduced the shocks to manageable proportions, Serena had no hesitation in deciding to continue her avoidance of contact with Peter Phillips; in fact, it was more essential to her peace of mind than before. She drifted off to sleep on the thought, but awoke more fatigued than when she had closed her eyes, by virtue of the fact that in her dreams she was frantically striving to gain some shadowy objective that continued to recede from her horizon while new barriers kept springing up in her path, and some vague pursuing threat drove her onward without rest or pause.

She opened thankful eyes on a prospect of soaking rain that would mean no riding that day. All gratitude at being safely in her room fled her mind while she considered her schedule over the next few days. Peter would certainly try to press his claims—what he imagined to be his claims, she amended—by seeking a meeting at the earliest opportunity. She would need to enlist the cooperation of her family in preventing this, though she had no intention of discussing the situation with anyone. She included Lord Whitlaw in the ban also, though she doubted he would have the temerity to approach her again.

Serena's hapless family had much to put up with over the next several days as she stalked around the house, chafing at the enforced inactivity and bitterly deploring the inclement weather whenever she chanced to glance out a window. The servants took to vanishing around corners when they saw her approaching, as boredom drove her to poke her nose into every aspect of household management, and her mother was heard to mutter that if she'd had any advance warning of her firstborn's stormy nature, she'd have called her Tempest over her father's objections, since his choice had turned out so singularly inappropriate.

In point of fact, Mrs. Boynton was not best pleased with either of her daughters that rainy summer. Serena, who could have Lord Whitlaw or, her parent suspected, Lord Phillips, by the lifting of her little finger, chose to give the cold shoulder to both and would most likely end up as one of those eccentric creatures in dowdy clothes who spurned the society of their peers in favor of doing good works among the undeserving poor. And Verity, for whose secure future this fatiguing Season had been undertaken in the first place, had willfully turned her back on an eminently eligible suitor, preferring instead to join her life to that of an impecunious country parson. Not only had she put her parent in the invidious position of having to deny her child her heart's desire, but she would, based on her current demeanor, no doubt subject her long-suffering mother to a winter of enduring her mopish behavior before making another expensive London sojourn necessary to get her settled. The only one of her children with whom Mrs. Boynton was in charity at the moment was her son, whose good looks and pleasing manners secured her many an envious compliment for her part in rearing him, and who seemed to be greatly enjoying his stay in town, unlike his difficult sisters.

Serena's unusual preoccupation with her own problems lifted as the week wore on, permitting her to recognize that, apart from her sister's general unhappiness over Mr. Selcort, there was a new aura of nerviness about Verity from time to time. For one thing, she froze each time the door knocker sounded, then hurried into unconnected speech if anyone noticed. Since Serena was absenting herself from the drawing room these days, she had no way of learning whom Verity was hoping or dreading to see—certainly it could not be Mr. Selcort, who had been given his *congé*. It would do no good to ask her sister if she were expecting a special caller, but Serena, being Serena, tried anyway, and received the denial she anticipated. What with the wretched weather, her self-imposed confinement, and her sister's worrisome secretiveness, Serena became more than a touch snappish as the uneventful days crawled past. She could not extend her imaginary indisposition much beyond a sennight without provoking comment and pointed inquiries from their friends, nor did she intend this. She'd had time to forget the effect of Peter's lovemaking by now, and her thoughts were far from charitable toward the author of her present predicament. It was all his doing that she was virtually a prisoner in her own home. She had absolutely no intention of marrying him, so it might be best for all concerned if she allowed him to declare himself so that she might make her feelings about marriage plain once and for all.

The crucial decision taken at last, Serena's restlessness subsided. They were to attend a musical evening at the Silverdales' tonight. She had sent the footman out in the morning with a large order for fresh flowers, and she spent a pleasant hour after lunch arranging the results of her prodigality and disposing the vases about the house. It was as she was setting a great bowl of sweet-smelling pink and white roses on the table between the windows of the drawing room that she glanced out of the window to the street below in time to see Lord Phillips handing Verity up into his curricle. She stepped quickly back from the window, but she need not have bothered, because they were too absorbed in each other to look up. Peter handed Verity a bandbox and mounted into his seat. Serena's brows contracted as she watched the sporting vehicle move smartly off.

She was nearly positive that Verity had indicated her intention of resting after lunch to try to get rid of a headache before the evening's outing. Of a certainty she had said nothing about plans to drive out with Lord Phillips. They might have made the appointment when he had called earlier in the week, but now that she came to think about it, she had not heard the door knocker in the last half-hour, though she had been using a room on the ground floor for her flower arranging. The room was at the back of the house, but the door had been open the whole time. Though she might not have been aware of someone on the stairs, she should have heard the loud, dull thud of the knocker.

Serena repositioned one of the roses in the bowl, bringing its face more fully into view while she mentally reviewed the scene outside. Why the bandbox? Her hand fell away from the flowers as a squiggle of fear made its presence felt in the pit of her stomach. She forcibly restrained herself from running as she headed upstairs to Verity's room, where she rang for her sister's maid before throwing open the wardrobe doors. By the time the girl arrived, Serena had determined that the only item that seemed to be missing was the new gown that had arrived just the day before from the modiste. She had closed the wardrobe and was facing the door when the girl who waited upon Verity came hurrying in.

"I thought you would be—" The words came to an abrupt halt at sight of Serena. "Good afternoon, ma'am." The maid dropped a little curtsy and glanced around the room before bringing puzzled eyes back to its only occupant.

"I'm sorry to have interrupted your rest period, Meggie. As you can see, my sister is not here. Do you know where she has gone?"

"Yes, ma'am, she went driving with Lord Phillips."

No hesitation in the girl's ready answer. Serena's stare was unwavering as she inquired, "Was the appointment of long standing?"

"I dunno, ma'am. She just told me today when I helped her to dress. Oh, we did meet Lord Phillips yesterday on Bond Street, accidental like."

"I see. Did she say anything to you about the new gown that arrived from Madame Vicennes yesterday?"

"Only that she thought as how one of the sleeves was too tight and she was a-going to send it back."

"I see," Serena said again. "That will be all, Meggie, thank you."

She stood undecided in the middle of her sister's bedchamber for a few minutes after the maid had gone. It was clear that the girl, a rather vacant-faced, sturdy creature, not given to curiosity or questioning the actions of others, was telling the truth as she knew it. Verity had not involved her in any conspiracy to conceal a meeting with Mr. Selcort. Indeed, there was no rational cause to suspect that her sister's engagement with Lord Phillips was anything other than the usual courtly behavior common among young men and women—except for the secrecy, that was. Verity occasionally drove out with one or another of her male friends, but this was the first time she had neglected to mention the arrangement to her mother or sister. Serena paused for a moment. Perhaps she had mentioned it to her mother. She glanced at the clock on the bedside table. Mrs. Boynton would be resting at this hour, and it really did not greatly signify whether or not Verity had spoken to her of an engagement with Lord Phillips. She would not have objected. Peter was a great favorite and trusted by her mother.

Serena closed Verity's door softly and walked with slow steps toward her own bedchamber. On the surface, all was in order, but she could not dismiss Verity's recent nervy behavior from her mind. She'd have taken her oath that her sister would never stoop to clandestine meetings; but Verity was in love, and from what she'd ever heard, there was no predicting the actions of persons under the influence of this disruptive emotion. Against her better judgment, and arguing with herself the whole time, Serena tied a becoming straw hat under her chin by its green ribbons and disposed a delicate crocheted shawl of the same soft green about her shoulders, catching up a reticule as she left the room.

Her exit from the house was as cautious as Verity's had been. Richford was polishing silver in the butler's pantry and Virgil, the footman, had departed on an errand an hour since. Serena wasted no time sending for her carriage, but set out on foot for Regent Street, where she would be able to get a hackney cab, having made up her mind what she intended to do while in her room. If Verity's conduct could be taken at face value, she must be meaning to return the new dress to the modiste for repairs. The presence of the curricle outside the dress-maker's establishment would reassure her that all was as it should be, and she could then drive on home in the cab with no one the wiser. Of course, Peter might have dropped Verity off and gone about some business of his own, planning to call back for her later. Serena bit her lip, debating whether she would enter Madame Vicennes' shop if there was no curricle waiting. Verity would know she had been followed, but how else was she to ascertain whether her sister was inside or had already called and left again? She would cross that bridge when she came to it, she decided, hurrying the last few feet to the corner of Regent Street as she saw a cab approaching.

She settled into the worn interior of a once-elegant vehicle after giving the jehu Madame Vicennes' direc-tion. She perched on the front of the seat, her glance sweeping the streets they passed on the short drive and her jaw tensed over clamped teeth. As the cab bowled around the corner into the quiet street where the shop was located, Serena's searching eyes picked out Peter's blue-coated figure sitting in his curricle pulled up to the curb on the opposite side of the street. Her jaw relaxed and she was about to sink back against the squabs when she noticed another vehicle standing behind the curricle. The second carriage, poled up behind a team of beautiful matched grays, was a luxurious traveling carriage whose brown and gold paintwork appeared spanking new; but this she assimilated with one corner of her brain. The rest of her intelligence was trying to comprehend that Verity had broken her promise to wait, that her quiet, biddable little sister was about to cause a scandal by eloping.

And Peter Phillips was helping her to ruin herself!

Serena was out of the cab almost before it stopped, propelled across the street by an explosion of fury such as she had never before experienced.

"You *Judas*!" she flung at Peter, who was eyeing her approach with openmouthed surprise. "How could you lend yourself to such a dishonorable enterprise? I ought to have you up on charges. Were you trying to pay me back for not falling into your arms by helping a seventeen-year-old to ruin her life?"

Long before this vitriolic speech was completed, Peter had mastered his original surprise—and every other emotion, seemingly. Serena had never known that periwinkle-blue eyes could go so cold in a face carved out of stone. She shivered a little at the look of disdain he bent on her from his perch in the curricle.

"Yes, you are shaking like a blancmange from rage, are you not? The only real emotion of which you seem capable," he observed as he climbed down from the curricle. He smiled nastily when she stepped back a pace as he confronted her on the flagstones.

"A little late to demonstrate prudence, isn't it?" he went on, his voice dispassionate. "You have nothing to fear from me, Serena, nothing at all. In my naiveté, I thought you merely a coward, guarding your heart from possible hurt; but you don't possess a heart, do you? If you did, you could not have treated your sister with such callous disregard for her feelings. No, you are going to hear me out for once," he said grimly when her lips parted to refute this charge.

"If I interpreted your ravings correctly, you think Verity and Nigel are about to elope, with my support and contrivance. Let me lay your fears to rest on that score by assuring you that you are mistaken. I have merely lent my carriage to Nigel for his journey back home and have done no more for the pair than to arrange a few moments of privacy for them in which to say their farewells, something you wold have done had you contained an ounce of compassion in your makeup.

"I see your driver approaching for his money. May I suggest that you return home and say nothing of this to Verity. In all likelihood she and Nigel have been too wrapped up in their own sad parting to have noticed your arrival. I will deliver her to Beak Street when she has recovered a little."

For once in her life Serena was left without a word to say. She cast a look of unconscious appeal at him, then turned away with what dignity she could summon when his face remained a stony mask.

"One more thing, Lady Whitlaw."

She looked back over her shoulder, pausing on the curb.

"You will be happy to know there will be no necessity to hide from me in the future. I'll trouble you with no more unwelcome attentions."

"Good," said Serena, pronouncing the defiant lie through lips that trembled, before she hastened across the street to the waiting hackney.

15

The headache Serena cited in her note to her mother begging to be held excused from attending the Silverdales' musical evening, was quite real. It was the result of an abandoned bout of weeping such as she had not indulged in since the crushing disappointments of childhood had passed. During the entire span of her unsavory marriage she had not shed more than a tear or two and was therefore both astounded and alarmed at the end of a session that had begun in fury the instant she had gained the security of her bedchamber and ended in desolation some forty minutes later.

Desolation because when her anger at Peter had been washed away by a raging torrent of tears, she was left with his harsh judgment of her. That it was also inaccurate, she trusted those closest to her would attest, but, being a fair-minded young woman, she had to admit that, seen from Peter's viewpoint, there was some evidence for his charge that she was heartless and lacking in compassion. It never crossed her mind that Peter's accusations might have had their source in a rage as consuming as hers had been. Her own nature being so volatile, she was unused to the icily controlled anger of a man slow to rouse and not given to histrionics or theatrical gestures. Serena accepted that he had meant each and every wounding word he had uttered with such apparently emotionless deliberation, and she wept bitterly for the loss of his good opinion.

None of this was thoroughly digested and comprehended until hours later, when, drained for a time of all emotional energy and readied for bed by a concerned

Betsy, she was alone again with a thinking apparatus that had begun to function once more. She owed this to her strong-minded maid, who had clucked over her unaccountably woebegone mistress and forcibly supervised the consumption of unwanted tea and toast by dogged persistence. After a soothing interval of hair-brushing by Betsy, to the accompaniment of a gentle monologue encompassing the doings belowstairs related in a purposely monotonous drone to which Serena hadn't attended, she felt almost human again and ready to disobey her young keeper's strict instructions to go right to sleep and leave any problems for the morning, when they would not loom so large.

She needed to make some sense out of today's events and her own incredible reaction. By the time she fell into a heavy slumber some few hours later, she was the unhappy possessor of a startling bit of knowledge that had come to her too late, and many regrets that she feared she would be unable to reverse.

Why had she not known until this moment that she was in love with Peter Phillips? Was she stupid or so unacquainted with her own emotional makeup that she had missed some vital clues along the way? Or had she perhaps been struck with the emotional equivalent of lightning at the very moment when Peter was declaring his disgust of her? She did not think she had been one of those fools who invite the retaliation of the gods by declaring their disbelief in the existence of love. She had merely accepted—on the basis of considerable experience of being wooed by some of the most-sought-after members of the opposite sex—that she was immune to that particular infection. Well, she knew better now, and the knowledge promised to bring nothing but misery in its train.

Recalling the cold disdain in Peter's eyes when he had dismissed her this afternoon, Serena shivered and blinked away two more tears. In the past he had looked at her in a quite different fashion. Even when teasing her abominably, there had been a light in those bright blue eyes that had invited her to laugh with him; and once in Lord

Sinderby's study he had gazed on her as if he would like to go on doing just that forever. Forever had not lasted very long, she reflected sadly, barely a week. She could not really blame him for his change of heart, for she had abused him like a fishwife today. What was more, now that she came to think of it, she had dealt him a deal of verbal abuse throughout their stormy acquaintance. That he had not long since turned his thoughts to a gentler, more amenable female was a blessing she now recognized after it had been withdrawn.

Thanks to a splendid constitution, Serena was none the worse the next day after her emotional spree, a trifle paler perhaps, but far from showing symptoms of going into a decline, she was ravenously hungry and eager to implement the plans she had made in her lonely bed. It was not in her nature to submit tamely to the harsh designs of fortune without a struggle, so she had not long remained in the depths of despair. Peter was disillusioned now, but he had loved her once. It was up to her to show him she was not the cold, unfeeling creature he thought her. Her father had been a rather coldhearted man, and "depraved" was the mildest epithet she could apply to her late husband, despite the surface charm that had blinded her at eighteen. She had never been privileged to know a man like Peter before. He concealed a heart as kind as his sister's beneath a sophisticated exterior and possessed an impish sense of humor that delighted her, often against her will. Now she knew he also possessed an intrinsic strength of character that would not compromise even to win the woman he loved. She skated over the question of whether his love for her could be reanimated. To think defeat was to invite defeat, and Serena was not about to get caught in that trap. Not yet, at any rate.

She pumped her sister at breakfast, to no good end. Lord Phillips had not been among the guests at the Silverdales' musical evening. Serena stood a bit in awe of Verity at present, if the truth were known. Only yesterday she had parted from the man she loved, without the comfort of knowing when she would see him again. Almost as hard to bear must be the necessity to keep her feelings to herself because the two persons closest to her had set their faces against the match. Yet Verity sat clear-eyed and self-contained, responding to their overtures with her customary gentle good nature. "Quiet heroism" was the phrase that came to mind to describe her sister's demeanor. One day very soon they would have a serious talk. Verity must be longing to defend her love for Mr. Selcort, and neither her mother nor her sister had wished to hear anything about it.

For the moment, however, Serena was eager to be out about her own tangled affairs. It was one of her exercise mornings and she set out for the Talbot house impatient for the physical release she had denied herself during her recent self-imposed exile. If she also cherished a hope of meeting Peter in his sister's house, she suffered disappointment, but at least she was able to expend a little of the pent-up energy that had had her stalking around her own house for days. It was marvelous to enjoy a friendly gossip with Natasha over a cup of tea afterward and to play with Justin, who could walk quite well now as long as some patient individual held his hands. Like all women newly in love, Serena longed to hear her beloved's name spoken, but Natasha didn't mention Peter, and Serena, unaccountably shy on that subject, could not mention him either. She did take heart, though, to hear that the Talbot household planned to attend the play in two days' time. Perry had agreed to escort his mother and sisters the same evening, so there was a real expectation of meeting Peter in the immediate future. His manners were too good to permit him to ignore their presence in the theater. He was bound to visit their box during one of the intervals, and she should be able to manage a moment or two of his company, enough time to see if he had regretted the terrible things he had said to her.

Only it did not work out that way. Having looked in vain for Peter at Almack's the day after her visit to Natasha, Serena took extra pains with her appearance on the evening they went to the play. Indeed, the patient Betsy was reduced to grumbling over her mistress's

uncharacteristic inability to make up her mind as to clothing or coiffure. She even dithered over the selection of a
necklet from her meager collection of jewelry, eventually
tossing everything back into the jewel casket with a fine
disregard for knotting chains, leaving her smooth white
throat bare of ornamentation.

Eyeing her mistress staring into the mirror, her pretty
mouth drawn down in lines of dissatifaction as she twisted
this way and that, Betsy said sharply, "There is no pleasing you tonight. Stop twitching that skirt; it looks fine as
it is. You'll only press creases into that thin muslin."

"Tell me the truth, Betsy, do I look fat in this gown?"

The maid's openmouthed astonishment should have
been answer enough, but seeing that the anxious look in
the green eyes did not fade, she replied with weary
patience, "Of course you don't look fat, how could you?
Your waist measures scarcely an inch more than Miss
Verity's, and she's just a little bit of a thing. Are you
sickening for something? You have been acting mighty
strange these past few days."

"Perhaps it's this way of doing my hair," Serena mused,
putting up a tentative hand to her shining tresses, to have
it seized and cast down again.

"Now, you leave off tampering with my work, my
lady, or you'll ruin everything and I'll have to start all
over again. You will be late as it is, with all this worriting
and staring into mirrors. You look just like you always
look—beautiful—and your hair, if I do say it as shouldn't,
is the envy of every lady in London. Now, give over,
do," the maid scolded, thrusting a pair of long white kid
gloves into her mistress's hands as she snatched up a
gauzy gold-spangled stole from the bed. She arranged
this lovely item in graceful folds across the countess's
back and over her elbows while Serena meekly donned
the gloves.

"I do not know why you put up with my crotchets,
Betsy." Serena flashed the girl a mischievous smile, the
charm of which her long-suffering abigail resisted, though
she had to purse her lips to keep back an answering
smile.

"Neither do I," she replied repressively, handing her mistress a gold-spangled reticule, an opera glass, and a charming gold-and-ivory fan before bustling over to open the door.

Her good humor restored by Betsy's bracing manner, Serena gave the girl's arm a friendly squeeze and told her not to wait up for her as she left the room.

Several of the gentlemen who visited the Boynton box during the course of the evening were happy to confirm Betsy's judgment that her mistress looked beautiful in her cunningly tucked and pleated white muslin gown with its gold embroidery on bodice and hem. Lord Phillips, however, was not among their number. Thanks to Serena's tardiness in dressing, the Boyntons barely got themselves established in their seats before the curtain went up. Serena's searching eyes picked out the Talbot box across the theater before she settled onto her chair with a careful show of unconcern. Her satisfaction in finding Peter there with Natasha and Cam was instantly eclipsed as she spotted a fourth occupant of the box, a very pretty girl with dark curls and what, based on a good deal of surreptitious observation over the next hour, Serena could only call a highly flirtatious manner. The fact that she had introduced Miss Morton to Lord Phillips a few weeks earlier in the hopes of diverting his attention from herself only served to exacerbate what she was appalled to recognize as pangs of jealousy at the unrewarding sight of her erstwhile admirer being more than adequately entertained in the lively brunette's company. Never had the realization of her wishes proved more painful.

None of this was allowed to show, however, as Serena chatted and smiled and murmured suitably in response to the many compliments she received from the visitors to their box, while still contriving to keep abreast of all the activity going on in the Talbot box without appearing to do so. Peter did put in an appearance toward the end of the last interval, though not before Verity had commented on his absence, attributing it to his obvious absorption in the sparkling Miss Morton.

"I hadn't noticed," said Serena, lying through her teeth.

She bestowed a particularly brilliant smile on a very dull admirer at that moment, thus missing the curious look her sister cast her.

Lord Phillips arrived just as this gentleman took his departure, quite set up after another beguiling smile from his goddess. The latest visitor bent over Mrs. Boynton's hand, complimenting her on the blue gown that deepened the color of her eyes and subtracted years from her age. He switched his glance to Serena briefly to say, "Good evening, Lady Whitlaw. I trust you are enjoying the play," before turning to Verity with a comment that evoked soft laughter from the young girl.

Serena had been given no time to utter a word, though it was doubtful if she could have managed an intelligible reply in any case, for her heart had set up a furious knocking against her ribs at his entrance, and the mockery in his glance during the split second it took to pass over her person had caused her throat to go dry. She averted her stricken gaze from the spectacle of Peter and her sister laughing together with the ease of old friends and concentrated on fanning herself with slow, deliberate motions in sequence with her labored breathing.

The rest of the evening was sheer penance. The voices of the actors reached her through a distorting buzz in her head and never registered over her own frantic mental activity. Peter's call at the box had been perfunctory, no doubt dictated by innate good manners, or perhaps a desire to see how Verity fared after her parting from Mr. Selcort. Serena had become "Lady Whitlaw" again, and she knew herself unforgiven. Her generally nimble brain tripped over itself in forming and discarding plans to meet again in circumstances more conducive to an honest discussion, in a fruitless attempt to postpone admitting that there were no such circumstances when a man did not wish to be a party to such a discussion. She applauded along with everyone else in the audience at the end of a well-received performance, having seen little and heard less of it since Peter had returned to the vibrant Miss Morton.

By now Serena had a raging headache and was longing

for her bed, but the furies weren't quite done with her that night. It was while they were standing among the milling crowd awaiting the arrival of their carriage that Lord Whitlaw appeared at her elbow wearing the confident smile that always made her palm itch. After the humiliation of Peter's calculated indifference, the earl's presence was the last straw. Hot words of protest rose to her lips. The only way she could choke them back was by clamping her teeth and turning her back squarely on him, an ill-conceived action that brought an ugly look to his face.

Fortunately for Serena's peace of mind, she did not witness Lord Whitlaw's reaction to her cut, but Lord Phillips, some ten feet away and seemingly occupied with his own party, did. Arrested by the virulence of the earl's expression, Peter tensed, ready to act if the latter should continue to press his attentions on Serena. He relaxed as Lord Whitlaw turned instead to Peregrine with a laughing remark. Peter had time to note that young Boynton was flatteringly receptive to the older man's overtures before he had to leave with his own party.

In the Boynton carriage there was a lively discussion of the merits of the play during the short drive back to Beak Street. Serena responded when directly addressed, though her critique of the performance was much less incisive than her family had grown to expect. She was not so vague, however, that she did not notice that Perry seemed to have no intention of coming in when he escorted his ladies to their front door. To her surprised question, he replied cheerily that Lord Whitlaw had invited him to join him after he had seen his family safely home. Her eyes flew to his carefree countenance and she bit her lip to keep from articulating her disapproval of his choice of companion. She had no desire to alienate her brother and no hope that he would attend to her either. She wished him a quiet good night and went in, adding a half-realized sense of uneasiness over Perry's ripening association with Whitlaw to her other problems. He called back a gay reminder to her to be ready to ride early the next morning as he ran down the steps.

Serena, entering her room after saying good night to her mother and sister, wandered over to the window that looked down into the street and pulled back the drapery. The street was wholly devoid of traffic, either wheeled or pedestrian, but she stood there for another few moments staring at nothing while she slowly drew off the long kid gloves. Her face wore an abstracted frown when she let the drapery swing back into place at last. She had divulged nothing of her last meeting with Lord Whitlaw to any member of her family, believing thankfully that his pursuit of her fortune had ended with the humiliating confrontation with Peter Phillips. Perhaps she should tell Perry the truth about Whitlaw in order to nip this dangerous association in the bud. On the other hand, she could not dismiss the possibility that Perry would think it his duty to exact an apology of sorts from the earl for the incident at the Sinderby ball. Her brother was big and strong and possessed all the foolhardy fearlessness of the very young, but she had a great fear of what could happen to him at the hands of a man like Whitlaw. She went to bed still undecided as to her best course of action, her poor aching head resounding with unattractive possibilities, on top of the heavy weight of hopelessness that bowed her shoulders like a physical burden whenever her thoughts turned to Peter.

Peregrine, happily going off to meet Lord Whitlaw, shared none of his sister's qualms about his association with the dashing earl. That an older man of such outstanding athletic ability and numerous sporting achievements should condescend to spend time with a callow youth was highly flattering. Of course he was not so green as to attribute this marvelous state of affairs entirely to his own raw charms; it was merely his good fortune to be Serena's brother at a time when she was being courted by two top-o'-the-trees Corinthians who were war heroes to boot. Lord Phillips, an even better athlete, had been equally gracious about taking him under his wing with sparring practice and helpful tips on boxing. Lord Phillips, however, did not extend his helpful interest as far as inviting Serena's brother to accompany

him to the more exciting sort of masculine entertainments to be found in the less salubrious parts of the city
after dark. Indeed, from what Perry had observed, Lord
Phillips led a rather boring social life, doing the pretty to
a lot of old biddies and dancing attendance on a bunch of
silly young girls so hedged about by rules and chaperones
they wouldn't know how to have a bit of fun and jollity.
Lord Whitlaw knew the places where the entertainment
was less inhibited and the females more forthcoming. He
agreed that the only way to gain town polish and experience of the world was to get right out in it and soak up
the atmosphere.

So Perry sent his sister's carriage off to the stables and
hastened to pursue his quest for experience in the company of that bang-up chap the Earl of Whitlaw.

The earl did not fail him. The neighborhood they
wandered into after dismissing the cab that had brought
Perry back to where Whitlaw awaited him was a world
removed from the well-maintained squares of the West
End. The refuse-strewn streets were thronged with milling people on a summer night, though a rolling din of
voices and music testified that large numbers of persons
were also inside the alehouses that abounded in the area.

"This place is a regular mumpers' hall," Lord Whitlaw
remarked of the tavern they entered presently. "Thought
you'd find it interesting to see how all those pathetic
crippled and blind beggars that arouse one's sympathy in
the daytime spend their evenings. This isn't the only
place of its kind, of course, but it is very popular. There
is a well-known ballad singer here who brings in the
customers. Look about you."

Perry did not have to be exhorted to use his eyes. They
were popping out of his head at the extraordinary set of
persons enjoying the hospitality of the Three Crowns
that night. He'd been to boxing matches and public fairs
where poorly dressed humanity was in the majority, but
even in the smoky dimness of the low-ceilinged room he
could not fail to discern that the motley collection of
dirty rags and tatters adorning his fellow drinkers was
beyond anything in his experience. It was only when his

eye fell on a collection of discarded canes, sticks, and crutches in a corner that it came home to him that beggars dressed for their profession in the same way actors dressed for their roles, and their props were no more real.

Certainly the liquor was flowing freely, and there were card games and dicing going on at some of the tables, with plenty of money changing hands. As his eyes grew accustomed to the shadows and his ears were able to differentiate among the various noises, he discerned a fiddler accompanying a female singer at one end of the large room. They moved toward this attraction, the better to see and hear, and found places at a long table loaded with tankards and glasses and awash with spilled liquids.

No very friendly looks greeted their appearance, and Perry felt accutely uncomfortable in his pristine evening wear. Lord Whitlaw dismissed his qualms airily, merely cautioning him to mind his valuables. He then ordered drinks for the whole table, largess that was accepted with little decrease in the sullen stares directed their way, but presumably ensured their safety for a time.

Poll, as the featured entertainer was styled, was a blowsy redheaded wench on whom the ravages of time and hard living had left their mark, despite her efforts to conceal her raddled complexion under garish makeup. She was dressed in cheap finery that aped the fashions in vogue among the wealthy, but this she embellished by eye-catching additions of feathers and glitter. Her voice must have been lovely once. Now there was a hoarse quality that yet held fascination. At least Perry was captured by her husky rendition of a sentimental ballad, so much so that he failed to notice that Lord Whitlaw left their table for a few minutes and subsequently became engaged in conversation with a female customer.

For the most part the interlopers were patently ignored, at least by the tavern's male patrons, but two such resplendent samples of well-favored masculinity were bound to catch the eyes of the female customers, none of whom were retiring by nature. Perry had not overcome his initial discomfort when he was approached by two young women eager to have him buy them a drink. Fortunately, one was not opposed to turning her attention to Lord Whitlaw when the other said something quick and sharp to her that Perry could not decipher. He was not averse to buying her company for a time. She was, as far as he could tell in the gloom, the best-looking girl in the place, young and possessing a prettiness that was not entirely dimmed by wild, unwashed hair and the inexpert application of paint on cheeks and lips. Large, heavily lashed dark eyes gleamed invitingly, and the lush proportions of her figure were amply revealed in an exceedingly low-cut gown of gossamer thinness. He didn't care for her perfume, but her teeth were pretty when she smiled, which she did nearly continuously, seeming to find his conversation amusing in the extreme. He found her comments largely unintelligible, but it did not seem to matter as he consumed quantities of ale. His lively companion, who announced herself simply as Maud, displayed a preference for gin, which she downed at a steady rate.

Perry was so entranced by the charms of his companion that he remained unaware of the considerable attention they were attracting from other merrymakers, until there was a stir at the other end of the room and an angry black-browed man came striding down the room to pull up in front of them with a rough oath. He grabbed Maud's arm and jerked her to her feet, then addressed himself to Perry.

"You ain't man enough for this dimber mort, young chub, and she's mine. We don't like yer sort around 'ere, do we, Maud?"

" 'E's no more 'n a bantling and 'e didn't mean noffink. Leave 'im be, Mick," implored the girl, putting her hands up against the newcomer's chest.

" 'E wants a good lick o' the chops, and so do you," growled Mick, grabbing her wrists.

"Say, now, you can't talk to my friend like that," Lord Whitlaw intervened, but Perry, who had remained surprised and silent so far, recovered his tongue and said hastily:

"Never mind, sir. If she's his girl, he has a right to be angry. Let's go."

Perry was in the act of rising from his chair when his antagonist, unable to remove Maud's clutching fingers from the lapels of his bright blue coat, landed an open-handed blow across the girl's face that set her reeling away.

"Why, you filthy brute!" Perry surged off his chair and lunged for the man called Mick, who stood his ground, though obviously surprised at the great size of the youngster.

"Watch out, Perry, he'll have a knife!" warned Lord Whitlaw.

Peregrine heard the words and was dimly aware of Maud wailing away and clutching her jaw, but his whole concentration was on reaching her assailant. His fist connected with Mick's unshaven jaw with a crack that could be heard all over the tavern. The victim was a fair size himself, but he was lifted off his feet by the force of the blow and knocked backward, falling against the stone inglenook.

For a second or two there was an uncanny silence in the public house before the noise level accelerated back to what it had been. Most of the gamblers went back to their occupation as though nothing had happened. A number of avid customers crowded closer, hoping to see more action. Perry stood with fists clenched, ready to resume the battle whenever his opponent should elect to do so, but it was soon apparent that Mick would be unable to engage in any hostile activity for some little time yet. Seeing her lover knocked out, Maud ceased wailing abruptly and turned on Perry, screeching abuse. Lord Whitlaw sauntered over to the prone figure near the fireplace and glanced down casually. A second later he bent down and examined Mick, while Perry, with rising unease, approached the small group clustered about the fallen man.

"Do not come any nearer, Perry," the earl said, rising to his feet and taking his young friend by the arm. "I'm afraid he's dead," he added in a harsh whisper. "Come, let's get out of this place." While he spoke, he was steering the boy away from the people crowding in to get a better look, but after a few more steps, Perry stopped and turned eyes huge with horror on his friend.

"Dead? How can that be? I hit him hard, but a crack on the jaw never killed anyone. He cannot be dead!"

Lord Whitlaw resumed his pull on the other's arm. "It was not the blow to the face that did it; he hit the back of his head on the stones when he fell. Come, we must get out of here before this mob turns ugly. We cannot fight everyone in the place."

Too stunned with horror to exert his will, Perry allowed himself to be led out of the Three Crowns. It was not until they had turned a corner and were hurrying toward Buckeridge Street that he spoke again urgently. "The police—we must tell—"

"Think, my boy. A hundred people in that place saw you strike the blow that killed a man. You and I know it was an accident, but that is not what the witnesses will say. We are outsiders, and they will band together against you. You would have to stand trial. Think of your family. It is better this way, believe me. There is nothing you can do. No one back there knows your identity. It cannot be brought home to you if you keep your head and stay away from this area. And now," he finished briskly, "I am going to get you home. You've had a most unsettling experience and will be better for a night's sleep."

"Unsettled" barely described Peregrine's state as he dumbly followed the older man's instructions, obediently getting into the first hackney cab they saw. He thanked Lord Whitlaw politely when they arrived home, and climbed down from the cab, barely heeding the earl's parting injunction to forget this night's work.

Alone on the doorstep, Perry came to a halt as though no longer propelled now that the earl was not there to see his instructions carried out. *Sleep? Forget?* Forget that he had killed a man? Peregrine pulled his hand back from the door and stumbled down the steps again. Without any destination in mind, he started walking, his footsteps echoing in his ears.

16

Serena awoke with the remnants of her headache but ignored it as she dressed rapidly in the new dark green habit with the matching narrow-brimmed hat that so complimented her russet mane, drawn smoothly back in a large knot at the nape today for convenience. She was unaware that this severe style had the additional advantage of emphasizing the perfection of her profile and the alabaster purity of her complexion. She did note the faint shadows under her eyes from a series of disturbed nights, but dismissed what she couldn't help with a shrug and headed downstairs. Perry was late, and when he still hadn't appeared by the time she had drawn on gloves of York tan, she sent Richford to hurry him along.

She was prowling about the hall, still wondering how much to tell her brother of her dealings with Lord Whitlaw, when Richford's voice at her elbow brought her out of her abstracted state with a rush.

"What did you say, Richford?"

"I said, my lady, I regret to inform you that Master Peregrine is not in his room, nor has his bed been slept in."

With a conscious effort Serena smoothed away the frown that had wrinkled her forehead at this announcement. "I see." She bit her lip and glanced at the blue sky through the fanlight over the front door. It was a glorious day and she could hear the groom outside with the saddled horses. Perhaps the best way to avoid questions was to go out as if nothing was amiss. "Richford, say nothing of this to my mother, if you please. If she should ask, we are out riding. Is that understood?"

"Yes, my lady."

"And don't look so disapproving," she chided in a rallying voice. "Did you come home every single night when you were young?"

"As to that, my lady, I really cannot recall," returned Richford, his expression even more disapproving if possible, as he handed her the crop she had placed on a table.

"Then I pity you," she retorted with a saucy smile that brought a tiny twitch to his lips before he donned his professional face once more as he opened the door for her.

"My brother will not be riding this morning," she informed his groom a moment later as he assisted her into the saddle. "We'll take Ebony back to the stables, and Jenkins may accompany me to the park."

There was a fair number of riders in the park on such a lovely morning, so Serena kept to a decorous canter, which was all to the good, since her chaotic thoughts occupied her to such an extent that her horsemanship was purely mechanical. She was not unduly upset by Perry's absence, but her inimical feelings toward Lord Whitlaw were increased if possible by this evidence of his bad influence over her young brother. She was less than gratified therefore to see the earl's tall military figure cantering toward her on a great rawboned roan a few moments after she entered the park. There was no avoiding him, but she kept up her speed, planning to acknowledge his presence and ride on.

Lord Whitlaw foiled this intention by swinging his mount around in front of her and fetching up at her side as she perforce slowed Dancer to a walk. "Good morning, Lady Whitlaw. I wish to speak with you. Shall we ride a little way together?"

"We can have nothing to talk about, sir, and your company is displeasing to me. Please ride on." Serena stared straight ahead, refusing to look at him, but his next words brought her head around directly.

"Displeasing or not, I fear you will have to endure my company because we do have something of a serious nature to discuss—your brother's predicament. Now, will you tell your groom to leave us, or shall I speak in his presence?"

Still distrustful, but sufficiently alarmed about Perry to obey, Serena dismissed Jenkins, telling him to meet her at the Stanhope Gate when he would have lingered just out of earshot. There were people enough in the park to afford her protection if necessary. "What have you to say, sir?" she prompted when the groom had moved off.

"Did your brother tell you what happened last night?"

"I have not seen Peregrine this morning," she replied, deciding not to speak of his absence just yet.

"Probably sleeping it off." After a pause that she made no attempt to fill, the earl went on, "Like most youngsters, Perry is eager to add to his knowledge of life beyond the, shall we say, restricted experiences offered boys of his station at home or school. From time to time I have accompanied him on his little jaunts about town, thinking to lend him the protection of my greater years and experience. Unfortunately, even my presence was insufficient to prevent him from coming a cropper last night. To be brief, he got into a fight in a rather unsavory tavern and in the ensuing melee he killed a man." Lord Whitlaw ignored Serena's involuntary gasp at this shocking statement and continued. "Needless to say, it was an accident. Perry was in his cups at the time and did not realize his own strength. It was just his misfortune that the lout hit his head against the fireplace when he fell. I have assured Perry that I will do all in my power to see that he comes safely out of this, but whether he does or not rather depends on you."

"I don't believe you!" Serena croaked, out of the depths of nightmare, her voice sounding disembodied in her ears.

"Perry will confirm what I have just told you. I got him safely out of that place last night and I have promised that he has nothing to fear from the law, but it is really up to you whether or not your brother's identity becomes known to the police."

Still ignoring his implication, she persisted, "Perry will not be prosecuted for an accidental death."

"I am telling you it was an accident for the sake of your peace of mind, and that is what I shall tell the magistrate, but the other witnesses will say differently. After all, the victim was one of their own. If your brother stands his trial, there is a chance he may be acquitted, but I somehow felt you would prefer to spare your mother the pain and notoriety of a public trial." Again he paused to let his threat sink in before adding, "Naturally, I would never permit my brother-in-law's name to come to light in a murder investigation."

Serena shuddered, and the eyes she raised to his handsome visage were dull and resigned. "Very well, since it seems to be a matter of no concern to you to have a wife who loathes the sight of you, I'll marry you, but," she added quickly, her nostrils flaring at the gloating triumph that swept over his features, "I shall never live with you. You may have your cousin's money, but I shall continue to live in the dower house."

"Do not be melodramatic. The law and the church will uphold a husband's rights."

"The law and the church will have nothing to say in the matter," promised Serena, meeting his gaze with steady purpose.

For a moment the earl continued to stare angrily down at his unwilling fiancée, attempting to intimidate her, but whether because he heard sounds of a rider approaching behind them or felt a disinclination to argue the matter in public, he said hastily, "We can discuss this question at a more convenient time, but I warn you, I am going to put the announcement in tomorrow's papers."

"You may announce it from St. Paul's pulpit if you please," Serena snapped, "but leave me now." She turned her shoulder on him with calculated rudeness and maintained a rigid unnatural posture, keeping Dancer unmoving. She could feel him debating with himself, half-inclined to stay and have it out with her; then, to the relief of her twanging nerves, he gave his horse a vicious kick and surged ahead of her along the path.

Once he was gone, Serena slumped in her saddle, no longer bolstered by pride and anger. She was shaking

with reaction, and it was only thanks to Dancer's beautiful manners that she was still in the saddle and moving at
a steady pace. She never heard a rider come up behind
her, and was almost unseated when a familiar voice called,
"Are you ill, Lady Whitlaw? May I assist you?"

For a moment there was no recognition in the ashen
face Serena presented to him, and Peter repeated with
rising concern, "Serena, what is wrong? What has happened?" He took Dancer's reins into his hand and brought
their horses to a stop. "Was that Whitlaw I saw disap-
pearing up ahead? What did that fiend do to make you
look like this?"

Some color had come back into Serena's cheeks as she
drew a long breath and responded to the urgency in his
voice. "Nothing, he did nothing. I am all right, truly I
am. For a moment I was a little faint, that's all."

Despite the brave words, Serena's voice shook and she
could not meet Peter's eyes for more than a second. He
sat still, watching the dark curling lashes on her cheeks,
then said with gentle derision, "I would be exceedingly
amazed to discover that you had ever felt faint in your
life. Despite what has passed between us, Serena, I am
persuaded you know that I may be trusted. Can you not
tell me what is wrong?"

"There is nothing." She shook her head, still not looking at him.

"You are very dear to . . . to my sister, and she would
wish me to help you if possible. I would like to help you,
Serena."

That brought shimmering green eyes up to meet his
briefly. Two tears spilled over but she still shook her
head. "Thank you, you are very good, but there is nothing to be done."

"Very well, if you will not tell me, then I'll find out
from Whitlaw. I know he is responsible. I'll beat it out of
him if necessary."

"Oh, how I wish you might beat him!"

Peter laughed at the venomous wish expressed with a
touch of her old spirit. "That's better. I intend to find
out what has happened, you know, if it takes all day.

We'll sit right here until you feel you can tell me what is wrong."

The flash of spirit had faded. She looked at him with eyes darkened with despair. "I said I'd marry him."

Peter expelled a breath and struggled with wild impulses to commit violence if only he knew where to direct his rage. It took a moment before he was enough master of himself to ask quietly, "Why?"

"Because if I do not, Perry will have to stand trial for murder. It would kill my mother, Peter, don't you understand?" She looked up at him again, and now the despair was turning to a wild rage to match his own. "I survived one marriage to a brute masquerading as a gentleman. But I'll never live with him. I told him so. He may have all the money unless my man of business can salvage something for me, but if he lays a hand on me, I swear I'll kill him! And do not think I cannot do it, either," she cried, her voice escalating into near-hysteria, "because I am a dead shot with a pistol. That's something I learned from the fourth earl when he was courting me. He was very proud of my prowess with a pistol too. He was used to tell everyone—"

"Serena, try to control yourself, my dear." At the risk of getting them both unseated, Peter transferred her reins to his other hand and flung a strong arm around her shaking shoulders. "Shhhh, my dear, someone may come along any minute. I promise you, you shall not marry against your will. Now, tell me about Peregrine."

Surprisingly, Serena's rising hysteria was checked almost at once by his matter-of-fact tones. She pulled away from Peter's comforting embrace, apologizing in an embarrassed manner, and was able to give him a coherent account of her meeting with Lord Whitlaw. Peter listened without interruption, saying as she finished, "Where is Peregrine now?"

"I don't know. He did not come home last night, but Whitlaw thinks he's home and I did not tell him otherwise."

Peter had been frowning, but now he produced a smile of encouragement and was rewarded by a lessening of the anxiety with which she regarded him. "You are not

to worry, and do not try to do anything about this yourself. I'll handle the matter." He looked around, and the
frown returned. "Where is your groom?"

"Waiting for me at the Stanhope Gate."

He nodded. "Good. I'll escort you there. Then I must
find Peregrine. If he should come home, send word to
me and keep him at home. Will you trust me to act for
you in this business?"

"Yes, but, Peter, he . . . Lord Whitlaw said he was
going to put an engagement notice in tomorrow's papers."

"I'll make him eat the words if he does."

Over the next few hours Peter feared he might be the
one to eat rash words as he embarked on a search for
Peregrine Boynton, but he would have said and done
anything to take that look of hopelessness from Serena's
eyes. She had achieved a fair counterfeit of her usual
composure by the time he had turned her over to her
groom so he might set about the daunting task of finding
a young man no doubt suffering from the aftereffects of
inebriation and afraid to go home.

His first stop was at his own home, where he gave an
order to his valet that would have confounded most
members of that snobbishly inclined fraternity. Fortunately, Marsden, who had been his batman for years,
was himself a Londoner and not unfamiliar with the less
refined areas of town. He never turned a hair when
ordered to canvass the used-clothing shops along Mon-
mouth Street.

Meanwhile, Peter and his groom scoured the meaner
localities, dividing up the taverns and hostelries between
them, thankful at least that Peregrine's great size and
well-favored lineaments made him conspicuous enough
to work to their account. It still took nearly four hours
and dozens of bribes to suspicious innkeepers and publi-
cans to run their quarry to earth in a disgusting establishment on one of the courts off the side streets near Drury
Lane, the like of which Peter hadn't seen since Portugal
for sheer filth.

Peregrine, shaken awake none too gently in the room
in which he'd simply fallen on the bed fully dressed, was

a lot the worse for wear, Peter decided, with bruised knuckles on his right hand and assorted cuts on his face. Understanding though Natasha was, he couldn't drive the boy to his sister's house in his present condition in an open carriage, and no respectable hotel would allow him through its doors.

It took the better part of two hours for Peter to make the young giant presentable enough to deliver to his home, what with having to dispatch his groom with a note to Serena to send along a change of clothing and a razor. By the time the boy was cleaned up, dressed, shaved, forcibly fed, and given something for a monumental headache, Peter had the whole sorry tale out of him, at least all that had occurred at the Three Crowns until Whitlaw had deposited him on his doorstep. Perry had no clear memory of the hours after he had made the maudlin decision that he was unworthy of his mother's home and had started wandering the streets in foggy despair, though the empty gin bottle on the floor shed some light on his subsequent activities. Peter was grateful to have found him alone and in one piece, though Peregrine had grumbled at the loss of his money and speculated on which of his recent acquaintances had napped his tick. A missing watch and purse were a small price to pay in the circumstances. His mouth took on a grim line as he watched his still-shaky protégé struggle into the Hessians Serena had sent with his clothes. It was up to him to see that the price went no higher, either for Peregrine or for Serena.

It was past midafternoon by the time Peter saw Peregrine into his curricle and shook his grateful hand, waving away the boy's shy but fervent thanks. He decided to walk for a while before hailing a cab to take him home. After several hours breathing the fetid air in the reputed hostelry that had sheltered Perry overnight, he needed to be outside under the blue sky, even in the insalubrious purlieus of Drury Lane and despite the presence of professional beggars and other wretched denizens of the area who jostled him frequently, no doubt hoping to pick his pocket should he prove unwary or inattentive. His

size and serviceable walking stick were sufficient protection for the short distance he had to travel to reach a
more respectable district where he could find a hackney.

The only course of action that had occurred to him was
to go to the flash-house where Whitlaw had taken Peregrine and question the patrons about the alleged killing.
The boy had confirmed the bare essentials related to
Serena by the earl, but his story of how he had been
drawn into a fight had aroused Peter's suspicions, mostly,
he admitted, because of Whitlaw's behavior at the theater. There was nothing to lose; Serena had already
accepted the earl's ultimatum, and she would keep her
word to save her family pain and disgrace.

From Peregrine's vague description it would seem that
the Three Crowns was located in the "Holy Land" section of St. Giles near Buckeridge Street—one of the
city's more notorious rookeries, breeding places of crime.
The neighborhood's inhabitants were predominantly Irish,
and its gin shops were gathering places for many of the
town's professional beggars of all ages. Peter sighed with
resignation as he contemplated the evening ahead of
him. Thank God for a hard head, but he'd best avoid the
gin sold in the district if he hoped to accomplish anything.

A warning echoed by his valet later as he cheerfully
assisted in the process of transforming his elegant employer into a figure that could blend in with the locals:
"Stick to ale if ye can, sir. The gin'll burn yer eyes out o'
yer 'ead, it will."

Peter, in the process of dragging on a pair of sleazy
trousers, part of the assortment of near-rags purchased
that morning by Marsden, merely grunted. He eyed with
revulsion the none-too-clean stockings provided by the
valet and tossed them aside, only to be brought up short.

"Now, sir, it wouldn't do to go prancing into one o'
them boozing kens wearing silk stockings—not if you was
wishful to get them wot goes there to snitch, that is." He
put out a hand for Peter's own stockings, and after a
pause pregnant with rebellion, the latter silently stripped
off his footwear and donned the offending stockings.

"Your mish, sir."

Suspicious blue eyes swept over his henchman's stolid features as Peter accepted the tatty shirt. "Enjoying yourself, Marsden?" he inquired silkily.

"Well, it does make a change, sir," the valet replied, holding out a badly wrinkled coat of a particularly bilious shade of green. "Your toge."

"Good God!" Peter closed his eyes for an anguished second before thrusting reluctant arms into the repulsive garment being offered him. "It's too small," he objected, displaying a length of shirt sleeve below the jacket sleeve.

"None o' the 'abitués o' them boozing kens patronize Weston," Marsden pointed out with a grin that he could not quite suppress.

Peter glared at his longtime servitor. "And I presume that deplorable object is my . . . er . . . clout," he observed testily.

"Yessir, or yer blow," the valet added helpfully as he folded a much-washed and no-longer-white handkerchief.

Wordlessly Peter accepted it and the cheap purse that followed and put them into a pocket. He slipped a few folded pound notes into his stockings and crammed his feet into a dilapidated pair of boots, wincing as he did so.

Marsden, casting a critical eye over his employer's reconstructed person, gave it as his opinion that he'd have done better not to shave that morning, and recommended that he tousle his well-brushed hair for a more authentic look. "Though that outsize shap worn on the back o' yer 'ead gives you a rakish touch, along wi' the scar."

"Thank you, Marsden," his lordship replied humbly. "May I take it, then, that I'll pass muster as one of the dregs of society?"

"Until yer open yer mummer. Sure, ye got a lot o' cant words in yer 'ead, but 'aving 'em at yer tongue's end, smooth-like, is another matter, I wish ye'd take me along to do the talking."

"You are too well-dressed," murmured Peter; then, in an entirely different voice, "Cast yer ogles on that peery cove over by the jigger. Wot's 'is lay? Curse me for a flat if 'e ain't a file meant for the nubbing cheat."

Marsden smiled reluctantly and allowed as how his lordship might just fool them long enough to find out what he wished to learn. "But ye will take a pop wi' ye, sir?"

"Certainly not. I intend to talk to people, not shoot them."

"At least a chive, then. Every cull in the place and some o' the morts will 'ave a chive tucked away out o' sight."

"I fear my education has been sadly neglected, Marsden. I can fight with a sword, a bayonet, a gun, or my fists, but I'd be quite useless with a knife. I promise you I'll keep my back to a wall, but I am, after all, merely seeking information, scarcely an aggressive act. Now, will you check the halls and give me a sign when it's clear. I'll find a hack once I'm well away from the square."

"Best yer leave that fam at 'ome, sir." The valet gestured toward Peter's signet ring, which was handed over immediately.

"What would I ever do without you, Marsden?"

"I can't think, sir, and that's a fact."

The Three Crowns was everything and more than Peter had expected. It was larger for a start, probably doubling as a brothel, and his imagination had been inadequate to depict the rancid smell compounded of spirits, mice, and unwashed humanity that assailed his nostrils on entering the huge public room. It was too early in the evening for many of the regulars, but the place was by no means untenanted. Two gray-haired men with eye patches, looking like mirror images of each other, were casting dice in a corner, watched by a small audience. At a table nearby, a singularly ugly gap-toothed woman was sitting in the lap of a grinning drunkard whose hands were roaming over her body while another man snored beside them, his head on the table. Peter averted his eyes hastily and met the incurious stare of the tapster, all alone near a keg.

"A pint o' yer best," he ordered, flipping a coin at the man, who caught it deftly.

"Hain't seen you 'ere afore, 'as I?"

"Been out o' the country lately." Peter took a huge swig of his ale and wiped the back of his hand across his mouth.

"Sojering?" inquired the tapster, eyeing his customer's flashy outfit doubtfully.

"Antipodes." Having established himself as a transported felon, Peter quaffed more of his drink, ordered another, and indicated that the tapster should join him, something that individual was more than willing to do.

"Not much life in this place," Peter observed caustically, letting his gaze range over the half-filled room.

"Early yet. Ye'll 'ave 'eard o' Poll wot sings 'ere most nights. She brings in the trade."

"A bloke I know says yer 'ad some excitement last night, a killing 'e told me, but I dessay 'e was too jug-bitten to know wot 'e saw."

The tapster grinned widely, displaying all four of his remaining teeth. "In a manner o' speaking." He jerked his thumb toward his left shoulder. "There's the corpse over yonder, nursin' a queer morley."

At this laconic remark Peter's face had gone completely still. Now he swallowed and allowed his glance to take in the black-haired man seated alone at a table a dozen feet away, staring glumly down into a tankard. The man's unprepossessing features weren't improved by a noticeably swollen jaw and a bloodstained bandage wrapped around his head. "I've seen deader corpses," he commented cheerfully. "My mate always was a doom crier. Wot 'it 'im?"

"A couple o' swells wot come in to 'ear Poll—leastways, the young 'un gave 'im a souse across the chops, an 'em 'ardly breeched." The tapster cackled evilly. "It seems the other cove, a bleedin' cully wot comes 'ere now and again, slipped Bawdy Maud a few bull's-eyes to make up to the chub. Black Mick considers Maud 'is, and 'e don't welcome no advances on 'is propity."

"Thus the fight," agreed Peter. "It's still a far cry from a fight to a killing."

The tapster shrugged incomprehension. "Next thing I knows, Maud's screeching that Mick's killed and the two

swell coves is whippin' away. It was nigh onto an hour
afore Mick opened 'is ogles.'' He jerked his thumb in the
direction of the solitary figure again. '' 'E's bin sittin' like
that all day.''

Out of sheer relief and thankfulness, Peter ordered
another tankard delivered to the fallen gladiator. He
made a point of ascertaining that Poll would be performing in an hour, promised to return in good time for this
treat, and parted from the garrulous tapster with mutual
expressions of goodwill.

All signs of goodwill were absent from his stern visage
as he hurried home to change out of his disgusting cos-
tume. There was no doubt in his mind that Whitlaw had
brought young Boynton to the Three Crowns with the
intention of obtaining some sort of hold over him. He'd
taken instant advantage of the lad's knockout of Black
Mick, and his improvised plan had nearly achieved his
objective. In fact, if the earl had succeeded in placing a
betrothal announcement with the papers for tomorrow's
editions, the Boyntons would still have to endure the
embarrassment of a retraction, but considering Serena's
state of mind when he'd left her this morning, she'd
count that a small-enough price to pay for her freedom
and Peregrine's safety.

Meanwhile, it would be Peter's great pleasure to spike
Whitlaw's guns permanently. In the pursuit of this laud-
able ambition he presented himself at the earl's lodgings
on St. James's Street an hour later and was gratified to
learn that his lordship had not yet gone out for the
evening. He refused to be fobbed off by the valet's
report that his master was dressing and therefore unable
to receive a guest.

"I'll wait here," he announced pleasantly, taking a
chair under the affronted eye of the manservant.

Lord Whitlaw, coming through the inner doorway some
fifteen minutes later, was also less than welcoming. "I
trust you'll state your errand quickly, Phillips, as I have
an appointment in ten minutes."

"Gladly, my lord. It is merely to inform you that the
game is over and you have lost. That fake killing you

held over Lady Whitlaw's head this morning has been proved just that, a fraud. I have seen the 'corpse' drowning his sorrows and nursing his sore head at the Three Crowns." Peter had risen when the earl entered the room, and he met the latter's astonished fury with an urbane scorn that brought dark color in a tide to the other's cheeks.

"You are after the fair, I'm afraid, Phillips. Lady Whitlaw has agreed to marry me, and the notice has already been sent to several of the dailies."

"Then, may I advise you for your own sake to prevent its appearance. If a retraction becomes necessary, I cannot guarantee that the story of your attempted fraud won't be all round the clubs by tomorrow evening, something that will do you no good in your quest for a rich wife. And if you dare to come within speaking distance of Serena or Peregrine in the future, it will give me great pleasure to put a bullet between your eyes."

That it would have afforded the earl a great deal of satisfaction to wreak vengeance on the man addressing him with a quiet and deadly calm was patent, and indeed his hands had curled into fists as he listened to his careful plans tumbling about his ears, but at this point violence would gain him nothing material. "Quite the gallant champion, aren't you?" he observed with a sneer. "I'd wish you joy of her, but she'll never have you, you know. I've never met a more stony-hearted b—"

Lord Whitlaw's unflattering description of Serena remained unfinished by reason of a powerful fist crashing into his open mouth. He went down like a felled tree, barely comprehending the soft words spoken by the man standing over him, flexing his fingers.

"If ever you should desire satisfaction, be assured that I shall meet you anytime, anyplace, and with any weapon you choose."

The pleasure of knocking Whitlaw down had been balm to his sorely tried nature at the moment, but it had long since dissipated by the time Peter knocked at the Boynton residence the next morning and requested a private interview with Lady Whitlaw. He had not been able to get the earl's prediction that Serena wouldn't have him out of his head. How could he, when that had been his fear all along? When had she ever given him reason to hope that she might be open to an offer from him? And after the way he had behaved toward her at their recent meetings, excepting yesterday's crisis situation, she had probably written him off for good and all, he decided gloomily. In any case, he could not ask her today; it would be tantamount to demanding a reward for services rendered after he related the events of the previous day.

It did not raise his spirits to realize that Richford, no doubt scenting romance, had unbent sufficiently to accord him a gracious smile as he ushered him into the small room at the back of the house with a comforting phrase about her ladyship not keeping him waiting above a minute or two. His own sober demeanor, he saw with a twist of wry humor, was accepted by the butler as a fitting attitude for a man about to put his hopes to the test. He tugged at a suddenly tight cravat, accepting that in essence, that about described the situation, though it was not as imminent as Richford supposed.

Serena slipped into the room while he was still lost in unsatisfactory musing, wondering if perhaps he should return to Devon for a time.

"I'm sorry to have kept you waiting, P . . . Lord Phillips," she said with automatic civility.

Peter's spirits descended still further as he noted the swift substitution of his title. That's what his wretched pride had earned him. "Not at all. It is I who have come at an unconscionably early hour, but I felt you would wish to hear my news as quickly as possible." Lord, he sounded like a damned prig! He mustered a smile which didn't reach his eyes and said gently, "Do not look so anxious; the news is good."

Her rigid composure softened a little and her eyes pleaded with him, but she continued to play the perfect hostess. "Won't you be seated, sir? Shall I send for Perry, since I presume this concerns him? He has endured a dreadful day, poor boy. I could not add to his remorse by telling him about . . . about my betrothal to Whitlaw." She faltered at the end and he said hurriedly:

"There will be no betrothal to Whitlaw unless you yourself desire it."

"Are you mad?" she demanded.

Peter smiled with more warmth to see her returning to her normal impatient self, and said lightly, "Do not send for Peregrine until I've gone. I don't think I could bear it if he should fall on my neck in gratitude, when I did nothing but discover a truth that already existed."

"What truth?"

"There was no death. The man Peregrine hit was in the tavern yesterday, somewhat the worse for his encounter with your brother, but alive and probably dreaming of revenge. Whitlaw seized on the fact of his being knocked unconscious to convince Peregrine he was dead so that he could use your fear for your brother to coerce your acceptance of his offer. I saw him last night and warned him to stop the announcement of an engagement. He'll not bother you again, or Peregrine either."

Serena had listened to his bare-bones recital with strained concentration, her hands gripping each other together in front of her. Now she exhaled a long breath. "You . . . are . . . sure?"

"Quite sure. It's over, my dear."

Her breathless little laugh held a touch of hysteria. "Do you suppose you could bear it if *I* fell on your neck in gratitude?"

"No," he replied shortly, and cursed himself for a fool as the color drained from her face, leaving her eyes dark and wounded. "I don't want your gratitude," he added, making bad worse.

She was in control once again, her back straight and her chin high as she said with quiet dignity, "Well, I am sorry to disoblige you, but you must allow me to thank you most sincerely on behalf of my whole family for the great service you have done us." There was an uncomfortable pause and she said with a hint of desperation, "Will you take some refreshment, sir? Coffee? Wine?"

"No, thank you. I must be going." For the life of him,

Peter couldn't come up with a single conventional phrase to get himself gracefully away, and Serena was silent now. He turned and walked toward the door, sensing that the bridge was on fire behind him but unable to douse the flames. He had his hand on the knob when her voice reached him, low but throbbing with the intensity of her feelings.

"Oh, Peter, I cannot bear it that you should think so badly of me!"

He spun around and read the distress in her eyes without comprehension. "I? Think badly of you? What nonsense is this?" His own voice sounded harsh with repression.

She was still gripping her hands together as the words tumbled out. "A-about Verity and . . . and being cold and heartless and without compassion. It was more thoughtless than heartless, really it was, and I have spoken with Verity, and . . . and Mama has agreed that if she and Mr. Selcort still feel the same way in a year, then they may marry. I . . . I want my sister to be happy," she finished in a whisper as he came close and possessed himself of her clasped hands.

"And you, Serena, are you happy?"

Her eyes dropped, unable to sustain the searching regard in his. "Of . . . of course, now that Whitlaw is defeated, thanks to you."

"Perfectly happy?" he persisted, and tightened his hold on her hands at the flicker in the green eyes as she glanced quickly up and down again.

"Is anyone perfectly happy in this imperfect world?" she asked with a little movement of her shoulders.

"*I* could be perfectly happy," he replied quietly, "if you loved me." She had grown very still. "Look at me, Serena." And when she had obeyed the gentle command, her eyes shimmering like jewels: "Do you love me?"

"Oh, Peter, yes, of course I do!"

There was nothing gentle about the embrace that followed this joyful admission. It was as if the doubts and uncertainties of the past could be exorcised only by a fierce declaration of mutual possession. Serena emerged from that kiss with her limbs trembling and her body tingling with desire. She looked at Peter in wordless wonder.

"Surprised?" He brushed back a lock of her hair with gentle fingers, and his smile was infinitely tender.

She nodded and said with difficult honesty, "I've never felt this way before, Peter. It's all new to me."

"I'm glad," he said simply. "It's new to both of us. We'll marry soon, beloved?"

"I think we'd better!"

Peter threw back his head and laughed. "I don't know what enchants me more, your delightful blushes or your uncensored frankness. I'll take you traveling, my darling, anywhere you wish to go, around the world if you like."

"You don't have to bribe me," she said seriously. "I'd live with you in a hut."

"Definitely the frankness." Peter caught her close again. They were drifting back into their private land of enchantment when Peregrine, impatient to know his fate, pounded on the morning-room door, calling to his sister.

"Oh, dear, we forgot about poor Perry." With palpable reluctance Serena freed herself from the haven of her betrothed's arms.

"There will come a time, very soon, my darling, when we'll be allowed to forget about the rest of the world."

Peter's fervent promise was rewarded by a spontaneous kiss from his beloved before, another blush mantling her cheeks, she crossed the room to open the door and fetch her brother.

SIGNET REGENCY ROMANCE
COMING IN FEBRUARY 1990

Norma Lee Clark
THE INFAMOUS RAKE

Mary Balogh
A PROMISE OF SPRING

Gayle Buck
HONOR BESIEGED